Intuition

By

Marala Scott
Alyssa M. Curry

INTUITION
Copyright © 2014 by Alyssa M. Curry, Marala Scott

Cover Design By: Alyssa M. Curry
Copyediting: Alyssa M. Curry
Cover Photo By: Gavin Mills
Author Photo: Gerry Garcia

ISBN Hardcover: 978-0-9911760-3-8
ISBN Paperback: 978-0-9911760-4-5
ISBN E-Book: 978-0-9911760-5-2

Library of Congress Control Number: 2014934503

For information regarding special discounts for bulk purchases of this book for educational, gift purposes, as a charitable donation, or to arrange a speaking event, please visit: www.seraphbooks.com

www.maralascott.com
twitter@maralascott
www.facebook.com/marala.scott

twitter@TheRealLyss
www.facebook.com/Lyss.curry

www.seraphbooks.com

Dedication

We've always said that we would praise your name to the largest audience we could find. Thank you for never leaving us. We dedicate this book to God.

Introduction

I couldn't always fathom why my mother was so protective over me. She knew who my friends were and where I was at all times. Most teenagers would consider her style to be domineering and overprotective. However, I'm different because I see it as necessary and a privilege to have someone love and care about me as much as she does. Although I'm accepting of her choices, many experiences allowed me to further comprehend why she shields me from any possible harm. What I found challenging was being able to accept that she is always right about everything when following her intuition. She's able to meet my new friends and immediately determine whether or not they were respectable or a positive influence on me. When she didn't approve, I would free myself of any potential issues. Sometimes, it would be a while before I was able to realize what a good choice it was. What I learned through these occurrences is that she uses her God given intuition to keep me safe. In fact, through her, God guided me until I learned to be in tune with him and his messages, without fail.

I prayed to God that I could receive the same beautiful gift she has. It didn't take long for me to understand that everyone is blessed with intuition and can have an unwavering bond with God if they choose. Intuition is a unique sensation, but sometimes we don't recognize when we already possess it. It could be a simple feeling telling you not to go out for the night or an odd discomfort towards an individual. Regardless, we get these feelings for a reason and that is what we are trying to share through this book. In this book, many of the conversations between she and I occurred. We are sharing these experiences and inspirational messages so all of us can continue to learn. Trusting our intuition is the key.

My mother is such an inspiration. I am very proud to work with her to help spread God's word. She is the most amazing individual and I love her with all of my heart.

With love,
Alyssa

One

Limited standing room in the dark Hill House Auditorium was all that remained. The packed crowd was overflowing with intense, radiating excitement. A calm Marala Scott was about to take the stage and leave them with a commanding delivery of her new book, *Intuition.* This book embraced the soul and inspired those who thought intuition was impossible to regain after they'd shut out any glimpse of hope. The horrific events once shrouding Marala's tormented life initiated an empowering thrust forward into a healthy existence as an alternative to remaining a victim. She was drained from fighting in a treacherous pool of unyielding quicksand. Marala exposed her tragic history as a way to share her triumphant method of healing in an attempt to help others.

Intuition was created from her benevolent heart and flushed as free as a songbird through her exposed soul in the form of compelling and compassionate expressions. The perception versus the true reality of Marala's life rendered her in favorable demand as a heartfelt inspirational speaker.

Patiently waiting backstage were Marala and Lyss as one of the professors at the university ardently introduced Marala, stating her list of accolades. Lyss's face was glowing as she listened to the words spoken about her mother. She was 5'6 but stood 5'9 in a pair of sexy black Manolo Blahnik shoes and a fitted black dress displaying a body women seek top plastic surgeons to obtain; only Lyss's was all natural. Her beautiful deep brown skin had a radiant glimmer as though against the reflection of the gently setting sun. Her almond-shaped, gorgeous brown eyes had a clear window leading to her insightful soul. The expression on her face mirrored the calmness and peace of a desert night. Lyss's brown hair had natural cinnamon highlights, which rested on her shoulders. Her layered bangs were gently swept to the right side of her face. Much like her mother, her flawless posture displayed an innate confidence.

"You'll be amazing as always," Lyss advised. "People love hearing you speak. It's as if you're slipping them the secret recipe to what they crave, especially when things seem to be so disparaging these days. I consider the topic of *Intuition* an excellent way to redirect adverse propensities. People can take in something enlightening, encouraging and faith based that'll be useful. Besides, this is reality."

"Oh, and you don't believe you're just a little prejudiced?" Marala asked, flashing a wide smile of her own.

"Mama?"

"Of course you are. You're my baby," she said running her finger down Lyss's pretty nose.

Lyss let out a soft giggle, adding in a self-justifying tone, "I'm not biased. I love being able to watch you give speeches every chance I get. Why do you think I'm here?" she asked shrugging.

"I don't know. Perhaps to escape the stalkers following you around campus pleading for a date," she replied cleverly cutting her eyes at Lyss.

Lyss waved her hand dismissively and laughed.

2

"Mama, I can spot them a mile away because I have a little of your intuition," she confessed with self-assurance. "I'm here because I learn something and what I'm learning can't be taught in a classroom. Your speeches are invaluable to me and they'll be useful to my patients soon," she added with three barely audible claps.

"Regardless, I'm glad you're here. I'm more relaxed on stage knowing I can look over and see you."

Marala kissed Lyss on the cheek as they shared a brief embrace. A moment later, a well-dressed young man, early twenties, with a clipboard in his hand approached them. Overflowing with zest he announced expressively, "The audience is full of spice tonight. We're all so excited to hear your speech. I love having you back here Ms. Scott."

"Parker, it's my pleasure. There's so much positive energy flowing through this place, I love it."

"Me too," he admitted eagerly. "A—lyss—a, feel free to wait back here during the show. But if you'd be more comfortable, I can seat you in the audience. Front row, of course," he added with a wink.

"Thank you. But if you don't mind, I requested one of the lower level private boxes on the left side. I'll have a perfect view of the audience for observation and a fabulous view of my mother."

"That's so not a problem, I can take you up there myself," he suggested.

"I'd appreciate that and you can call me Lyss if you'd like, Parker."

"Lyss," he restated touching his index finger to his chin, deliberating. "Okay, I like that." Parker gave a polite smile and spun around to Marala. "I'd say they're about ready for you. Let's switch on your microphone." She turned her back to Parker and he moved the tiny button to *on* and then adjusted the volume. Unable to hide his spark of excitement, he announced, "Ms. Scott, I'd say you're all set." Taking his cue from the audience, Parker made a shooing motion with both hands sending her on stage at the conclusion of the introduction.

Marala took a deep breath and headed for the stage from behind the heavy red velvet curtain, exhaling slowly. All of a sudden, she paused as though she'd forgotten something significant. In a smooth fleeting motion, she twirled around and blew her daughter a passionate kiss with both hands. Radiating with grace and a quiet confidence, she took to the center of the stage. In moments, she illuminated the auditorium with warm vibrations of truth and passion. The enthralled crowd listened with clear enthusiasm as her words encountered their soul. Marala remained careful to make certain the message she shared was conveyed in a way they'd easily remember. She wanted them to be familiar with intuition and discover how to trust their own.

"Hello everyone," she began in a welcoming tone. "Thank you for taking time out of your schedules to share this wonderful afternoon with me." Applause sounded throughout the auditorium. "Additionally, I'd like to thank this university for bringing me here to distribute this powerful message. I truly pray that it will impact your life in the extraordinary way mine has been." Again, applause roared across the room. "Okay are you ready?" she asked with a commanding yet, energetic tone.

The crowd shouted in an echoing unison, "Yes!"

"Are you sure?"

"Yes!" the crowd repeated eagerly.

"Well then—what I'm going to share with you, I can unconditionally guarantee it's going to change your life in one aspect or another, if you trust it. So, let's make this time together extraordinary," she shouted causing a thunderous applause. She took a few calculated paces across the wooden stage and continued with an evolving passion emanating from deep within her soul. "You know—" she began, before yielding in thought. "There's something we all have in common and it's something we make the choice to use or not to." Light laughter spread across the room. "No, no, no," she said, shaking her finger shamefully at them. "Not that," she teased. "This is not a sex education presentation." The crowd had a sudden outburst of uncontrolled laughter. "What I speak of is more powerful than what you may realize because it can protect you from—*you*," she said offering a smooth wave of her hands across the audience. "Since many of you are smiling, I'm going to do you a favor and save you from your own little embarrassing guesses and just tell you." Marala took a few more paces across the stage and paused after returning to the center; revealing with confidence, "It's your *intuition!*" Without hesitation, the audience passionately applauded and nodded in agreement as she continued. "I rely on mine as a first resource and this should be a vital part of your instinctive survival mechanism. *Intuition* is a direct perception of the truth or fact independent of any reasoning process. It's a quick, keen insight," she explained, snapping her finger one time into the microphone. "That insight can help you make a good choice over a bad one and it can save your life or that of someone else's. Most people call it their gut instinct. But I—*I* call it my God given intuition as it rises above reason and defies science. *Intuition* operates outside of conscious awareness and is a natural resource or gift, in itself. By the time this speech is over I want you to trust with conviction, that you have it, too." A soft approving moan evolved from the audience. "When I hear that voice inside of me say, *no*, I trust it. When I feel uneasy about something, I automatically understand. Should I meet someone and my intuition warns me something's not right—without hesitation, I leave the individual alone because I'm *not* a collector of trouble!"

Once again, the crowd let out a deafening uproar of laughter while Marala shared a brief series of her own. Her eyes shifted up towards her daughter sitting in the box and she smiled. Lyss nodded while returning an expression denoting approval. As Marala continued speaking, Lyss's eyes responsively scanned the room surveying the crowd for a dissertation she'd later write. Immediately, her attention was captured by a middle-aged woman in the third row sobbing into a white handkerchief, in what appeared to be an uncontrolled temperamental release. The redheaded woman behind her was busy taking notes; writing more than she glanced at Marala. In particular, she distinguished the ratio of men to women and studied the reactions of both. It was typical for her to focus on a handful of people in the audience to examine their expressions and reactions to what Marala communicated.

Out the corner of her eye she spotted a man, in his late fifties to early sixties with an even mixture of black and white hair, sitting fifteen rows back. He appeared to be studying Marala the way Lyss observed him. His posture was erect and he seemed totally immersed in what she way saying, as though he were a psychologist or professor at the university. Several rows behind him sat three young men each sitting between three women. They applauded and returned frequent nods while making approving gestures to one another. The crowd's enthusiasm escalated as Marala's message continued to strike at their core. It always did.

Lyss noted the audience's widespread approval of her mother, which made her smile broaden. As she picked up her bottle of water, she eyed a young man about six-foot-two, standing in the back of the room exhibiting an ardent demeanor visible by his movements. He was too far back for Lyss to capture the details of his face, but his head moved from the crowd to Marala, much like a reporter. Regardless, he seemed to be taking in her every word like everyone else.

The penetrating delivery of *Intuition* continued.

~~~~~~~~~~

Two

A few hours later, Marala was leaning against the sophisticated wrought iron balcony in her hotel suite overlooking the Pacific Ocean. The serene expression blanketing her face seldom disappeared. A wave of fresh ocean air drifted throughout the room, carelessly blowing the white sheers. A moment later a cell phone began ringing. Lyss answered it and after a few words, she pressed the mute button on the phone and walked out on the balcony wearing a vanilla colored, flowing t-shirt and a pair of comfortable, khaki linen pants.

"Mama, Mrs. Carson's on the phone. She'd like to know if you want to join them for dinner this evening. She has a few people she wants you to meet that have been raving about your speech."

Marala let out a deep sigh of disinterest and gave a fleeting look to Lyss before returning to the view across the glistening ocean. Lyss left the balcony and finished the phone conversation while Marala's eyes marveled at the largest ocean in the world. She loved the ocean. In fact, both of them did. The day had already been long and she knew when to draw the line between business and personal.

Lyss returned to the balcony and slipped her hand into her mothers, locking their fingers together.

"Why'd you decline dinner with Mrs. Carson? I thought you liked her?"

"Oh, I do," she replied truthfully. "But it's easy to get caught up working and forget what's really important. Look out there," she said nodding towards the stunning coastal view. "What do you see?"

"Only one of my favorite places," Lyss admitted revealing her flourishing excitement.

"Yes," Marala agreed, looking directly at Lyss. "And what I see is my beautiful daughter who works her butt off on all my speaking engagements. You've done a lot of work with me instead of enjoying your vacation the way most kid's do."

"I really don't mind at all."

"I know you don't. That's why I've decided, since you'll be returning to school soon, tonight we're going to enjoy one of *your* favorite places. Will dinner suffice? Afterwards, we can comb the beach for a few shells."

"Absolutely!"

"Okay, let's get out of here," she said, heading into the room.

Marala shut off her laptop and grabbed her phone.

"I think seashells are like a collection of art."

"And who's the artist?"

"It's God's creation and the artist is the ocean itself," Lyss explained.

Marala ran her fingers through Lyss's soft hair and replied, "Beautifully spoken," she agreed, with her eyes twinkling. "As you know, I love collecting shells but if that's a little too boring for you, perhaps we'll go sightseeing for gorgeous guys instead," she added playfully.

"Oh yeah! Let's go," Lyss replied, mixing her words with excitement and laughter. "I'm just teasing Mama. I love finding unique shells. I'll get a bag to put them in. Do you want me to grab your purse, too?"

"No, thanks. I can throw my stuff in yours and keep my hands free," she said while dropping her phone into Lyss's purse, "in case I need to keep any undesirable guys away from you. Just remember I said *sightseeing*."

Lyss continued laughing as she slipped on her brown leather sandals and then grabbed her matching purse before heading out.

"I'm sure we'll find exactly what we're looking for right on the beach."

Three

The subtle evening breeze enhanced the already superb ambiance. Marala and Lyss relaxed on the patio of a restaurant overlooking the ocean in Newport Beach. The breathtaking view displayed a reflection of vibrant colors melting into the ocean as the sun leisurely set.

Lyss reached for her mother's hand and blessed their meal. Lyss broke off a small piece of whole wheat bread, dragged it through the herb infused olive oil and slipped it into her mouth. Her eyes smiled while tracing the details of Marala's face as she began chewing.

Lyss's devotion to Marala while working on her Ph.D. was touching. During the summer months she traveled with her mother to assist with speaking engagements and maintained the experience was invaluable. Analyzing the responses to her mother's books captured her interest in learning more about her. The first book, a shocking memoir, *In Our House*, displayed the power of forgiveness. Her second book, *Surrounded By Inspiration* revealed how she fought to emancipate herself from her past using inspiration. The latest, *Intuition* turned into another spiritually arousing experience about trust in God. Lyss guaranteed readers would love it, even before the release. The book disclosed reasons and benefits for following your God given intuition. Marala trusts this to be the internal voice, which warns, advises and protects.

Lyss picked up a thin slice of lemon and with gentle pressure, squeezed the juice into her glass. After giving the glass a light swirl, she took a sip of water and said, "Mama, can I ask you a question?"

"Go ahead," Marala replied casually.

"This might sound odd but do you mind if we talk about something?"

"Why are you asking? We're here to spend quality time together, which I believe includes talking. Don't you?"

Lyss laughed and replied, "Yes, but I'd like to talk about you."

"Oh no! Are you bored or something?" she asked with her cheeks rising as the corners of her mouth lifted into a smile.

"No," she answered enthusiastically leaning in towards her mother. "I think you're fascinating. It's just that sometimes I don't take time to delve deeper into things I've seen or wanted to ask about you."

"What type of things can you possibly be intrigued with, in regards to me?" she asked laughing a little more. "My life's become—excuse the cliché, but literally, an open book. Anything you'd want to know is practically in there."

"You said practically, but not everything," she added shaking her finger at her mother.

"Is that so?"

"Yeah. I love what's shared in your books because it brings up things I remember happening."

"So now you want to ask me questions about *your* childhood?"

"Exactly."

"Go right ahead. You can ask whatever you want, but you'll never be able to fix me," she teased.

"I'm not trying to fix you because I love you the way you are. I want to learn more about my Mama and see if I'm becoming more like you."

"In what way? Or should I ask, relating to which book?" she questioned with her eyes narrowing suspiciously.

Lyss's childhood landed nowhere in the vicinity of Marala's first two books. However, *Intuition* would logically be where her curiosity fell.

"As a kid, I kind of sensed you had something unique about your character."

Marala released a slight laugh and replied, "I can't disagree with you."

"Quite honestly, I loved the way you were protective of me and definitive in your decisions."

"Are you serious?"

"Yeah."

"Interesting," Marala replied.

"Why?"

"An overprotective parent is something most children don't like having."

"Do you consider yourself overprotective?"

Beaming delightfully, Marala paused to reflected and said, "No."

"In light of some of the things I protected you from, I'd do it again. The choices were necessary. But I can understand if *you* think I was overprotective."

"That's my point. You weren't overprotective because you were simply resolute in your decisions. When you made one, you wouldn't reconsider."

"Not too often," Marala agreed. "In case you can't tell, you're the same way."

"I try to be."

"Okay, continue."

12

"When I was a teenager, I'll admit, I had a little difficulty with you being right about what seemed to be everything."

"I wasn't right about everything."

"Come on, Mama. Regardless of whom I dated, you knew if he was good for me or not, and long before I did."

"Okay. You've got me there. But that's just the way mother's are Lyss."

"No, it wasn't just that. You could tell as soon as you met them. You'd identify specifically what their problem would be *and* how to handle the situation. You read people with such precision."

"Don't be mistaken, I've made plenty of decisions based on my heart just the same as anyone else. Naturally when I was wrong, sometimes it hurt. Eventually, I learned to trust my intuition because it remained accurate and caused me less pain. I didn't know as much as you thought, but God did."

"I get it now. I'm disappointed because I didn't understand you until I matured. Not until then, did things begin to fall into place. You're very intuitive, Mama. I spent years trying to figure you out."

The server came to the table and sat two white plates in front of them. He placed a palatable seafood assortment on ice in the center and then asked, "May I get you ladies anything else?"

Marala deferred the question by nodding towards her daughter and said, "Lyss?"

"No, thank you. This looks great," she answered, while her eyes feasted on the delicious display.

The server gave a slight nod and walked away.

"I love this place," Marala stated with a refreshed sense of awareness.

"Yes, it's perfect," Lyss, agreed without hesitation, sharing the spectacular view.

"Just like you."

"Thanks, but I'm far from perfect Mama," she said, picking up a fresh forkful of crab. She lightly dipped the tip of the fork into a lemon butter sauce before eating it.

"To you perhaps, but you're perfect in my eyes, sweetheart. Perfection has the highest of standards and people have been taught to think it's not obtainable. I believe *perfect* means, more than enough. It's precisely the way *I* like it. God created everything—the ocean, sun, moon and you. So to say you're not perfect means *He* made a mistake or did something wrong. For some reason, *I* don't quite think that's the case."

"I get your point," Lyss conceded.

"How's the appetizer?"

"Oh, delicious," she replied, picking up an oyster and scooping the meat out of its shell on to a cracker topped with tangy cocktail sauce.

"Does it need anything else?"

Lyss placed it into her mouth and savored the delectable taste with every bite. After swallowing the appetizer she answered without reservation, "No. It's perfect."

Following the realization of what she said only a slight pause separated her from heartfelt laughter.

Marala reached for an oyster and said, "*And so are you.*"

"The emphasis that society puts on perfection is so tremendous. It's hard to believe something as insignificant as the taste of an oyster can be considered perfect. But when it comes to people, our critical valuations of them reinforce imperfection."

"Imperfection is good for business. It's important to love yourself before someone convinces you that you don't have enough of the right thing to love. That alone can shape you into seeking something that you'll never attain if you didn't believe you had it to begin with. Billions of dollars are spent each year from people trying to achieve perfection."

Lyss let out a long sigh, followed by a brief silence between them before she spoke, carefully weighing her words.

"Do you remember when I was about twelve and I asked you if I could take our dog, Domino, for a walk? You told me I could but after I hugged you and said *goodbye* you became alarmed."

"I remember," Marala conceded.

"Well, so do I. Because out of nowhere you suddenly changed your mind and didn't let me go."

"That time you didn't need to," she replied, delicately preparing her oyster the same as Lyss had done.

"And that's what I'm talking about. You changed your mind without further consideration and you were extremely calm about it."

"People change their mind all the time."

"Is that your justification? Really Mama? I understood there was more to the situation, but you maintained that you wanted me to stay with you."

"I did. I enjoyed having you with me. However, things felt a *little* different then," she said sliding the oyster into her mouth.

"I didn't understand why I couldn't go because we lived in a beautiful community and kids were always outside. Mama, you were absolutely convinced about having me stay home. To this day, I recall the expression on your face when I said *goodbye*. A light switch flipped on in your head and you saw or felt something happen. Am I right?"

"Yeah," she agreed, after taking a sip of her cranberry juice.

"Ironically, on the evening news, a man abducted a little girl around the same time I would've been out walking, Domino."

"Yes, however, you *didn't* go." Marala reminded, shrugging nonchalantly.

"No, you didn't *let* me go because you were protecting me. What if that was me? It could have been."

"It wasn't."

"What are the odds of that happening in our neighborhood? You stopped me from being at risk on that specific day and time."

"Sweetheart. I can't tell you because I don't gamble; I play it safe and follow my intuition. I've been this way for as long as I can remember and I'm not exactly sure how far back it goes. Sometimes I was aware of it and others, not so much. I had to learn to trust it and now, I do. Unwavering trust ascends from me."

"That much I know. As far as timing, I think it began when you were about ten or eleven and everything transpired with Grandma. Those women weren't who they claimed to be; it was strange the way you came to that conclusion."

"I don't think it's something I would have known but my God given intuition brought clarity to reality."

"I'd agree. You were convinced they were going to hurt your mother because you never stopped revealing things to your father."

"I wish he'd listened from the onset. Things would have been different."

"And I believe that. You knew something was seriously wrong, although you couldn't explain how or why it was happening."

"Honestly sweetheart, the situation was so inexplicable, I don't think anyone would've known what was happening. The *why* part is still a mystery."

"Maybe, but where I'm lacking comprehension is I thought your father would have contemplated something was wrong before you or anyone else. Frankly, as intelligent as Grandpa was, he should have been the one to figure everything out. Instead, you did. You discovered something was wrong with *his* wife. It doesn't make sense."

Marala shrugged.

"*I* wasn't right sweetheart, my *God given intuition* was. There's no explanation as to why I was able to sense deception and evil at such a young age. That's why I keep insisting that intuition rises above reason. It's not me."

Marala paused, lending her attention to the tranquility of the vast ocean as Lyss studied her mother's face. Her light brown hair was neatly pulled back into a shoulder length curly ponytail that would swing with the wind. Her colorless, diamond hoop earrings sparkled with brilliance from the light. A peaceful glow rested in her transparent brown eyes. Barely distinguishable chestnut freckles dotted both sides of her nose atop of her caramel complexion. No one could entirely decipher the components of her ethnic mixture, although the African American and Indian were detectable. The first noticeable feature about Marala was her peaceful smile rising from her soul. She hadn't always been this way but when her true evolution surfaced, her life changes allowed it to remain.

"I want to understand what it's like. I've always sought to identify with what you see or somehow sense. I've even prayed for God to let me be like you more often than you'd imagine."

"Really?" Marala asked, with an abrupt glimmer of bewilderment.

"Absolutely. Why are you surprised?"

"Sweetheart, how many times do I have to tell you? You're already like me and you've always been. Intuition's more about connecting to God than anything. In reality, it's something very personal to you and to everyone else."

"You're able to discern a lot about things in a way most people don't," Lyss said.

"To you perhaps. Don't forget to consider my age and experiences."

"I already have."

"Remember, we're not privy to what most people are knowledgeable of either."

Lyss conceded with an agreeable nod and added, "Sometimes I actually believe I'm connecting except I'm not certain if it's the same way you do."

"So you sense it's working?"

"Yes," she proclaimed with wide eyes, "I do."

"Okay. Well, then you have it. I want you and everyone who cares to listen to use what's saved me every time. Pay attention to your intuition because it'll warn you first and if you're in tune enough, it'll protect you or whomever you share the warning with, *if* they listen."

"I get that part but—"

"I'm not psychic. I don't mess with tarot cards or anything else. I'm connected to Gods communication and that's all. It's simple."

"Mama. Simple?"

"Sure."

"We share the same faith and beliefs," she stated, sounding slightly frustrated, "I should be consistent in following it by now if it were simple."

"You need to be consistent in trusting it first."

"How?"

"By understanding the distractions in this world can keep you from hearing Him. Everywhere you go you'll hear noise. Take into account; I'm speaking of both external and internal noise. We're never completely still in a mental or physical capacity. Even when we're asleep our minds are extraordinarily active. Noise can cause a lack of focus or concentration because your attention's divided. For example, when I listen to a cd for the first time, I like to close my eyes. I don't want to focus on anything but the music. I'm able to hear most, if not all, of the instruments and lyrics. It's easier and I enjoy the music more."

"I've seen you do that," she acknowledged. "Sometimes your eyes are closed when you're listening to someone speak. I thought you were trying to connect with the meaning of their words."

"It's the same way with my spirit when I'm praying. I don't focus on anything so I can receive God's message or hear things more distinctly. When I worry about things it contradicts my faith in God. Internal noise generally means I'm worrying about something."

"How do you stop worrying?"

"By praying for one thing in particular."

"What?"

"Peace—to let things go so I can have clarity to receive what I need."

"Yes, but how do you discern what you're hearing, Mama?"

"Intuition. Sometimes logic goes against what I want or think is best. Should I try to resist, I have this nagging tug forcing me to focus more intently."

"And you get a—"

"Firm yes or no; don't do this or do that. I know when I'm being warned because an inescapable sensation surrounds me. If I decide to disregard it; consequences will likely occur."

"Okay. I'm wondering how you know for sure if you would have had consequences or not?"

"I'm not the curious type to want to find out by being stubborn and going against it. The answer to your question's easy. How many times have you done something that went against what you initially felt and afterwards you said, I knew better? I should have followed my intuition. I should have listened to myself."

"Quite a bit."

"That's how. We all have lucid examples of what happens when we don't follow our intuition yet; we neglect to pay attention to it. People know what it is but they don't entirely understand what to do. Some are afraid and others—"

"Ignore what they don't comprehend. Better yet, they aren't acquainted with how to be consistent in following it either."

"So you *do* understand," Marala acknowledged affably.

"Your intuition is truly your guide. It's irrefutable that you pay attention to yours," she conceded with a smirk.

"Yes it is," Marala, admitted, grinning with pride.

"Over the years, you've warned me about numerous things. You'd tell me what not to do or places I shouldn't go on specific occasions and I didn't. Later on, I'd find out something unexpected happened. You never seemed to want me to find out the hard way."

"Why would I—you're my daughter."

"Like I said, at times I wanted you to be wrong."

"I know. What child *wants* their parent to be right about certain things when it opposes their choices? Not many. I hope you understand I never sought to be right, I only wanted you out of harm's way. If following my intuition helped accomplish that then evidently it worked for me. I'd rather have you upset with my decision but safe."

Lyss reached across the table and placed her mother's hand in hers.

"True, but it was difficult to grasp the constant accuracy of your insight. You didn't give me a standard explanation for things; you always provided details of what would happen. The few times I went against your advice, what you said would transpire, did. Oddly, exactly the way you described."

"What did you think?" she asked suggestively, trying to understand her daughter's perspective.

"I couldn't find any logical rationalization so it remained inconceivable."

"Because intuition—"

"I know. Is above reason."

"I don't have anything more than a quick keen insight."

"And?" Lyss asked, petitioning the balance of the recipe.

"Total trust in following it." Marala released Lyss's hand, picked up her glass and took a sip while reflecting on what her daughter said. She put the glass down and circled back to a previous statement. "My intuition *does* go back to my childhood. Without it, I wouldn't have survived what happened in our house. Besides, what's to say it wouldn't have gone on longer than it did? I exposed something that was anomalous," she said, exhaling heavily. "After what I went through, would you doubt your intuition if you were me?"

"Of course not."

"Alright then."

"I think it's fascinating how in tune you were at such an early age."

"So do I."

"Mama, you're the reason I listen to my intuition; at least I try to."

"Don't try. Commit to trusting it completely."

"If I learn to trust my intuition, I'd be able to save myself time," Lyss said, before tasting another forkful of fresh crab. "When you meet someone, what is it that tells you if you can trust them or not?"

"The first thing I do is look into their eyes and study them. The old saying that the eyes are the key to the soul is as accurate as you can get; trust me. Some people have beautiful eyes full of peace and tranquility. You can tell they're inherently content. Then, I've seen others that have dark eyes. I'm not talking about the color either. They're incredibly mysterious or threatening, which implies their soul is dark or concealing something. The people you want to avoid have eyes as dark as a midnight sky. Their behavior and words match their objectives."

"That's creepy."

"I'd say so. If you're not investing too deeply into a person's external appearance you can see the truth about them by paying attention to their interior and what they say versus what they do. That's what people need to look at because who they really are can't be contained; it cuts through. We choose to ignore the signs because we want what we want. We make conscious decisions to see exactly what we desire or even *need* to see. Warning signs about a person's true character are always present."

"And that's where our intuition comes into play. Listen," she said perceptively.

The song Warning Sign, by Coldplay was playing in the background. Marala smiled and continued, "Sweetheart, your intuition's working just fine."

Their time together was treasured and the conversations, meaningful. After dinner they took a lingering stroll along the beach, taking in the subtle breeze of ocean air in silence. Both collected pieces of art until the heavy clusters of twinkling stars appeared.

~~~~~~~~~~

Four

A few days later, Marala was home sitting comfortably on her sofa with a piping hot cup of Earl

Grey tea, returning emails. Her inbox was mostly full of comments about her books while several of them were questions on how to make personal life changes because of them. Regardless of who wrote her and what they asked or communicated, she replied to everyone, even if only to say, thank you.

Marala opened the next email from a woman that had been writing her since the release of, *In Our House*. The woman had been in an extremely brutal marriage. Marala inspired her to trust that she could rebuild her life into something healthy and beautiful that she'd be proud of. Not long after exchanging a dozen emails or so, the woman left her violent husband and continued to send Marala updates on her progress.

Marala,

I hope I'm not bothering you too much although I wanted to thank you for sharing your inspirational words with me. I wake up anxious to read them because they help shape my day. After reading your message I make it a point not to let people get to me and to stay positive. I've been thumbing through Intuition for the third time and I can't tell you how on point you are with your words. I enjoy quoting you and try to share your messages because intuition is powerful. I know you're busy but I wanted to say thanks, again. Is there any chance you're coming my way to speak? I would love to hear you talk about Intuition because yours definitely helps me. Have a blessed day!

Love,
Danielle

Marala took a sip of tea while staring at the screen thinking of what to say. She sat her cup down and began typing.

Beautiful Danielle,

Thank you for taking time to read the inspiration I post. I'm happy to hear it's beneficial to you because sometimes it serves as a reminder for me, as well. I won't be in your city anytime soon, but I will let you know when I am there or anywhere nearby, if just to have a fabulous lunch.

Have another extraordinary day. I'm sending you lots of hugs. Give your handsome little boy a big hug from me.

xoxo
Marala

She pressed send and then scrolled down to read the next email. It was from a man named Garrett that had been writing her for a few years.

Good Morning Beautiful,

I've been thinking about the advice you've given me concerning forgiveness along with everything else. For some reason, I wanted to thank you. The communications we've shared have changed my life in ways only God could imagine. I never thought I'd be able to move out of the negative state of mind I was in or forgive the person that subjected me to the pain induced life I suffered through. Admittedly, some days are still difficult, causing slight emotional setbacks, but they're nothing like before. At this point, I've gotten back on track with staying focused on my career and I'm progressing in a healthy manner.

On another note, I received the promotion I was telling you about in our last communication. I owe you Marala, because my outlook on life is now one it hasn't been for many years. It's finally positive. I realize I can't change the past but I can save the future from being negative. Your selfless ways of sharing your personal experiences have touched me greatly. I think of you often and love looking at your smile. Keep making a difference. Intuition has impacted me greatly. I appreciate you explaining the benefits of intuition as I'm learning to follow my own. I'd love to talk more about it with you soon.

Thinking of You Fondly,
Garrett

Marala's face flushed as she began tapping on her keyboard, lightheartedly.

Garrett,

I'm extremely pleased to hear you received the promotion. Congratulations! You deserve it. I have a huge smile on my face. I'm sorry for everything you've been through. Take time to embrace the changes you've made and accept you're far beyond your history. Be proud of who you really are as I'm incredibly proud of you. Share what you've learned and use it to protect or help others. We can discuss *Intuition* whenever you're ready.

Much Love,
Marala

Marala scrolled down to another email from someone she didn't recognize.

I hope your INTUITION is as good as you think!

There was no signature.

She pressed reply, smiled and typed two words.

It is. ;-)

She nodded approvingly and sent it. Marala deleted the email just as Lyss walked through the front door. After kissing her mother on the cheek, she tossed her purse on one end of the sofa and plopped down beside her.

"Returning emails again?"

"Yeah. It's become part of my daily routine these days."

"I'm impressed with the way you write everyone back."

"Yeah well, it's time consuming, but worth it. If someone reads my books or quotes, ask me a question, or writes to say hello that means they're thinking about me. It's important they know I appreciate it and care about them too."

"I don't know if I could write everyone back, but at least I'd try," Lyss admitted.

"You'd write them back because you're like me. So what are your plans today?" she asked, turning her attention from the laptop to her daughter. Her lovely brown eyes studied her mother as she spoke.

"You have a doctors appointment in forty-five minutes and you should already know I'm going with you."

"Lyss I'm—"

"I know. Glad I'm coming. I can tell something's going on with you and I want to make sure my Mama's okay. You don't think I can sense when you're keeping things from me?" she asked, raising one of her perfectly shaped eyebrows.

~~~~~~~~~

Five

Marala and Lyss walked into the neurosurgeon's beautifully decorated office and took a deep breath before signing her name on the clipboard resting on the receptionist desk. She reached in her purse and pulled out a yellow envelope. The receptionist hung up the phone and glanced at the neatly written name.

"Has any of your information changed, Ms. Scott?" she asked.

"No, it hasn't."

"Is your insurance still the same?"

"Yes, it is," Marala, replied kindly.

"And did you happen to bring your film?" Marala handed her the envelope. "Okay, great. You're all set. You can have a seat anywhere on the left and you'll be called back shortly."

"Thank you," Marala said, as she followed Lyss to a seat.

Lyss studied Marala's eyes before putting her arm around her mother's shoulder.

"How are you feeling?" she asked, with a trace of uneasiness spreading through her voice.

"I'm fine sweetheart."

"Do you want something to drink?"

"No thanks. I'm good."

"Are you having any pain or headaches?"

"Nope."

"Are you sure you're okay?"

"I hope you aren't going to be like this with your patients. You'll make them believe something's wrong with them for sure," she said jokingly.

"Mama, you know if they're coming to see me then something is," Lyss responded delicately before laughing with her mother.

Minutes later, a short, pleasant looking woman came out into the waiting area and called, "Ms. Scott!" Lyss sprung to her feet.

"Yes," Marala answered in an even tone," as she stood. She glanced over to find, Martha.

"The doctor is ready to see you. Follow me dear," Martha offered, leading them through the double glass doors.

Marala and Lyss followed closely behind her.

"Is this beautiful young lady your daughter, Lyss you told me about?"

"Absolutely," Marala said, proudly.

"Hi. It's nice to meet you," Lyss stated, politely extending her hand.

Martha paused and shook her hand before leading them into a very orderly examination room.

"Nice to meet you, too. I'm Martha."

"Thank you," she replied, wondering how often her mother had been there.

"Well dear," Martha began, after turning to face Marala, "Do you have any questions?"

"Not just yet, but I'm sure I will."

"And how have you been feeling?" Martha asked, tenderly rubbing Marala's right arm.

"Not too bad. I'm just a little anxious to get this over with."

Lyss cut her eyes at her mother, hosting a grand look of confusion.

"I understand. Make sure you ask him anything you want to know. You're in very good hands with Dr. Gesner."

"Thank you."

"Let me get your blood pressure, dear," she said, wrapping the black cuff around Marala's arm. She placed two fingers on Marala's radial artery and pumped the bulb, filling the cuff with air. After the cuff deflated she frowned and said, "I see why you're here."

"Same issue?"

Martha glanced at Lyss noting her concern and didn't reply verbally. Instead, she quickly nodded, *yes* while removing the cuff.

"Dr. Gesner was reading your film. He should be finished any moment."

"Okay, great."

"Well, I have to say, *In Our House* was really something. I could hardly put it down."

"You read it?" Marala asked.

Martha nodded and responded enthusiastically, "I sure did. I went online and read the reviews. They were all favorable so—I bought it."

"What chapter are you on?"

"Oh! I finished *In Our House* since the last time I saw you. Let's see, *Surrounded By Inspiration* and *Intuition* came in the mail yesterday. Can you believe I'm halfway through *Surrounded By Inspiration* already? The first few pages just pulled me into it and I kept reading to see what was going to happen next. I mean it pulled me right in."

"I hear that a lot. I hope it's a good thing."

"Oh, of course. I've already recommended your books."

"Wow, thank you. I appreciate you telling people about them."

She leaned over and squeezed Marala tightly.

"I know I've asked you before but I want to make sure. Are you allergic to any medicine?"

"Not that I know of."

"Has anything changed since you were last here in regards to pain or headaches?"

"Nope."

"Okay, dear, he'll be in shortly," she said, pulling the door closed behind her as she left the room muttering, "Talk to God and you'll know what to do with the surgery."

Lyss turned to face her mother and questioned with a controlled hint of disappointment, "You've been here before?"

"Uh-huh."

"Martha knows about your book and the two of you were talking as if you've been here a few times."

"I have been," she admitted nonchalantly.

"Why didn't you tell me?"

"Look how worried you are now."

"I thought this was your first visit."

"I know," she admitted, coyly. "I'm pretty good at not worrying you, huh?" she boasted.

"Mama, how long has this been a problem?"

"I've had issues for a while sweetheart. My blood pressure medicine isn't helping anymore and I think it's time to face reality."

Lyss stared at her mother with her mouth agape and her eyes deadlocked. She couldn't believe she didn't know what had been going on with her. Marala always said there were warning signs but Lyss couldn't see them because she was away at school. Guilt swarmed through her lean body.

The doorknob began making a slow turn. Lyss quickly tried to regroup when it swung open. A distinguished looking doctor about five-foot-eleven, with a smooth baldhead, in his mid-forties entered the room and firmly shook Marala's hand followed by Lyss's.

He cocked his head to the side and narrowed his eyes, analyzing her disposition.

"How are you?" he asked sternly.

Although it was a routine question, his sincerity was well received.

"I'm good," she offered, hesitantly. "Thank you."

He took in a deliberate and slow breath, exhaling even slower.

"I reviewed your film and your aneurysms have grown *significantly*. Did they share the film with you at the time of the angiography?"

"Yes."

"So you're aware of what we're dealing with?"

"Pretty much," she admitted, trying to avoid Lyss's gasp.

"Because of the size and location, I'd recommend surgery," he said flatly.

Marala bit down on her bottom lip before letting out a sigh and then replied, "Dr. Atwater told me you probably would. When?" Marala questioned, making an unsuccessful attempt to maintain her composure.

"I'd say immediately," he replied. "Did Dr. Atwater explain the problem with the aneurysms and why surgery is necessary?"

"Yes. He was extremely thorough."

Lyss squeezed Marala's hand to gain her attention.

"You were aware of this, Mama?"

"Please sweetheart, let him finish," Marala requested, rubbing Lyss's leg to quiet her.

Dr. Gesner yielded in thought to Lyss's uncomfortable demeanor before elaborating further. Since it was his first time meeting her, he was trying to be careful with his words.

"You're already aware they can't be stented or coiled, correct?"

"Yes."

"What I can do is clip the aneurysms."

"Are you sure you can fix them?"

"I never give a guarantee when it comes to this type of surgery but, yes, I'm confident I can. The one in the cavernous area behind your eye, I'm going to *attempt* to clip. It may not be possible but *I am* going to try."

"Just for the record," Marala confessed, "I've seen several neurosurgeons and none of them would touch my aneurysms. The size and location, in addition to being in my speech and memory area isn't a good thing I guess," she said with a trace of sadness.

He shrugged apathetically and with poise replied, "They're not me."

A smile returned to Marala's face as her eyes darted up at him.

"How long will the surgery be?"

"Three to four hours, without complications."

"Will I be awake?"

"No."

"Are there any risks?"

"Yes. Brain surgery is quite serious. You do have hypertension. Although it's hereditary your blood pressure is a negative. Other than that you're in good health, which helps your odds. But when going into a delicate area such as the brain, you're at risk for things such as a stroke, heart attack, brain damage, memory loss—"

"Would you have this surgery if it were you?" Marala asked, interrupting his list of risks.

"I would have already had it. The risk of having surgery and surviving are greater than not having it and surviving."

"Okay so, you're recommending I have the surgery soon."

"Correct," he stated resolutely.

"As in a few months," Marala asked in jest.

"No, as in immediately," he replied with a stern grin.

"Seriously?" Marala questioned.

He nodded.

"Okay well, I have to think about it and digest all this before I make a decision. Is it alright if I call you when I decide?"

"Of course. It's important you're comfortable with your decision." He reached into the left pocket of his white jacket and handed Marala a card. "Here's my number in case you have any questions or further concerns you may want to discuss. Martha's number is on there as well. You can call her to schedule the surgery at any time."

Marala slipped the card into her purse and draped it over her shoulder preparing to leave.

"Thank you," she said standing.

"If you don't mind, before you go, I'd like to explain the entire procedure so you understand what will happen. We need to discuss the risk before you make your decision final. Okay?"

Marala glanced at Lyss and without saying a word, sat back down.

Dr. Gesner covered all of the details before they left his office. The drive home was quiet. Lyss drove with red, watery eyes while Marala closed her eyes and prayed. As soon as Marala finished consulting with God, without hesitation she pulled out Dr. Gesner's card along with her phone. When Martha answered, she scheduled the appointment to be done five days later.

Lyss gently bit down on her bottom lip and turned the corner at a slower pace than usual. A few seconds later, in a soft, firm tone she asked, "Do you mind if I research other neurosurgeons so we can get another opinion?"

"Intuitively, I knew something was wrong and I've seen several neurosurgeons. For months, no one could find anything abnormal, but that feeling wouldn't subside. In fact, it grew stronger. Finally, I was referred to Dr. Gesner and he found the aneurysms. I've had other opinions since then, except they *wouldn't* do the surgery."

"Are you comfortable with Dr. Gesner? I thought he was extremely professional but a bit unemotional."

"Which is good. I wouldn't want an emotional neurosurgeon working on my brain. I've done a lot of research on him and he's one of the best. I trust him."

"Are you sure you want to do this so soon?" Lyss questioned delicately. "Don't you want *the best*?"

"I already have Him. God is and He just told me to *get it done*."

~~~~~~~~~~

Six

Four days later, Marala observed her reflection in her bathroom mirror. She leaned in closer and looked deep into her eyes and whispered, "You'll be fine." Seconds later, she picked up a sharp pair of scissors, grabbed a handful of her hair and randomly cut chunks of it, tossing it into the small wastebasket. When it was short enough, she opened the new package of clippers she purchased earlier that day and began cutting the rest off. She remained unflustered. After her hair was cut as low as she could get it, she filled the basin with warm water and then lathered her head with shaving cream. She picked up her razor, dipped it in water and took short even strokes to shave her head completely clean. When she was done, Marala turned her head from side to side and admired her work in the mirror.

"Okay, I'm ready, Father," she mumbled, before gliding her hand across her smooth baldhead. *"I'm ready because I trust you."*

After a long hot shower, Marala climbed into her comfortable bed and closed her eyes to pray. A single teardrop rolled down her cheek and onto her pillow. As her spirit submitted to her prayers, she grew calmer. The night was quiet and Marala peacefully surrendered to the calling of sleep.

The next morning at five-thirty, Lyss was dressed and nervously waiting to take her mother to the hospital. The constant pitter-patter of rain fell against the SUV and loud crashes of thunder refused to yield to a serene day. Marala and Lyss had brief bouts of barely audible conversations regarding surgery and recovery on the drive over. Lyss's failed attempt to be unobtrusive while asking questions was paired with her apprehensive tone.

"Why didn't you tell anyone about the surgery? You must know there are a lot of people who love you. They'd want to be here. The way you worry about others is how they'd worry about you."

"The way I see it is why should I allow people to worry over nothing? There's enough worrying about things we can't control already."

"This isn't *nothing*," Lyss snapped, sounding irritated by Marala's dismissiveness.

"Sure it is sweetheart. God told me I'd be fine. So why should I get anyone upset and crying if I'm going to be better than I am now after the surgery? It doesn't make sense to me. Besides, you know how private I am."

"What about your family, shouldn't they be told? Or at least your agent."

"I told Adam. He's already there," Marala said, flashing a brilliant smile.

Marala noticed Lyss's mood beginning to descend so she returned the conversation to a discussion about her business matters. She explained what she needed Lyss to handle while she recuperated.

"There's really going to be a lot of follow-up on things. You'll be so busy you won't have time to do much else."

"I'll be fine, Mama. Did you write down everyone you want me to communicate with and the dates I should reschedule on your upcoming tour?"

"I did. I placed the list next to my laptop in my office."

Marala reached in her purse and pulled out a tissue.

"Then, don't worry. I can handle everything. I know your passwords."

Marala leaned over with the tissue and lightly dabbed the tears escaping from her daughter's eyes.

"If you have time, can you keep up with my emails, too?"

"I already planned on it. I've got this."

"Don't forget to write everyone back and continue to post my daily inspirational messages."

Lyss nodded, affirmatively and then said in a shaky voice, "I can't write inspirational messages the—"

"Sure you can, sweetheart. Besides, I made it easy for you. I've given you enough to post for the next several weeks and you can respond to my emails the way you think I would. Better yet, respond however *you* think is best. Read their previous conversations so you have an idea of what we were discussing."

A few minutes later, Lyss pulled into the hospital garage and parked. She pulled the key out of the ignition no longer struggling to fight back her tears.

"Mama?"

"Yes, sweetheart?"

"You're the best mother anyone could have and I *really* mean it. You've taught me so much and you've always been here for me."

Marala reached for Lyss's hand and replied, "You're the best daughter any mother could *ever* have and I *really* mean it. You've done the same and more. After surgery, I'll still be here for you."

Lyss nodded, as though she wanted to say something but couldn't get it out.

"I'm not going anywhere yet, so stop acting like I am. Let's get this done so my hair can start growing back," Marala teased. "I love you sweetheart. I'll be fine."

There was a brief silence with an unspoken dialogue between them.

"You know how much I love you, right?"

"Of course I do. I need you to understand that *I am not* afraid and there's absolutely no reason for you to be," she said, getting out of the car. "I promise, because *He promised*," Marala insisted, pointing up with a sincere smile.

Alyssa grabbed the suitcase out the back seat and tightly held her mother's hand as they walked inside the hospital. Marala had an elegant black scarf draped over her baldhead and wrapped stylishly around her neck. They approached the registration desk and signed in for her surgery. As she finished, a handsome, well-toned, medium-brown skinned man walked up behind them. He was five-foot-ten and had gentle brown eyes. It was her agent, Adam.

"Hey Lyss," he said kissing her on the cheek. "How's my Goddaughter doing?"

"Hi Adam," she replied, still sounding somber. "You beat us here. Thank you for coming. I know Mama's always happy to see you," she told him, while wrapping her arms around him.

"No problem baby girl. I'm just glad she told me," he said with a light chuckle. "You know how private she is. It's hard to get anything out of your mom if she thinks it'll worry someone."

Lyss forced a weak smile and partial laugh. Her concern for her mother wouldn't subside.

Adam was always upbeat and joking around. He went through so much as a kid that as an adult, he found no other recourse than to let things roll off his back. He had a good heart and fought to make a difference in the lives of others by working with Marala. Creating a strong platform for Marala to share her story was one of the things he did best. Adam often said he felt Marala was sharing a part of his story too.

"It's about time you took care of yourself. We need you," he said to Marala. "How are you feeling? You okay?" he asked, massaging her shoulders.

"Yeah. I'm ready to get this over with," she said observing the large, open waiting area full of bright colors and mixed patterns on the furniture.

Lyss sat next to her mother and Adam was seated on the other side of Marala. He wore dark blue suit with a crisp white dress shirt. His typical business face didn't work with Marala. Adam was always transparent to her and this time even he was worried.

"I know what you mean. Look, if anyone can make it through this surgery and come out just fine, it's you," he said, trying to conceal his concern. "You're a tough lady," he admitted, hugging Marala firmly followed by a peck on the cheek. "You've always been."

"Thanks Adam. I've had these aneurysms for six years and I've exhausted my credit with God so—"

"So you'll be fine," he affirmed, confidently.

"I know. I'm not worried about surgery. I don't like seeing my daughter this upset," she whispered.

Lyss listened to their conversation with red puffy eyes. She kept turning her head and wiping her tears as if no one could see her crying.

"She'll be fine. I'll see to it," Adam assured Marala convincingly.

"She tries to hide it, but this is tearing her up. She's more worried than anyone would be able to tell, but she forgets how well I know her."

"I can tell. She's crying," he said with light laughter. "All joking aside, I'll keep her occupied talking a little business so she's not thinking about the surgery. Before you know it, it'll be over."

"I appreciate you being here."

"I wanted to be here. Nothing's going to happen. I promise. God won't let anything happen to you."

41

"I know. He told me."

"Mama, I'm sorry I'm upset, but I'm always going to worry about you."

"I understand sweetheart. I need you to be okay because worry doesn't accomplish anything. It detracts from your faith. I have to get this done so we can get back to our life. We have a lot more to do together. Everyone has choices and right now mine is between life and death. I choose life so I'm getting this out the way before it's too late and death chooses me."

"I get it, Mama. I do," Lyss said, choking up. "It just hurts to watch you go through this."

Marala wiped Lyss's eyes and kissed her on the cheek again. "Well, when I get home, I'll be able to have you spoil me while I rest. Don't worry."

"I'm sorry, Mama," she cried, "Who wants to see their mother go through something like this? I don't want anything to happen to you."

"And it won't. I might look a little strange when this is over but, hey."

"Mama, don't joke."

"It's true," Marala said, laughing.

"As always, you look beautiful," Adam interjected, trying to change the subject.

Lyss nodded, still unable to hide her uneasiness and said, "Adam's right, Mama. You are beautiful and you'll be the same when this is over."

"You might want to hold that thought," she confessed, eyeing Adam, "You haven't seen my head. It's bald."

"Come on. Nothings changed. Its just hair; you're still beautiful. I'm bald," he said rubbing his hand across his head. "Yours will grow back, but mine won't."

Marala smiled, "It's more important for people to see inside me. As for adversity, it'll only make me stronger and wiser."

Approaching the waiting area was a tall and very large gentleman in green hospital scrubs with a clipboard in his hands. He glanced around and yelled, "Scott!"

Marala stood up along with Lyss and Adam. He moved closer towards her.

"Yes," Marala answered proudly as if she'd won a prize.

"Marala Scott?"

"Yes, sir."

"Can you verify this information?" he asked, displaying the form on his clipboard.

"Everything's correct," she replied.

"Okay Ms. Scott, I'm going to take you upstairs to prep for surgery. They'll start your IV, the anesthesiologist will talk with you and Dr. Gesner will be in to see you."

Marala hugged Adam and kissed him on his cheek. He hugged her tightly and said, "I'll be right here when you wake up. I love you."

"I know. I love you too. I knew you'd be here." Adam smiled. The initial worry that was in his eyes had slowly dissipated. Marala took Lyss in both arms and said, "I promise, I'll be fine. Actually, I'll be better when this is over." Lyss's tears fell liberally, "Stop crying or you'll make me cry. I know you don't want to do that."

"I love you Mama."

"I love you too baby girl. I'll see you in a few hours. I promise. Have faith!"

"Okay, Ms. Scott, time to head upstairs," the man in the scrubs, insisted politely.

Marala shouted as she walked away, "I'm ready to rock 'n' roll! Let's get this over with!"

She whipped off the black scarf and sat in the wheelchair exposing her baldhead with a gigantic smile. He wheeled her over to the elevator, pushed the button and she was gone.

~~~~~~~~~~

Seven

The waiting room was unusually quiet. It was like walking into a library with only a few quiet whispers drifting through the morbid air. Everyone in the room seemed tired or worried. Some sat holding their beaded rosary while others gripped the crucifix hanging around their neck or clutched their faith filled hands together in prayer. There were people in intimate gatherings conversing nervously over coffee, as others paced the floor sharing updates over the phone. A few bibles rested on the laps of relatives or friends of those in surgery. The streams of water flowing into the fountain several feet away in the lobby could still be heard. That's where pennies were tossed for a wish.

Each passing hour seemed like a week as Lyss sat waiting impatiently to hear if the craniotomy was successful. The thought of her mother's head being cut open and screwed back together remained unsettling.

Four hours later, Dr. Gesner solemnly entered the waiting room. Lyss apprehensively stood, gripping her stomach tightly as he approached her with slow movements.

He clasped his hands together, took a deep breath and stated routinely, "The left pterional craniotomy and clipping of the left posterior aneurysms were successful. Your mother's going to need a lot of rest but you can see her when she wakes up. She's tough. She did well."

Lyss's clammy hands went into prayer position as her joyful tears dropped silently to the heavily waxed floor. "Thank you," she told him.

Adam extended his hand and shook Dr. Gesner's, "I was positive she'd make it through just fine. Her entire life has been about faith and she's literally living proof that having it works." Adam turned to Lyss and said, "When your Mama believes, you can believe too. Your mother has faith because she recognizes His miracles."

~~~~~~~~~~

Eight

A week later, Marala was at home recovering from surgery. While she was asleep, Lyss sat quietly in a comfortable right arm chaise, next to her mother. She worked on her iPad rescheduling engagements and returning emails. Until now, she hadn't fully realized how much time it took writing everyone back. Once she began reading some of the accounts of what people were sharing with her mother, she understood. Many of them simply wanted to thank Marala for her inspiration while others sought to keep learning more from her while disclosing extremely personal issues.

Lyss rubbed her sleepy eyes and then clicked on the next email. She settled back in her chaise and took a deep breath after reading it. It was clear her mother had been giving more of herself to these people than anyone could have considered. They viewed her as a friend and even family. Some of them had been following and writing her for the past five years or longer and many of them made strategic changes in their life to improve it because of her steady encouragement. There were several significant and loving bonds communicated in her emails.

A woman named Caroline wrote her faithfully every few months. She had been in an abusive relationship but was able to break free and start over with her two young children. Marala's mentoring pulled Caroline through some dark hours. An overview of the accurate yet, eerie intuition of Marala's was spread throughout their exchange of emails. Marala cautioned her of things that would happen if she didn't make crucial modifications to protect herself and children. At first, Caroline seemed to dismiss the fervent advice, according to Marala's intuition, but over a period of months her situation grew worse. Month's later she humbly returned to Marala, sharing additional abusive accounts, requesting more encouragement and guidance. The only advice Caroline received were the exact faith filled words originally given, steering her to God. Until she took the advice, Marala made it clear that she couldn't help her any further. She knew Caroline was waiting for a solution that was more favorable and one she could accept more readily. Instead, Marala took care in explaining that change for the better wasn't always something convenient or easy to do.

Shortly after that communication, Caroline decided she had enough of her isolated and abusive life. In a heartfelt dialogue with Marala she chronicled her departure from her situation. Finally, Caroline was able to return to a peaceful state by stepping into the arms of God's love, grace and mercy instead of the arms of a vile abuser. Lyss was moved by her powerful and tearful journey.

Caroline's current communication was providing a brief update intertwined with several heartfelt words of appreciation. She wanted to know if she could visit, Marala.

Lyss, pressed reply and mumbled, while glancing up at her mother, "What would you say?"

In a low, faint tone, Marala questioned, "To whom?"

Sounding surprised, she replied, "I thought you were asleep?"

"I was," Marala mumbled.

Lyss sat the iPad on the table beside her and helped shift her mother to a comfortable position. Marala released a series of brief moans from the awkward movement.

"How are you feeling?"

"Lethargic. I wish I could turn over on my side to sleep but I can't with all these staples in my head," she said, wincing sorely.

Lyss observed apologetically knowing there was nothing else she could do to ease her mother's pain. Each time her mother groaned or moved painfully, Lyss responded with her own internal discomfiture.

"I'm reading and replying to some of your emails. This one is from Caroline, the woman—"

"From Richmond?"

"Yes."

"She ah—finally left her husband," Marala uttered sluggishly.

"How'd you remember?"

"They didn't take my brain out," she teased. "They just fixed it. I have regulars on there, but only one Caroline. She writes me often, so I figured it was her."

"Did you know she wants to visit you?" Lyss asked perking up with curiosity.

"There are a few that ask to meet at some point."

"That's pretty neat."

"Yeah. I think it is too."

"What should I tell her?" she asked, picking up her iPad and positioning her fingers on the keyboard.

"Tell her I'm a bit tied or rather stapled up for awhile, but to stay focused, positive and prayerful. Just inform her that she does visit every time she writes."

Lyss released a soft giggle as she typed in her mother's reply, omitting the stapled up comment.

"Anything else?"

"Is there supposed to be?" she asked sounding worried, as though her memory had failed her.

"I don't think so."

"Well then, no, not today. Thank you sweetheart."

"Hmm. What's this, Mama?" she asked deliciously. "There's a message from a guy named, Garrett."

"Really?"

"Yeah. I've noticed he's in here quite a bit and—"

"And nothing," she sighed unable to smile. The staples caused pain at the slightest movement. She was careful with her words when speaking.

"You sure have a lot of guys that write."

"The majority of them write after reading one of my books. They usually start with the first one and get to know me from there."

"That's interesting. It's been my experience that men don't open up that easy, but to my Mama they do," she tittered.

"Once they know you're going to be a doctor, they expect you to analyze them."

"Surprisingly, they ask pretty straightforward questions."

"What about?"

"Forgiveness, intuition or my inspirational messages."

"Garret writes you the most."

"You think so?"

"I know so," she said with a grin. "What's his story?"

"What makes you think he has one?"

"Because they all do. That's why they write you."

"Honestly, it's sad, but Garrett's been through a lot."

"How so?"

"Well, society thinks it's predominantly women who suffer through abuse and violence, which is true, but there are scores of men that have and continue to endure abusive situations. Think about all the little boys that suffer from some form of abuse."

"Yeah."

"Well, they grow up and become men. And their stories are rarely heard until tragedy strikes them or someone else at their hands. Unfortunately for Garrett, he's experienced more than even I could've imagined."

"Is he still dealing with it?"

"No. I mean, kind of. It happened during his childhood but he hadn't dealt with the issues until a few years ago."

"When he met you."

"No. Some of the people I communicate with come to hear me speak but the majority of them, like Garrett, I've never met. More than likely, I won't meet most of them either."

"That's sad. Why not?"

"They live all over the place including other parts of the world."

"Where's Garrett?"

"I think he lives in New York. Well—" she began, sounding unsure, "I guess I forgot."

"That's okay, Mama. How did you get to know him?"

"Someone sent him a copy of *In Our House*. When he read it, he was reminded of his childhood. He found me online and we've been writing one another ever since."

"I think it's shocking that anyone has similarities to your childhood," Lyss conceded, as she turned away from her mother.

One of the reasons Lyss chose to become a psychologist was to have better comprehension of her mother. Marala's natural insight and strength to overcome the childhood horror she suffered through was perplexing. Although Lyss knew about her mother's childhood, she couldn't imagine the hatred and horror paired with it.

"So do I. In reality there's a lot more people that have similarities than those who don't," Marala mumbled groggily.

"It may seem hard to believe but I agree. You have numerous layers to your life and people will identify with one of them for some reason or another. It might be as simple as having a friend or family member that's experienced some semblance to what you have. At some point in their life, everyone has to make the choice to forgive. Whether or not they do is another story."

"When Garrett understood I was able to forgive my father and move on with my life, I think it made him curious."

"In what way?" Lyss queried.

"He was able to understand exactly what was keeping him in a place of anger and pain. He needs to forgive the person that hurt him so he can get his life back on track. I don't think he has yet but–"

"Back on track? What happened?" she asked, sounding intrigued by his history.

"Oh, sweetheart, it's a long story. Read the exchanges, it'll help you understand what he's been through, at least in part anyway. From what I've gathered, Garrett's extremely intelligent. You'll like reading about him. The—the people who write me—most of them have tragic accounts. They share them with me because they know I empathize with how they feel or what they're going through emotionally. Others simply want inspiration, advice or to discuss one of my books."

"Yes, I see. I've found that you actually give prudent information based on your opinion or personal experiences."

"Thank you."

"And I like your disclaimer."

"Huh? What disclaimer?" Marala asked with her eyebrows painfully arching together.

"When you respond to someone's issue or problem you make sure they're aware you're *not* a psychologist."

"Yeah. Well—I'm not and I want people to be clear about it. I'm leaving that job for you and the professionals. I don't try—nor do I desire to get into their head or tell them what to do. I basically share my own experiences, which are detailed in my books. I share what worked for me and offer my perspective, if they ask. To be cautious, I typically advise someone with a problem to seek out a psychologist or therapist to talk with."

"I like it. I think it's fascinating that you have people writing about such personal issues and more importantly, they want help," Lyss said.

"I agree."

"And you have a plethora of potential clients right here," Lyss suggested, tapping her iPad in jest.

"It's heartbreaking to communicate with people that are going through so much. Several of them really don't have anyone to talk with about it. And not everyone can afford a psychologist nor do they trust one enough to talk to either," Marala explained.

"Trust is important and unfortunately, it's hard to come by."

"I've asked if I can write about their situations on my blog to encourage others. Most of them are okay with it and if not, I simply delete their emails to avoid breaching their trust."

"I know you're big on confidentiality."

"Absolutely. I wouldn't allow you to read their emails otherwise."

"I know Mama."

"If they're seeking to make a difference in anything, I tell them to begin with the truth about everything. The truth brings clarity and revelation to some things they may not be ready or willing to accept; but need to. This is where people stand face-to-face with how they'll shape their future."

"Once they look at things from a well-defined and honest perspective, they're prepared to make the choice to see reality."

"A lot begins right there."

"It's good you're so available for them. I can tell you're making a difference."

"I'm trying, sweetheart," she said, reaching to loosen the silk scarf wrapped around her head. "What did—um, Garrett have to say?"

Lyss opened Garrett's email.

Good Morning Beautiful,

I heard you've canceled some of your upcoming speaking engagements. A friend of mine read your new book and was planning to see you speak in South Carolina. She let me know it was postponed. Is everything okay with you? Now you have me worried!

Fondly,
Garrett

After reading it, Lyss clicked on his profile picture and smiled. Her escalating interest led her to click on his photos to see the rest of him. Garrett had dirty blonde hair. His eyes were a brilliant blue and his smile was as sexy as a man's could get. His tanned body was chiseled to perfection exuding good health and confidence.

"Oh, Mama. This man is really handsome."

"Yeah, I'll give him that. Some of those guys are," she agreed, sounding indifferent.

"Have any of them ever asked you out, such as, *Garrett*?" she asked, with a giggle.

"Sometimes they do."

"He called you *beautiful* and said he's worried about you as though you guys have a *close* relationship."

"He probably says that to most women. That's why I keep a definitive line drawn so they all know I'm not interested or available."

"Too bad, Mama. He's nothing less than completely gorgeous. I could pick him out of a crowd easily. You don't forget a face like his."

"Remember sweetheart, I indicated, Garrett's making a transition through a few challenging issues. Don't get too caught up on that desirable exterior of his, the interior still needs work."

"So you're serious about that?"

"Yes, very."

"Well I wouldn't care," she teased, still looking through his pictures.

"Actually, I think you would."

"Aww," Lyss pouted, sighing heavily in disappointment.

"It's a little odd that he's worried about me. I deliberately go out of my way to try and keep my communications focused on what's going on with him, not me."

"Since he's clearly focused on you, how do you want me to respond?"

"Tell him I'm fine, but I had a little more on my plate than I could handle for now.

Thank him for me," Marala said, closing her weary eyes.

"Anything else?"

"I need some rest. Use your judgment. You can say whatever you want to him," she responded feebly, with her words trailing off, "as long as it's inspirational and compassionate."

"Remember you said that."

Marala's head shifted to the right side as she involuntarily drifted to sleep. Curiosity was already tugging at Lyss. She wanted to know more about the type of people that wrote her mother and their thought-provoking situations.

Later in the evening, Lyss decided to curl up with a cup of tea and read Marala's emails—starting with Garrett's. If she were going to respond appropriately to these people she needed to be aware of the initial conversations and how they developed. Every one of them had a reason they communicated with her mother and her interest had peeked into the cavernous realm of finding out why.

The next morning, with slow movements Marala went into the kitchen and put on a kettle of water for tea. Afterwards with careful steps, she made her way into the family room to turn on the news. She found Lyss leisurely stretched out on the sofa with her iPad on her lap, tapping away."

"Late night?"

Lyss adjusted her beige Tiffany glasses and finished typing her sentence before moving the iPad aside.

"Good morning, Mama. I didn't know you were up already," she said, cheerfully. "What do you need?"

she asked, covering her mouth before letting out a long yawn. She stood up, stretching out her arms before cracking her back and then neck from side-to-side.

"I don't *need* anything, but I *wanted* a cup of tea, which I'm quite capable of getting myself," she answered proudly.

Lyss smiled and said, "Sit down, I'll get it."

It looked doubtful that Marala could manage the small task on her own yet.

"Thank you, sweetheart."

"How are you feeling?" Lyss asked, carefully planting a kiss on her mother's cheek.

Marala grabbed hold of Lyss's arm and used it as support to lower herself onto the sofa.

Her words were slow and calculated when she replied, "It may sound improbable at this stage, but I'm feeling much better."

"I'm glad, Mama."

"My head still aches at times, but um—Dr. Gesner told me I'd feel it for a while."

"I'm really sorry."

"I'll get used to it. The fact that the surgery was successful is worth this. I'm still here," she confessed, trembling lightly as she coddled the left side of her head. "Have you been up all night?"

"Almost," Lyss replied. She lifted her glasses and rubbed her eyes sluggishly like a little kid.

"Why?"

"I started reading your emails," she stated.

"I seemed to have gotten pulled into them like a good book. I've already responded to several people."

"You don't waste time," she answered, sounding surprised Lyss had indulged so quickly.

"Not really. I think the communications are pretty interesting. The aspect I find abnormal is when they ask a question. It appears that regardless of what your response or opinion is, they work with it."

"Yes, but I don't tell them what they should do. I explain what worked for me. Why do you find that abnormal?"

"Because they've never met you and the things they're asking about, some of them are personal."

"People read self-help books, never having met the person who wrote it and they attempt to do what's instructed or suggested. There's not much of a difference really. If people want help, they have to share the truth," she began. Her sluggish words gradually faded in and out, "Communicating something painful or embarrassing is easier to do with a stranger than it would be to you as a psychologist."

"Why do you believe that is?"

"Because there's no authentic degree of embarrassment. They know in communicating with me, whether or not they think I'll judge them, doesn't really matter."

"Why not?"

"If they don't like what I have to say, they can delete or block me. They'd never have to talk with me again. The likelihood that I'd recognize many of them if I passed them on the street is slim anyways."

"They definitely attempt to accomplish the things you propose with an inimitable commitment."

Marala let out a weak groan and replied, "Yeah, well some of them do."

"Surprisingly, quite a few of them have. I've been reading these messages all night and what I've deducted is people aren't in the least bit reluctant to confide in you about their private matters. I don't know if I'd share that kind of information through an email with someone I'd never met. But these people share personal things, which some of them admit, they've never told anyone about. They really trust you," she stated with conviction. "Why?"

Marala took in a measured breath and then released it before replying, "My first book was where I bared the truth that's been hiding in *my* soul. If they wanted to know more about me they had to accept or identify with what I went through before they could trust me. In some way or another, because of my experiences, they're better able to connect with certain layers of my life. After they've read my reality they associate it to something that's happened in theirs. It's like they say, okay—she told me her secrets so I'm comfortable entrusting her with mine. Once they realized how much I had to overcome, they want to rip me apart to find out where the strength came from that got me to where I am now. And—"

"That process helps them."

"You've got it."

"From what I'm reading, you explain the same thing you've always told me."

"Correct," she conceded, proudly. "It comes from, God."

"After everything you went through and the powerful way you revealed it in your memoir, I'd want to learn how you got past everything and turned out to be as strong as you are, too. Who wouldn't? I'm doing it now."

The teakettle began to belt out a piercing whistle.

"What kind of tea would you like?" Lyss asked, heading for the kitchen.

"I'll have a cup of—Oh, the usual," she said, forgetting what type she drank. "Thank you love."

Marala picked up the iPad and noticed Lyss was still in her emails. She clicked on her inbox and scrolled through the names and then clicked on Sabrina's.

> Hi Marala!
>
> I read your status today and believe you put it up for me. Thank you! I have to repost it because you know where I am in my life and once again you posted what I needed to hear to make it through the day. I appreciate your inspirational words more than you know. I bought Intuition on the way home today. I'm so excited to be digging into this one. Talk to you soon. By the way, you forgot to put my hearts on the end of your last message. <3
>
> Love you lots,
> Sabrina xoxo

Marala clicked on Sabrina's profile page and read the reposted status message.

> Everyone you love isn't going to love you back, so don't expect you will and can make someone love you. You already have the greatest love from God, which is more than enough. Celebrate being who you are by loving and protecting yourself. You're stronger than you know.
> -Marala Scott

A few minutes later, Lyss entered the room carrying a wooden, decorative tray with a steeping cup of green tea and two pieces of whole-wheat toast topped with a thin layer of strawberry jam.

"I know you didn't want anything besides the tea but it's almost time for you to take your medicine," she insisted, setting the tray on the coffee table.

"Thank you, sweetheart. This is perfect. Where's yours?"

"I was thinking I might catch an hour or two of sleep before I start my running for the day. I have a lot to do. Last night I wondered where on earth you find time to write people back."

"It can be challenging." Then she remembered the response Lyss shared with Sabrina and smiled with a hint of excitement. "I almost forgot. I read today's inspirational message. It's beautiful and powerful. I love it."

"Really?"

When Marala looked up, Lyss was already smiling.

"Of course. Have you seen how many people commented?"

"Not yet."

"When they comment or *like* it that means it's hitting home. Who believed you could do this?" she asked, playfully.

"Thanks, Mama," she replied. Her face displayed an appreciative radiance.

"Was the inspirational quote for, Sabrina?"

She reached for the cup and slowly lifted it to her lips, taking two small sips.

"Actually, I did have her in mind. Her previous messages were predominantly about her being taken advantage of. After I read them I thought it was kind of sad."

"It is. There are a lot of good people who've been hurt and taken advantage of repeatedly. The typical result causes them to either become bitter because of it or passive allowing the cycle to persist. I've heard so many inscrutable accounts of injustice and pain; it hurts my heart. Sometimes a little inspirational lift from a positive viewpoint can help people see things more clearly." She placed the cup back on the tray, "Another perfect cup of tea," she said, flashing a smile with a tinge of uncertainty. "That is how I like it, right?" Marala let out a sweet giggle.

"Stop it, Mama. You're not funny. You remember more than you think," Lyss insisted.

"One thing I recall is how much time it takes to keep up with these emails."

"Yes, it does," she agreed, taking a well-deserved bow.

"As insignificant as it may seem, doing this means a lot to me because I didn't want to share anything about my surgery. You'd be surprised what happens if I don't post anything. A couple times I didn't have anything to say and I was hit with a barrage of messages."

"Really?"

"Oh yeah. They'll write to say—Hey, I need the quote today or where's my inspiration Ms. Scott. It's cute though."

"How do you handle the request?"

"Are you kidding? I post one. Why do you think I have you doing it?"

"I don't think you're getting the point, Mama. This is helping me too. I'm learning a lot about people by

61

what they're willing to disclose and why they choose to share it. I consider the way you see people to be a fascinating perspective. They make immediate and even drastic changes, by such simple suggestions. That provides me with an incredible angle that's not always contemplated. They hear *something* from your experiences and words of inspiration. It seems to stir their spirit or wake them up. I don't know what you call it but I think the personalization you have with everyone is remarkable. I'm certain that has something to do with it."

"Okay. Give me an example."

"Sabrina. She wrote and stated, you forgot her heart at the end of the message. What's the heart about? I've noticed you give one to some people but others you don't."

"It's completely random and the same as when I send a hug, blessings or love. Some days I know when people need to see my little heart. They can feel my sincerity in sending a touch of love by the tone of my message. It's easy for a message to be grossly misinterpreted."

"I agree. And it's a thoughtful way to personalize your communication."

"Nice observation."

"Yeah. The funny thing is I've noticed you've never given Garrett a heart. Why not?"

"Oh, because he already has a very good one."

~~~~~~~~~~~

Nine

Two months later, Marala was restless and looking forward to getting back to her regular schedule of speaking and promoting *Intuition* before the dust settled on it. *Intuition* had taken off, building a remarkable fan base, which made it necessary for her to reappear and take it where it was intended. Physically and mentally everything was almost normal but the few things that were off only she'd notice. The long worm-shaped scar from the surgery had healed so well; it was barely detectable. The deep, dark bruising that spread from the base of her ear up to her left temple had finally vanished. Her long, curly hair easily covered the titanium plate and screws that left a slight protrusion beneath the skin. The only visible physical remnant was a two-inch indentation on her temple.

Since the surgery, Lyss kept the press and everyone at bay. However, it was becoming difficult to keep Marala away without sprouting suspicions of something being wrong. Lyss worked with her mother's agent on the itinerary, which was cautiously created and awaiting Marala's approval.

Marala was relaxing on the patio in a comfortable espresso colored armchair with a thick white cushion, taking in the mild breezes of fresh air tickling her nostrils. Her eyes darted between the pages of her book and quick glances of the three squirrels playfully chasing one another on their imaginary high wire, the upward diagonal branches of the tree. She locked her fingers together and stretched out her arms yawning dramatically; ignoring the phone ringing in the background.

"Oh, it feels good out here," she said, noticing Lyss headed her way. "I think I'm about ready," she added joyfully, gazing at the swaying gracefulness offered by the ornamental weeping willow tree in her yard. "Although the scenery is beautiful, sitting here any longer is going to age me."

Lyss put her coffee mug down and gently kissed her mother's forehead.

"Then you'll like this. I have some kind of timing. Here's the contract and itinerary for your next few events." She handed her mother the manila folder containing the schedule. "The stats of where your book is selling best are in there, too," she added, in a witty tone. "I thought you'd like to see it since you made *The New York Times Best Sellers List.*"

Marala's jaw dropped open. Her brown eyes widened and clouded with tears as they shifted up towards Lyss.

"Are you serious?"

"Of course I am! Congratulations! A few minutes ago your agent called confirming it, except I'd already read about it online. There were hundreds of congratulatory comments posted everywhere this morning."

"Goodness. This is simply unbelievable."

"Why? You've earned it. *Intuition* is something everyone should be receptive to learning more about. The statistics are evidence that people feel the same way I do. You're *my* mother and your words captivated me to an infinite—boundless realm. I've seen you do firsthand what you're recommending others consider," she whispered, majestically. "But there's a wealth of information in your book and the examples have already helped me. I'm still gaining wisdom from you because I refuse to stop learning. I'm working towards having intuition as strong as yours," she admitted, decisively.

"Yours is every bit as good as mine. I've seen it, firsthand." Marala's eyes returned to the schedule and a few seconds later an infectious concern shaded her face. "New York and Chicago are fine but—"

"But what, Mama?" Lyss questioned, peering over her shoulder at the schedule.

"I'm not sure about this one," she stated, tapping her index finger on the paper. "Minnesota. Perhaps it's because I've never been there before. I—I don't know."

"Adam worked really hard to put this together. This tour is designed to take you a lot of places for the first time. The purpose of it is to continue opening up your demographics so your message is exposed to as many people as possible."

"I understand. But the fact remains that these are significant numbers they expect from Minnesota. I'm not totally convinced I can pull them off there."

Lyss sensed her mother's swelling apprehension and jumped in sharply.

"Mama, I've never known *you* to be afraid of speaking anywhere. If you want to look at numbers then take a look at all of them," she insisted, pulling a spreadsheet from behind the itinerary. "They're great! Your statistics are off the charts in most of these cities. Minneapolis and St. Paul's are only two of them. The numbers are large because we're expecting to pull from the Twin Cities for this one event."

"As impressive as it sounds you have to remember they're projections that I'm being held accountable for. If the theatres aren't filled the way they need to be, it could hurt any future events we plan. Sometimes, I think more intimate crowds allow me to have a better connection with people."

"I'm not worried and you shouldn't be either after having made, *The New York Times Best Sellers List*. Furthermore, you have some very large sponsors from Minnesota supporting the event and the title sponsor practically begged to get you. I mean, this guy fought really hard and was relentless in his bidding," she explained, defensively. "Mama, he met all of the request thrown at him, which were far more than usual, because *I* wasn't sure about going there either. I don't know why, but I felt the same way about Minnesota as you do."

Marala had a tingling sensation crawl up her spine and began stumbling over her words, "I—I admit I find it exciting, but—"

"You had brain surgery a few months ago and I know you must be a little nervous about speaking; I'd be too. Don't forget to take under consideration that this is *you*. It's who you are. You know this topic like the back of your hand and there's absolutely no reason for you to be worried about anything," Lyss reminded, while softening her tone. "I'm not going to let you stop doing what you love, which is making a difference by helping people. You can be a little guarded and that's okay, but I'm not going to sit by and watch you let go of your passion. Sometimes, after traumatic experiences such as surgery, people change. They're uneasy about doing things they used to do prior to surgery. You can be certain I won't dare let you fall into that category. This is who you are, Mama."

"I know and perhaps, that's all it is."

"Look. You have another month before these tours begin and of course your health comes first. If we need to cancel, we'll cancel. If you don't want to do it, we won't."

Marala leaned forward, picked up the black ballpoint pen and signed the contracts.

~~~~~~~~~~

Ten

Once Marala's *Intuition* schedule was finalized, Lyss posted it online. Enthusiastic emails flooded her inbox while tickets sold out at all three venues in less than two weeks. Many people shared favorite restaurants, places to shop and things to see in the cities she was speaking. Some sent simple request to meet her. Even Garrett joined in and recommended his favorite hotel. He mentioned it had a long walkway adjacent to the Imperial Theatre, which hosted the best events in the Twin Cities.

The New York speaking engagement was an enormous success. Every seat was filled to capacity and the crowd's fervor, said it all. While recovering, Marala's, *Intuition* had been making it's way from one set of eager hands to another, allowing her to open to impressive numbers. Even though she was unusually exhausted after speaking for two hours, she had agreed to do an autograph signing. This time, scores of people who followed her online were anxiously waiting to say, hello and steal a moment of continued insight as they got their book signed. Others either read the book or heard about her and came to hear the *Above Reason* commentary for the first time. It was an electrifying night in the grand city of New York for, *Intuition*.

The next day Marala and Lyss caught a late afternoon flight to Chicago. By the time they arrived, the blanket of overcast clouds hovering above New York was miles behind. The brilliant sun lit up the sky leaving no sign of a cloud or trace of wind. The temperature was inviting for mid-September. They settled into the posh hotel on the Magnificent Mile to get ready for that evenings speaking engagement. Upon entering the impressive suite, Marala walked directly over to the large window and drew the curtains, revealing an extraordinary view of the city. Generous sunlight poured in and drenched the suite.

"God is everywhere," Marala insisted placidly.

"He sure is. This view is just another piece of evidence," Lyss agreed. "Progression is powerful but when it's not done with the right plan it can be devastating."

She unzipped her large oversized purse and pulled out her faithful iPad.

"Are you ready to grab dinner?"

"Actually, I like that idea. Would you mind if I checked some emails first? I'm sure your mailbox is packed right about now."

"Of course not. Go right ahead. How's that going?" Marala asked, walking over to her suitcase resting on the walnut luggage stand in the corner.

"Surprisingly, very well. You have a lot of women that contend they're making better choices because of what they gain after reading your books. Since I've been responding to your emails I feel more connected with some of them. You're empowering these women in so many ways—I'm learning from them in addition to learning a few moving things about you. It's intriguing to see how other people view you. It's ironic for me to read things about my mother that I may have taken for granted."

"I wouldn't say you took things for granted."

"Are you kidding?" she asked sarcastically. "Of course I have. Not everyone appreciates everything. If they did, we wouldn't have something known as complaints," she explained, with an outburst of laughter.

"My daughter the comedian. Okay, that's funny," she replied with a wide smile.

"But seriously, we wouldn't live in a world like this if complete appreciation existed. And we certainly wouldn't take life and the scarifies Christ made, for granted."

"Excellent point," Marala admitted, admiring Lyss's quick wit. "Just remember growth consists of evolution."

"That's true too," Lyss acknowledged, politely. "One thing I've noticed is that you have a lot of men writing. They've been expressive in communicating how much they value the honesty you share in your messages. They seem to like them because they're not one-sided. You know, for women only. I guess you leave a little something that touches everyone. Often, the painful issues that men are subjected to appear to be disregarded. In my opinion, they need to receive the same positive counsel, information and help as women. Nevertheless, I think it's pretty impressive the way they view you."

Marala unzipped her garment bag and laid it across the bed. After pausing she modestly stated, "You should know by now that what matters is how *you* view me." She pulled an elegant burgundy dress out of her garment bag and added, "The reason I do all this speaking is to help people look at themselves, not me. I want them to learn how to create better situations by acknowledging and responding when God is speaking directly to them. If they've been hurt by someone, I want them to unearth the power they'll regain when they forgive that person. It releases them from the pain they're choosing to carry. Sweetheart, there are so many things that can make us better people and enrich our lives if we keep learning and growing in positive, progressive ways. When I speak to people using words full of inspiration what they really don't know is that I'm still speaking to remind myself, as well. I post the messages for me and if others benefit from my lesson, great. Progress can't be accomplished by forgetting the lessons we've had, regardless of how difficult or painful they are. There's something to learn from every single one of them whether we like it or not. Once we do, the pain from our past will begin to dissipate, like melting snow."

Marala opened the beautiful French armoire with hand woven cane doors and hung her dress inside.

"It's evident through all of these personal communications, you've made a difference in a lot of peoples lives. It's a blessing to have you as my mother."

"The blessing is having *you* as my daughter. Think about everything you've done to keep me on task

70

over the past few months. You've been taking care of me, handling my schedule, returning emails. Baby, you've accommodated me greatly. I mean you're still handling everything. I wouldn't be able to heal as quickly if you weren't here. And it's impossible to adequately express how much I appreciate you taking off this semester to help me recuperate," she said, dropping her head. "I'm really sorry."

Her humble words made their way into Lyss's heart. Marala closed the doors to the armoire, walked over and wrapped her arms around her daughter.

"You know I don't mind and it doesn't feel like work. I love helping out. Do you realize how much I'm learning by communicating with these people? Besides, I can't wait to share this and most of my professors read your books."

"Thank you sweetheart."

"No problem, Mama."

Lyss went into the sitting area and relaxed on the sofa. She pulled her iPad out of her bag, turned it on and logged in. When Marala's inbox popped up she had several messages. Lyss clicked on the first new message.

Hi Marala,

I had dinner with some friends the other night and we were discussing Intuition. What a powerful conversation the word alone caused. The funny thing is all of us agreed with your perspective, but only a few of us actually follow our intuition as much as we should. We realize we can save wasted time on the wrong man, friends, or situations if we pay attention to our intuition more! Again, you've shared something to make a major difference in the way we live by the choices we make. I'm looking forward to your Chicago engagement. I'll be there with a few friends.

Hugs!
Tara

Lyss continued to the next message.

Marala,

I was so excited to see your show in New York. I loved it! I was finally able to meet you and get my book signed. The line was so long and there were too many people around to say much other than thank you and tell you where I traveled from to hear you speak. I was wearing one of your black Intuition (Trust It) t-shirts. I have more of a reason to trust it than most and I wanted to share it with you. I read your inspirational messages daily and they've helped me in ways no one else could possibly know.

After a friend recommended your first book, I was captivated by the strength you displayed as a child and it motivated me to take control of my life. The forgiveness part is coming along a little slowly because I was in an abusive marriage. Much like your mother, what I went through was brutal and demoralizing. I'm grateful God brought your words of encouragement into my life giving me the strength to leave. My husband boasted his children watched him kill his ex-wife in Wisconsin over fifteen years ago, except they never found her body or had evidence to charge him. After arrogantly admitting he'd gotten away with it once and would do it again, I knew I had to leave him. No one would believe this man could ever do something as sick or even entertain the idea. I told him I should have trusted my intuition in the beginning because there were several distinct signs warning me something was wrong. I've since moved to Connecticut to live with a friend he didn't know about. I pray to God I never see him again.

Your schedule is taking you to my old hometown. There are a lot of people that need to hear your message. Thank you for changing my life and inspiring me to make modifications so I can finally breathe and be happy again. In Our House helped me realize I had to get out of the abusive relationship. Surrounded By Inspiration opened my eyes to my own self-discovery. Intuition made me aware of how to trust God so I don't end up in another horrible situation. I owe you so many thanks Marala. You've been a blessing. Keep sharing because I look forward to your inspirational messages. xxoo

Love,
Sharon

Lyss took in a deep breath, completely stunned by what she read. She pressed reply, exhaling with a poisonous taste of lingering disgust.

"Mama," she called out.

"Yes?" she replied, exiting the bedroom.

"Are you busy?"

"I was preparing notes for this evening," she admitted, as she pulled off her glasses and rubbed her eyes.

"I didn't mean to interrupt."

"No problem, sweetheart. What's on your mind?"

"I just find this difficult to fathom," she said, pointing at the iPad screen.

"What exactly?"

"It bothers me to read so many blatant accounts of women still running and hiding from the reality of their life. We have remedies and solutions for a lot of things but oddly, not abuse."

"Unfortunately, it's one of the topics people write me about. There are resources available and people need to use them."

"Yes, but the coinciding problem is that the laws haven't changed enough to save lives. It makes no sense how abuse could still be so prevalent in this country, let alone, any. Reading these emails makes it apparent that little progress has been made from Grandma's era, up until now. And abuse towards men is steadily climbing yet, that's still overlooked. Mama, I read emails from men trying to get out of abusive relationships, but insist they have nowhere to turn."

"Yeah, well there are more than a few who write me. Many of them were abused as children and it pains me to see that cycle keeps spinning. So, what's your question? I can tell something's bothering you?"

Lyss leaned back against the sofa trying to determine how to respond.

"I just read a message from a woman who heard you speak for the first time in New York. I know you signed a lot of books so I don't expect you to remember everyone. She mentioned she was wearing one of your black *Intuition* t-shirts."

"Hmm," Marala huffed.

"I'm sure that's too vague because a lot of people were wearing them," Lyss sighed.

"Did she say she was from Connecticut?"

"Yeah, and—"

"Okay. I think you're talking about, Sheryl, Sherrie—No, no, Sharon," she acknowledged, quickly correcting her mistake.

"How do you remember her?" Lyss asked, quizzically.

"Because this woman seemed like she had something to tell me, but was aware it wasn't the time nor place. Her eyes let me know she needed to talk. So writing me would be the logical thing to do. Besides, I got the sense her fatigued spirit was still being—battered. I forget a few things but I remember, Sharon from Connecticut," she said proudly.

"Really?"

"Yeah, really. It's heartbreaking, but I'm only speaking the truth," Marala replied, plopping down comfortably on the sofa next to Lyss.

"Well, in the message, she explained what happened and why she went to see you speak.

Marala perked up a bit and responded instinctively, "Most likely, it was an abusive situation—and she probably reached the point where she finally gathered the courage to get out."

"You're right," Lyss agreed, sounding surprised.

"She mentioned her recent move to Connecticut. Given her spirit and eagerness to talk with me, I thought that might be the reason. So what's your question?" Marala asked, inquisitively.

"You already answered it. I wanted to know if you remember her, which you do, so I can tell her."

"Very nice."

"Like I said, you personalize your messages, so I want to be consistent."

"I try. Anything else?"

"You have a lot of emails here, quite a few are because of your engagement in New York."

"I usually get them after I speak somewhere. I appreciate you returning these for me. I should be able to get back to it soon. Hopefully, before I've worn you out. If you receive anything personal that I need to address, I'd prefer to respond to those."

"There's no reason for you to push yourself because I'm fine with this. Just so you're aware, I expected this would take a little time before you were able to get back to it so I made concessions. Mama, when I tell you I'm fine, I am."

"Okay, I trust you've got it handled, but I want you to know how much I appreciate it." She softly pinched Lyss's cheek and said, "I'm going to finish my notes and then rest until you're ready for dinner. For some reason, my head's starting to bother me again."

"Do you need me to get you anything?" Lyss asked, with concern taking the form of little wrinkles across her forehead.

"No thanks. I think a nap will help."

Marala got up and disappeared into the bedroom. Moments later Lyss began typing.

After returning several emails a new message notification popped up on the screen. It was from Garrett.

Marala

Good luck tonight with your speaking engagement. You impact lives with your positive message and disrupt those that want to keep others bound to their pain and misery. Inspiration spreads truth and perpetuates healing. Some people don't want to heal! Use your intuition to keep yourself safe.

Fondly,
Garrett

Lyss stared at the screen with a tinge of unexplained fear. She didn't know what to make of his words but thought they sounded cryptic. Without hesitation, she wrote him back.

Garrett,

Why would I need to be safe? If there's something you want to say, please feel free to be more direct.

Lyss continued returning messages however; nearly an hour later there was still no response from Garrett. She was uncertain as to what he was implying, if anything at all. However, she viewed the communication as somewhat alarming. She didn't know whether or not to tell her mother or keep a close eye on her to avoid causing unnecessary stress right before her speech. From what Lyss knew about Garrett, this type of exchange was unusual. Perhaps he was having an off day or someone had upset him, causing a setback with one of his issues.

Lyss was about to log out when another message alert popped up.

She shook her head and said, "Enough of this for now," and turned off the iPad.

Marala woke up a half hour later feeling and looking rejuvenated. Her head was no longer bothering her so she decided to shower and change before heading out to enjoy dinner at the trendy new restaurant, Reasons, prior to the evening engagement.

"I'm not willing to ruin these babies for a salad," Lyss admitted, lifting her leg to prominently display the strappy wine-red stiletto. "Do you want me to hail a cab?" she asked, as they stepped out of the hotel's revolving door.

"You don't need to do that because you won't ruin them." She grabbed Lyss's hand and confidently crossed the street. "It's right there," she stated, nodding at the illuminated sign on the beautiful rustic brick building with round arched windows.

Lyss giggled once she noticed it was only a few businesses away.

"Are you ready for tonight?"

"Absolutely. New York was fun and I enjoyed the people. It's easy to share a message when the audience is open to receive it," she replied, speaking carefully.

"True, but what I meant by *ready* is how are you feeling? Are you physically able to do this again? Do you have any strange or intuitive feelings about tonight?"

"Not at all, I'm fine. The crowd has a way of energizing me."

"I've noticed you've been a little more reserved on stage than usual."

"Yeah. I'm trying to slow my pace so I'm not overdoing it."

"Any headaches or pain? Is there anything or *anyone* you're worried about?" she asked, still probing.

"No, no and no. Now stop worrying. I'm fine," she claimed persuasively. Then she abruptly halted at the entrance of Reasons and asked, "Do I look like something's wrong?" She placed her hand on the side of her head and tenderly felt along the shape of the scar, concealed by her sweeping banes.

As the host weighted his body against the heavy metal door, politely holding it open, Lyss replied, "Actually, you look great in that dress Mama."

She sighed and dropped her hand to her side, appearing relieved.

"Then stop worrying!"

~~~~~~~~~~

Eleven

Eager crowds of attendees assembled in the inimitable ambience of the hotel lobby, which hosted an alluring luxurious beauty. The crackling of wood and earthy smell of burning oak emitting from the imposing stone fireplace provided warmth. Like a magnetic force, it drew people near for comfortable conversations. An influx of wind-generated waves flushed positive energy into the minds of the audience before the commencement of the speech. Marala found splendor in the variation of ages, from mature teens extending beyond the sage sixties, along with a brilliantly blended potpourri of ethnicities.

Lyss kept a watchful eye on the crowd throughout the evening. Many of the women were wearing the trendy *Intuition* t-shirts with radiating pride, enjoying a lively girl's night out. Chatty little clusters of friends spoke freely, allowing their bonds with one another to strengthen.

The audience's enthusiasm to learn more about the book is what crammed the theater; allowing Marala's fervent passion to feed off their burning vivacity. Marala had uniquely woven together key inspirational words of encouragement that derived from her many personal accounts of pain. Her energetic speech resonated with triumphant expressions and examples of sheer faith, creating another overwhelming success. The pulsating delivery of *Intuition* rang true to the testimony of faith. What remained was the residue of a humbling and life-changing affect for anyone choosing to trust it.

Marala ended her speech by restating, as a reminder to her audience, the crux of the message. She wanted it to be the last declaration to envelope their thirsty souls. Faithfully clasping her hands together, she exclaimed, *"Trusting your God given intuition is trusting God! Your faith is proven by your actions!"*

By their reaction, the crowd's acceptance of her message was beyond measure. Lyss accompanied her visibly fatigued mother off stage, leaving a surge of trailing applause. Marala made an unsuccessful attempt to hide a slight tremble creeping through her lean body.

"Mama, what's wrong?" Lyss asked tightening her grip around Marala's waist.

"I guess I got too excited tonight," she explained, forcing a weak smile.

"Careful then. Grab hold of the banister," Lyss instructed as Marala cautiously went down each step, trying not to tumble.

"Are you cold?"

"Not really."

"I didn't think so. Let's find a quiet place to sit down for a few minutes."

Lyss walked her mother over to a lounge chair in a private sitting area. When she grabbed hold of her hand she could feel the increasing tremors now racing through her mother.

"I can feel it. Your trembling's getting worse. Would you happen to know why?"

"Not really."

"Your blood pressure may be elevated."

"No. I took my pill before the speech," she said, letting out a long sigh. "Speaking must have worn me out more than I thought it would. I'll be fine though," she claimed, patting Lyss's arm. "Let's sit for a few moments before the signing. I need to recharge. I'm exhausted from standing and talking so much," she said, forcing a frail smile.

"Are you sure?"

"Yes, baby girl."

Marala leaned her head back, closed her eyes and prayed.

Twenty minutes later, Marala appeared to be feeling better. Lyss escorted her mother to sign books and socialize at her private meet and greet. When Marala and Lyss entered the beautifully decorated room they were impressed by the tremendous effort put into it. Fragrant floral arrangements and small table lamps with dim lighting were strategically placed throughout the room, adding an extraordinary touch. Marala was humbled to see the large *Intuition* banner prominently displayed behind the palatable display of hors d'oeuvres. The soft and melodious music was a compilation of her favorites and the final touch pulling everything together perfectly. *Intuition* was the avenue that created phenomenal sparks of conversation.

Lyss detected a few individuals watching her mother attentively so she kept a close eye on her while networking. Marala received offers to speak at additional corporate events and a handsome, single professor from Northwestern University invited her to dinner. Marala was quick to use her typical diplomatic decline, "Due to my schedule." However, he was insistent and left the offer standing when her schedule allowed. The remainder of the evening was simply delightful.

The next morning, Lyss went to awaken her mother but found her dressed and sipping on a white mocha latte listening to the heavenly sounds of Andrea Bocilli flowing effortlessly from her laptop.

"I thought you'd still be asleep after last night," Lyss remarked.

"Oh, I'm sorry," she said, hitting the mute button. "Did I wake you?"

"No, I'm ready to get moving. I wanted to check and see how you're feeling because you were unusually drained last night. I was worried about you. In fact, I still am."

"I've been up since a quarter to three," she said, using her hand to smooth her hair back off her face. "I suppose it's because I have a lot on my mind."

"What's wrong?" Lyss asked sympathetically, moving closer to her mother.

Marala folded her arms defensively across her breasts and stated adamantly, "I've been thinking about canceling the speech so I can take a break. I think it was somewhat premature for me to return to all this traveling and speaking. It's—too much for me."

"They've already put a lot of marketing into tonight's event."

"I'm sure they have sweetheart. It's certainly not my intent to disappoint anyone but I don't think I should be doing this one. In fact, I know I shouldn't."

Lyss pushed a Persian blue leather armchair closer to her mother and sat directly across from her. She studied the fearful expression her mother could no longer conceal. Marala had never opposed any part of her itinerary other than going to Minnesota. Lyss could clearly discern the undeniable trepidation in her mother's eyes. It was boiling out of her perceptive soul.

"We have a break before the next set of dates begin—"

"I know, but I'm not feeling right?" Marala insisted.

"About the event?"

"Yes."

"Mama," she began, reaching for her hand. "Look at the outcome of the last two events. Your speech is so good it's hard to believe you had brain surgery, let alone a few months ago. Even the doctor said you're way ahead of schedule. I'm sure you're pushing yourself because it's a part of what you do, but I don't think the surgery is what's affecting you this way."

"I think it has something to do with what I'm feeling."

"You forget how well I know you. You've been tired before, yet you never quit anything. You've been adamant about stopping this tour before this Minnesota date in particular," she added, waiting for a response.

"Can you hear the problems with my speaking? I can, when I pronounce certain words."

"How can you tell?" Lyss questioned.

"I stumble over them."

"The only reason I hear a slight difference is because I know about the surgery."

"That's good then."

"I'd say so."

"But I still have trouble with specific words."

"Yes, and I've noticed how well you avoid the words you typically have difficulty with. Your speaking isn't the problem."

"Okay."

"Okay, what?" Lyss questioned.

"I've made up my mind."

"So we're good. We can get this done and you'll stop worrying?" she asked, letting out a sigh of relief.

"Not exactly. I still don't want to do it."

"Are you having any sort of problems standing or walking on stage that perhaps I'm missing or don't know about?" Marala shook her head, no. "What about shooting pains anywhere in your head?"

"They're not as distracting as they were," she confessed.

"I recall you teaching me something about fear. Oh yeah, you said, '*Fear can paralyze you and keep you exactly where you are.*'"

"And that's true."

"Then what, Mama? What are you afraid of?"

"I'm not afraid of anything. I just don't want to do it. I think that something's—"

"Nothing's going to happen. Your audiences are as good as they get. They love the book and the way you explain it. This message is something everyone can relate to and quite frankly, need to hear. Mama look, if you don't want to do it at least give me a reason I can share with the media and sponsors as to why it's canceled. That's all I need."

"Sweetheart, I can't."

"What?" Lyss's eyes narrowed with total disbelief circling her pupils. "You can't? What do you mean, *you can't*? That's not a familiar word to you. Now I know this is about *your* intuition? What are you so afraid of that you don't want—No, I mean you *won't* share with me?" she asked fretfully getting out of the chair. She knelt in front of her mother staring into her eyes, connecting with the hidden fear. Marala's facial expression mirrored what her eyes revealed. Without delay, Lyss reached into her pocket and pulled out her phone. "If that's what all this is about, we're *not* doing it. I'll make the calls," Lyss announced, quickly standing as she began dialing Adam. "How could I have missed this? How could I not hear you warning me! Ugh!"

Marala's mind was suspended as it took in all of the fear being generated because of her unwillingness to continue the tour. She knew whether it was tonight, tomorrow or the day after, the reality of what was going to happen was inevitable. When she saw Lyss's worried face she grabbed her hand pulling her down on the sofa.

"No sweetheart," she said, taking the phone from her. "I'm just tired and really believe I came back on tour too soon. It doesn't feel right. Not yet. I mean the surgery has me challenging my abilities in regards to speaking."

"It shouldn't. You're doing an amazing job. The precision in your message comes across without any confusion or reservations."

"To you maybe."

"No, to everyone because their response tells you. Have you read any of your reviews?"

"I haven't."

"Well, maybe you should. They're raving about it."

"Perhaps it's going to take me a little getting used to. I'll do this engagement because I know these people need to hear this message, possibly more than anyone knows. But—"

Lyss finally sensed what her mother was reacting to. After looking into her mother's eyes the same turbulent reaction Marala was having plunged into Lyss's core. Something bad was going to happen and her mother was searching for a way to avoid it without alarming Lyss.

"Mama, I get it. You've been telling me the same thing repeatedly but I've been ignoring what you've said. I get it," she expressed with sincerity.

"What?"

"That you're being led to fear because your intuition's warning you about something. I don't know if it's your health or what but—"

"No sweetheart. My intuition doesn't lead me to fear it's leading me to my reality. I simply haven't dealt with it yet."

"Mama, whatever that reality happens to be, it unquestionably has you afraid. It's what your intuition's been trying to protect you from. And *I*, of all people, shouldn't be pushing you to do something that goes against it. I know better," Lyss said agitatedly. "Ahh," she screamed, clinching her fist in the air. "I don't believe I've been forcing you to do something you absolutely shouldn't! That's what you're speaking about and here I am ignoring it."

"Sweetheart, I don't know what it is yet, because I can't pinpoint it. I'm not certain if it has anything to do with my speech tonight either. It may be I'm worried about my health or a combination of a few things. Until the situation plays out, I don't know what's wrong. I'm sorry I've been so preoccupied with not wanting to do this engagement."

"You have every reason to be."

Marala took a deep breath and exhaled gradually, "After this engagement, cancel the next set of dates. I won't be able to do them. I'm positive I'll need to take a break afterwards."

"Now that I understand, can you share with me exactly why or what your intuition is showing you to make you this definitive?"

"Not yet."

"Mama, I really need to know."

"Let's get through tonight and we'll figure out what's going on at that point. Okay?"

"Are you sure because—"

"Promise me you won't schedule anything after Minnesota. Nothing at all."

"That's not a problem. I promise. I'll handle it this morning and it'll be done before we head to Minnesota."

Marala nodded approvingly.

"Is there anything you want to talk about now? Should I be watching out for anything in particular?"

"We'll talk about it later."

"Alright. But I'm not going to let you forget because I want to know what's going on."

"That's fine. You'll know soon enough."

Lyss wrapped her arms around her mother and whispered in her ear, "I know you're hiding something. You can't protect me from everything."

Marala looked at her with grave eyes and a heavy heart before replying, "I can try."

Lyss ran her hand down Marala's arm knowing the discussion was over. Her mother's muddled patchwork of excuses didn't work although she was sure the explanation was near.

"Do you want to go down to the restaurant and have breakfast with me or should I order room service?"

"I don't have an appetite for anything. Go have breakfast while I try to get a little rest before we head to the airport."

"But I want to have breakfast with—"

Marala waved her hands dismissively, gently sending Lyss away, "Go on sweetheart, I really need to rest."

Lyss picked up the room key and headed down to the hotel restaurant. Marala put her hand up to the left side of her head where the scar was and shut her eyes.

"Okay," she mumbled to herself. "I know it's time."

~~~~~~~~~~

Twelve

The turbulent flight through looming dark clouds and squally weather caused Marala and Lyss a delayed arrival to Minneapolis. They barely had enough time to get to the hotel, do a brief walk through at the Imperial Theatre and then shower and change for the reception hosted by the sponsors.

Lyss was wearing a sleeveless, Marc Jacobs, chocolate and back trim dress with a pair of attention-grabbing black stilettos. Her loose curls were pinned up with soft sweeping bangs to her right side. When she entered her mother's room, Marala was wearing a pair of wide leg black dress pants and a soft pink blouse rummaging through her jewelry case deciding which earrings to wear.

Lyss calmly reached in the leather case and pulled out a pair of diamond hoops and said suggestively, "These, they match your belt."

Without protest, Marala put them on. Lyss had an undisputable eye for fashion and never seemed to miss her mark.

"Thank you sweetheart. They're perfect," she said, void of emotion as if her words came from an abyss inside of her. Her mind was wrapped around something else.

"Are you feeling any better? You still seem slightly out of it."

"I'm fine," she replied, turning towards Lyss. "You look beautiful, as always."

"Thank you, Mama. So do you."

Marala smiled sadly as she took Lyss's soft face in both hands and stated firmly and leisurely to make sure she heard every word.

"Following my intuition has kept you safe. We both know I've taught you more than enough to understand how to trust *yours*. Let it guide you, as it *is* God speaking to you. Don't become emotional in times of crisis. Baby girl, I love you more than I can *possibly* show. I want you to know what a brilliant light you've been and always will be."

Lyss's eyes welled with heavy tears and Marala gently wiped them with the back of her hand as they escaped.

"Mama, is this about—"

"We spoke about that this morning and I told you we'll know soon enough."

"You never want to tell me anything so I don't worry, but I can feel it, right here," she said clinching her fist and placing it on her stomach.

"No, no, sweetheart. I'm here to help people by sharing an encouraging message and I've prayed it's well received. Depending on their level of faith and receptiveness to learning something above reason, some will receive it better than others. That's just the way it goes," she said picking up the hairbrush. Marala was noticeably hiding something. She ran the brush through her hair several times looking blankly into the mirror. "Remember, you reminded me that *I* said, fear can paralyze you and keep you exactly where you are?"

"Yes and I agree with you."

"I know. But the rest of it was, others use your fear as a stepping-stone for themselves. Don't let this negative state of mind hold you hostage so you don't progress. Your mind is a powerful tool that can sometimes confuse you. So use your faith and intuition instead of worrying about things. Move past fear."

"That is the rest of it," she conceded surprised at her mothers accurate memory. The surgery seemed to cause a trace of forgetfulness at times, but her recollection of her inspirational words was unscathed.

"Always keep that in mind. Use your faith and move past fear." Lyss's tears turned into heavy sobbing. "Thank you for always being here for me sweetheart. You've done a lot of work over the past several months allowing you to get to know *everyone* I've been communicating with. You've inspired them with your own powerful words of faith. Can you believe all of those communications are on my laptop? I keep *everything*. If you can't find what you need in there, you won't find it."

"I know. You have messages going back a few years."

Lyss handed her mother the pink hair clip from her jewelry case. Marala took it and held it in both hands smiling sadly at Lyss before pulling her hair back and clipping it. She sat on the end of her bed and let her hands rest on her lap.

"There's a lot of information in there," Marala said pointing at her laptop. "I keep it because sometimes it provides me with clues on how to help someone based on their history. And everyone has one."

"Which is why I thought I needed to read them." Lyss's cell rang twice before she answered it. "Thank you," she replied politely. "We're on our way." She picked up her purse and announced with artificial excitement, "Let's go, Mama. After this we'll have plenty of time to hang out together because I had Adam clear your schedule. I think you're right about needing a break. I don't know why, but I guess it's my intuition. Oh—" she reminded herself, "Do you want your wrap? Sometimes the room gets a little cool."

"No thanks. I'm fine now, but remind me to grab it before I speak. I'll take it with me then," she replied giving her daughter a quick kiss on the cheek.

"Why?" Lyss asked appearing confused.

"In case the theatre is a little cooler than it was earlier," she answered holding the door for Lyss.

The reception was far more crowded than anticipated. Marala was off in a corner talking to four women when a very well-dressed, middle-aged gentleman interrupted and announced he wanted to introduce her to the title sponsor. The sponsor's confident stride over to Marala appeared as if every step was calculated and measured. He was strikingly attractive regardless of the small but notable scar on the right side of his face. His demeanor was incredibly grim to be at this type of upbeat event. It didn't appear it was his idea to sponsor or attend but more than likely, his business associates recommended it as they had been raving about the content of the book since the reception began.

"Thank you for coming to this part of the country to share your message Ms. Scott. You had a lot of people in support of your being here."

"I most definitely appreciate their support. What about you? Are you one of those people in support of my being here?" Marala asked candidly.

"I must admit that someone else convinced me to bring you here. They believe your message, for lack of a better phrase, is a life-changer and has opened their eyes to the truth," he stated mockingly.

"Well, it only happens if they're receptive to the message."

"Do you think everyone has this, *intuition* Ms. Scott?"

"Absolutely," she answered without wavering.

"Do you think your intuition is accurate or are there times you're, shall we say, off?"

"Robert, my intuition has never been, let's say, *inaccurate*. Therefore, it's never been, *off*. I trust it explicitly as it's my direct pipeline to God," she explained with a confident smile. "And what about you? Do you believe in intuition?"

Robert folded his arms securely across his broad chest and took a deep breath, allowing his bitter tasting response to escape his mouth.

"No, I don't. Those are weak individuals who *hope* their lives can change by believing intuition can guide and protect them. I don't believe in giving people something they don't deserve when it is they who contributed to making this world, hopeless. I don't believe in hope."

"We agree on something."

Robert frowned angrily.

"What could that possibly be?" he asked gawking at her scornfully.

"I don't believe in hope alone."

"You must," he spewed.

"In my opinion Robert, I believe genuine hope will lead you to pure faith. Ultimately, you won't need it if you have complete faith. Hope is an avenue."

"To what?" he snapped.

"To God. I have complete faith in God. Out of curiosity, why would you sponsor this event given your disbelief in intuition?"

"Look around Ms. Scott," he said lifting his wine glass as though sarcastically toasting her. "You've created a following of people who want to learn how to trust their *God given intuition*, hoping they'll improve their lives in some form or fashion. But they really shouldn't trust in God if God can't put His trust in them, now should they? What happens when they make Him angry? You're highly regarded for your inspirational messages and while I don't agree intuition is real, I'm in the business of giving people what they want. From a business perspective, bringing you here keeps me relevant," he stated condescendingly.

"Robert, thank you for putting together such a well-organized event. The room looks amazing and the people are wonderful. They don't appear to hold your sentiment either. Although it wasn't your intent, you did a beautiful thing by bringing this assembly of receptive people together to hear an empowering message."

"I instructed my associates to do whatever was necessary to get you here. I think your message is one a lot of people are beginning to grasp. I simply wanted to see your work in person," he replied with a charitable grin.

"I guess we're clear on your disapproval of my inspirational message?"

Robert handed the gentleman who introduced them his wine glass. He studied Marala's soft expression and released a lingering smile.

"Well Marala," he began sternly, adjusting the Salvatore Ferragamo tie resting beneath the collar of his crisp white shirt. "I lost my beautiful wife because of a situation that is still—very difficult for me to discuss. Much like you, she believed in her God given intuition and trusted it dearly. But, because of my lack of faith, I convinced her to trust me and it cost my wife her life," he shared coldly.

"We all make difficult choices at times."

"That time," he said leaning in to whisper in Marala's ear, "I relied on logic and made a choice according to what I considered best."

Marala stepped back and locked eyes with him. Robert's eyes were beyond dark and below sinister.

"I'm truly sorry for your loss," she announced dryly.

He replied unemotionally, "Some things God can't foresee."

Marala countered him and said, "God see's everything. He will reveal it to those with faith because they trust and believe in Him."

"I had faith once. Does your intuition tell you if I'll ever have it again?" he asked snidely.

Marala didn't respond. Lyss walked up and stood beside her mother.

"Excuse me, Robert," Marala said, turning her attention to Lyss. "Sweetheart, I'm going to head up to the room to rest before my speech. I have nearly two hours so can you manage here?"

"Of course."

"Thank you."

Without another word, Robert nodded and walked away.

"He's tormented," Marala mumbled.

Lyss grabbed her hand and led her to a private corner.

"What I meant was, of course I can stay here but I'd prefer going with you. You don't look well. What's wrong?"

"I'm a little tired," she said reassuringly, "But I'll be fine. I've talked to quite a few people."

"Hold on a minute."

"Lyss I'll—"

"Mama. Wait, please," she snapped, streaming with irritation. "Let me grab my purse and we're out of here."

Lyss disappeared briefly and returned with her chocolate colored purse stashed under her arm. After thanking a few people, they slipped out of the room and headed down the long hallway towards the elevator.

"You didn't have to leave," Marala insisted.

"I've already met everyone I needed to and even managed to get the Grim Reapers business card so we can send him a thank you gift."

"Who? Robert?" she asked, surprised Lyss had met him.

"You've got it," she said sliding his card into her purse. "He's what I call creepy."

"To say the least."

"Now *his* eyes—they were as dark as a midnight sky. What did you make of him?" Lyss asked inquiringly.

"He has a lot of secrets I'd prefer not to know about and he's unquestionably carrying a lot of luggage."

"Yeah. I definitely thought there was something uncomfortable surrounding him and I heard about his wife. I'm sure that helped shape his morbid personality."

"For some reason I think it was more difficult for his wife," Marala uttered under her breath.

"What?"

"You seemed to be having a good time," Marala remarked in an effort to change the subject.

"Not really. I thought the vibe was a tad off tonight. Especially after Chicago."

Marala glanced at Lyss with concern and asked, "How so?"

"It doesn't feel like it should. I don't know exactly how to explain it because I can't put my finger on it yet. At any rate, the people are nice and—"

"I agree, the people are extremely welcoming," she replied lowering her head.

They reached the elevator and Lyss pressed the button going up. The doors immediately opened and five people got off smiling and nodding at the both of them. Marala and Lyss got into the empty elevator and as the doors closed, Lyss pressed twenty-six.

"You've been off tonight, too. I can tell when something's wrong. You probably aren't feeling well again and I know you've been trying to hide it for the past few days. You don't think I've been aware of it, but I am. I'm convinced all the trepidation you've had about coming here is affecting you."

"Perhaps," she agreed with a sigh.

"Oddly enough, I wish we hadn't," Lyss admitted.

Marala's eyebrows scrunched together as she cut her eyes inquisitively at her daughter.

"Why not?"

"It's like you've been saying, it doesn't feel right."

"Take it as a lesson. Sometimes that happens and it's exactly when you—"

"I get it."

"Well then, never deviate from following your God given intuition. You do believe you have it don't you?"

"You already know the answer. I wouldn't be here supporting your book if I didn't fully believe in it."

"And you understand there are signs to validate your intuition as long as you're in tune with it."

"Why are you bringing this up?"

"Probably because I talk about it so much," she said trying to diffuse Lyss's trending uneasiness. "You're always saying you want to be like me so I want you to realize how much you already are. There are certain things that fly above reason and that's where you have to go to figure it out. Words are powerful so take time to learn from what's written, but do it with patience and without losing control," she demanded shaking her index finger at Lyss. "Relying on others to figure out what God is trying to show you isn't wise. *Always* trust God! You have to—"

"What's all this about? Why are you worrying so much again?"

Unsure of how to respond she offered, "I'm not worrying. I'm thinking about elaborating on the topic of intuition a bit more tonight. I may dive deeper into its power."

"No, Mama. I am like you and I'm following my intuition. Something's wrong and you're still keeping it from me!"

"Sweetheart, calm down and listen to me. You know how passionate I am about this subject and how important it is to me, right?" Lyss nodded agreeably. "So it's been on my heart to go deeper. I want people to not only believe in, but understand how to use the beautiful gift God's given them."

"Are you sure?" Lyss asked appearing quite uneasy as she narrowed her brown eyes suspiciously at her mother.

"Yes," Marala replied adamantly.

The elevator doors opened at thirteen.

"I wasn't aware hotels had a thirteenth floor," Lyss stated.

Marala and Lyss shared the same staid expression.

"They don't," Marala replied.

The elevator door stayed open longer than usual but no one got on before it closed. A few moments later they reached their floor. Marala grabbed Lyss's hand securely and headed toward 2643. There was a man in the hallway swiftly walking away from their door. He made a sharp right turn down the corridor and his silhouette disappeared before Marala could call him back to see what he wanted.

"Were you expecting someone?" Lyss asked charily.

"No, I wasn't," Marala replied guardedly, observing the hallway.

"I wonder what that was about."

"Probably a guest trying to get into the wrong room. He had some kind of backpack with him like he just checked in."

Upon reaching their suite, Marala slid the key in and pulled it out. Once it flashed green, they went inside and Lyss locked the door behind them. Marala removed her shoes and stretched out her arms yawning as if it were long past her bedtime. She walked over to the oversized sofa and sat down in a relaxed position, curling her legs up.

"Come sit with me for a bit," she insisted, patting the seat next to her. "I need to rest for a little while. If I doze off, wake me in an hour," she warned.

Lyss grabbed a pillow off the bed, slipped it under Marala's head and set her phone alarm as a reminder before curling up next to her mother. Lyss watched Marala's eyes close. Only minutes later, Lyss drifted off to sleep. Marala's mind was restless; she plunged deep into her vast pool of thoughts, revisiting her intuition.

~~~~~~~~~~

Thirteen

Two hours later, Marala kissed Lyss on her supple cheeks, hugged her tightly and headed towards the stage. Once again, she turned around and threw her daughter a kiss with both hands before confidently walking out on stage where the spotlight picked up every step she took. Heavy applause rang out at the conclusion of her introduction. For the next hour and a half, Marala captivated the audience with one of her most prolific and riveting speeches about *Intuition* sweetly blended with her opinion on the power of forgiveness. Lyss's eyes danced between the audience and her mother, paying close attention to anyone seeming out of the ordinary. Energy was striking throughout the night like heavy bolts of lightning being drawn to the attentive capacity crowd.

Lyss welcomed the considerable presence of men in the crowd and was delighted to find the audience becoming broader. They were fully engaged in learning how some things are simply, above reason. In spite of the impressive turnout, Marala's disposition was unquestionably tainted. Even as she spoke, she appeared somewhat guarded and disconcerted, which was contrary to her typically warm and balanced spirit. It appeared as if someone in the crowd was causing a concentrated debilitating force of negativity that was affecting her. Evidently, the uncomfortable feelings she had about Minnesota, resurfaced. Something was definitely wrong. She couldn't shake the feeling that there would be consequences following her choice to continue the tour.

In addition, Marala's surgery was somewhat of a troubling enigma to Lyss because she was unsure if her mother had more going on with her health than she was aware of. The underlying notion of Marala hiding something was tearing into her. Pushing for an answer didn't help. It would be revealed only when Marala was ready.

"Mama, you were awesome," she said greeting her with a heartfelt embrace. They walked off stage, down the side steps and out the back door to the hallway heading into the hotel from the theatre. "You added a lot more tonight and—I totally get it."

"Good. I was praying you'd hear the underlying message too," she replied.

A short, thin man, with dark brown hair combed neatly to the side, in his mid-twenties approached Marala and announced enthusiastically, "Ms. Scott, you had more men in the audience than I expected. I wish my mother could have heard this speech," he continued, rambling freely. "I believe in intuition. I always have. But we don't pay enough attention to it. Anyways, I'm glad I was able to hear you speak. I hope everything was to your expectations."

"Thank you. Everything was very nice."

"Can I get you anything? Water, juice—"

"No thank you. I'm good."

"Well, you look a little wiped out, you know, flushed. I think you might want to have a drink of water at the very least."

"Thank you, I'll take that under consideration," Marala added politely.

"Now, I know this isn't on the schedule but apparently there's a book signing that's been arranged."

"By whom?" Lyss questioned sharply.

"Um, one of your sponsors for the event. He said he was a bit embarrassed to ask you to do it so last minute himself, but—"

"I'm sorry," Lyss began defensively. "I certainly didn't approve of the book signing and due to our schedule we can't just toss it in—"

"I don't blame you, but he *really* looked embarrassed," he insisted.

"Didn't you say my mother looked wiped out and flushed? Well, you're right, she's exhausted."

"I understand. All I'm saying is after that memorable speech I think a whole lot of people are expecting to get their books signed," he cautioned, singing the last few words, like he was in a Broadway production.

"Mama, I don't want you doing this. I'm sorry. I already said it's not—" Lyss argued.

Marala threw her trembling hand up to silence the both of them. "It's okay. These things can happen. Why don't we do this? I'll sign books for about forty-five minutes and not a minute longer. Alright?" Marala suggested benevolently, rubbing Lyss on her arm.

Lyss vehemently shook her head disapprovingly.

"Ms. Scott, that's more than appreciated. I'm sure he'll be elated. Thank you," he said graciously. "One more thing. Do you mind signing my book? Um, I'm one of those *whole lot of people!*"

Lyss couldn't help but to smile at the way he slipped his book in front of Marala and supplied her with a black marker, like a magician.

"I'm making this out to you?" Marala asked.

He nodded approvingly while pulling his nametag closer towards her, so she could read it. After signing the book she handed it to him. He smiled affectionately and held it snuggly against his chest and sighed dramatically.

"Let's head to the signing so we can get you in and out," he insisted, snapping his finger gleefully.

"Okay, let's make it happen," Marala agreed unenthusiastically.

"Then, follow me this way," he instructed. "Back to the hotel."

Marala stopped and turned to Lyss after a deep chill streaked through her body and said, "It's a little cool sweetheart. Would you mind getting my wrap? I think—I think I left it folded up on the little shelf inside the podium?"

"I'll grab it for you. How are you feeling?"

"I'm fine. I appreciate you being here."

"It's always worth it. Besides, it's the last one for awhile."

"Very true," Marala responded dropping her head.

"Excuse me," Lyss began. "Jordan, is it?" she asked reading his silver nametag.

"Yes."

"Jordan, I'm Alyssa. Where's the autograph signing?"

"Oh, I'm sorry. It's in the State Room, Alyssa. Follow this hallway all the way down the long corridor," he said pointing straight ahead of him. "It's the third room on the left and the name's on the door. You'll see it as soon as you cross into the hotel."

Lyss leaned in and whispered in her mother's ear, "Before I forget, here's your purse. Your prescription refills came in and were sent to the front desk so I put them in there along with your phone. I'll get you a bottled water after I grab your wrap so you can take your medicine."

"Okay, thank you sweetheart," Marala replied planting a heartfelt kiss on Lyss's cheek. "I love you."

"I know. And, I love you more." Marala's eyes followed Lyss until she was out of sight. Lyss returned to the theatre to get the wrap and a composed Marala followed Jordan down a long empty corridor into a large empty banquet room."

"Why isn't it set up, yet?" Marala asked upon entering the room.

"I don't know, Ms. Scott. Wait here and I'll find out where they've moved the signing," he suggested. He stomped his foot like he was throwing a tantrum, sulking childishly and said, "He must have given me the wrong room. I'll get this handled."

Jordan left the room and less than a minute later, Marala heard the door swing open. She turned around and found a man standing directly in front of her. It wasn't Jordan. Once her eyes met his, she clasped her hands over her mouth.

"You know who I am?" he asked, barely tipping his hat up off his face. Marala nodded slowly with a trace of uneasiness making its way through her. "Then you should know why I'm here," he acknowledged sternly. In a single swift move towards Marala, he locked her into a forceful embrace between his arms; quickly pressing a sweet-smelling white cloth, laced with chloroform firmly over her nose and mouth. She tried to pull away but he tightened his firm grip as her eyes fluttered shut. In a low raspy voice, he warned, "Marala, *don't* fight me. If you do, you'll die painfully. Trust your intuition."

Marala's body fell limp into his muscular arms. Seconds later, heavy smoke filled the corridor with a loud chorus of screams echoing from the lobby as the fire alarm blared. Marala was unconscious. With her purse draped over her shoulder, he lifted her into his arms and carried her out of the fire exit at the opposite end of the room. He put her into the front passenger side of his truck, got in on the driver's side and quickly pulled away from the hotel as three fire trucks raced towards the hotel from the opposite direction. He entered the highway ramp and headed east.

Within seconds, Marala's phone began ringing. He reached down inside her Louis Vuitton shoulder bag and pulled it out. The name on the display was, Alyssa. He committed the number to memory before answering it.

"Mama!"

"Listen, without interrupting! I have your mother. If you call the police and they try to locate her, she *will* die. As long as you do as you're told Alyssa, she won't get hurt."

"I want to talk to my mother," Lyss demanded. Her heart sank deep into the empty pit of her stomach, causing an excruciating ache.

"You will—in a few hours and from another phone. She's—sleeping."

Lyss struggled to catch her breath and wrapped her arm across her stomach to buffer the persistent pain.

"How do I know you haven't hurt her?"

"You don't. Remember, *not* to contact the police. It's for her benefit. If you're anything like your mother you'll trust your intuition and keep your mouth shut. Tell no one she's missing. I mean, no one! I'll call you shortly from another number. No police or she's dead."

"Don't hurt her! Please, I'm begging you! She's recovering from—"

He put the window down and hurled the phone out onto the highway.

Lyss quickly analyzed the situation surmising the fire was nothing more than a timely and clever distraction allowing her mother to be taken. Confusion settled comfortably into her mind as she tried to understand who would take someone like her mother. It didn't make sense.

After the fire department authorized a return into the hotel, she rushed back inside to find the last person she saw with her mother, Jordan. She spotted Jordan making his way across the lobby headed towards the front desk and ran over to him, nearly pinning him against the wall.

"My mother! Where did you take her?"

"I—I—I took her to the room you know, the State Room. The guy—"

"What guy?"

"The guy who told me to get Ms. Scott for the book signing. I tried to tell him she didn't have one scheduled."

"And?"

"And he said he was one of the event sponsors. He said they advertised the signing but they forgot to tell, Ms. Scott. He asked me to see if she'd do it and if she agreed, I was to escort her to the book signing in the State Room. That's what I did. I swear. I didn't do anything else," he said breaking out into a thick layer of perspiration covering his forehead and nose.

"What did he look like?"

"Um—six two, six three maybe with wavy, dark blondish hair and blue eyes. No, he had *gorgeous* vibrant blue eyes and he was very attractive."

"Any scars—marks on his face or anything distinguishable?"

"No," he insisted, shaking his head. "He was perfect," he threw in, admiringly, "Maybe on his— Oh, I'm not sure."

"How old was he?" she snapped.

"It was hard to tell with him."

"Guess!"

"Mid to late thirties."

"Wearing? What was he wearing?"

"Blue," he blurted out nervously, "A blue ball cap."

"Any logo?"

"No—maybe—but I don't remember," he replied in a frightened, whiney tone.

"What else?"

"Dark Armani jeans and a fitted white t-shirt under a brown Bluefly jacket. He's nicely built."

"How do you know?"

"I could tell because his jacket was only half-zipped and I worked in a men's designer store prior to here."

"Anything else?"

"Dark brown boots."

"Earrings? Tattoos? Chipped teeth?"

"No. No, and perfect."

"But you don't know if he had any scars?"

"No. I'm sorry. Do you think he *kidnapped* your mother?" Jordan probed eagerly, trying to solicit noteworthy gossip.

"No!" Lyss yelled defensively. "I haven't seen her since the fire and I need to make sure she's okay," she claimed finally taking two steps back from him. "And you, *you* were the last person I saw her with," she stated crossly.

"I didn't do anything to her! When I took her into the room it wasn't set up for a signing and no one was in there. Nothing was in there!"

"So what did you do?"

"I told her I'd go check with the guy and make sure I had the right room."

"Did you find him?"

"No."

"Was there anyone with him when he approached you?"

"I don't think so," he replied sounding confused.

"I need to find out what happened to her," Lyss complained sighing heavily.

"It's a big hotel," Jordan explained. "She could be anywhere."

"Well, she's not anywhere!"

"Come on," he stated enthusiastically, slipping past her. "I'll have security show you the surveillance video and you can see where she headed when she left the State Room. I swear I don't know what happened after I left. Hey, have you checked her suite?"

"Would I be here talking to you if I hadn't? Jordan, just take me to your security."

Jordan walked behind the front desk and spoke to a tall, attractive gentleman with short brown hair. He was wearing a blue security uniform, in his mid-twenties, lean and built like he worked out on a regular basis. Jordan motioned animatedly with his hand for Lyss and she followed them into the security office. The largest wall above a long desk was plastered with small monitors watching every entrance, hallway, restaurant, bar, kitchen, housekeeping and banquet room in the hotel.

"Alyssa, this is Christian. He should be able to help you from here. I'm sorry about all the confusion. I hope you find Ms. Scott. She was really,

really nice to me," Jordan added gleefully. He left the office, shutting the door behind him.

Christian's serious green eyes indulged on Lyss's sexual beauty from head to toe before adoringly returning to her breasts prior to addressing her.

"Hi Alyssa, I'm Christian. I handle security for the hotel," he said politely, extending his hand.

"Thank you for taking time to speak with me," she replied, receiving his firm hand in both of hers. His flirtatious grin extended, displaying his perfect teeth.

"Would you like to have a seat?" he asked pulling out a chair.

"Oh, no thank you. I need to ask if you have any way of seeing what happened in the State Room this evening, right before the fire?"

"For clarity, Jordan said you think your mother's missing?"

"Correct."

"He believes you were separated because of the fire. Is this accurate?"

"Yes," Lyss agreed hesitantly.

"I caught part of her speech and I really connected with what she was saying. She's impressive, like you," he admitted scanning her body again.

Lyss noticed Christian's roaming eyes and was used to reactions like that, but chose to ignore them instead of becoming upset.

"Is everyone okay? Did anyone get hurt?" Lyss asked compassionately.

"No. The fire wasn't as bad as it seemed. It was more noise and smoke than anything."

"Do they know what caused the fire? Was it intentional or an accident of some sort?"

"Not yet. They're not sure if it was electrical, accidental or even arson at this point. The police took some of the surveillance video to review so—"

"How will I be able to tell what happened to my mother if they have the video?"

Christian's calm narrow eyes focused on Lyss's face and saw the sadness spreading across it.

"I don't have everything here," he admitted. "But let's take a look at the State Room where your mother was last seen and find out what happened in there. The police didn't inspect that area." Lyss let out a sigh of relief as she moved closer to Christian. He turned to inhale the alluring scent of her perfume and shook his head. His attraction to Lyss was distracting him and noticeable to her.

Christian nervously punched a few buttons. When it showed the State Room he stopped and pressed play from the point Jordan entered the room with Marala. Jordan was right; he led Marala into the empty State Room and looked around, appearing baffled. He said something to Marala, threw a slight tantrum and then turned and exited the room leaving her alone. Moments later, dressed exactly as Jordan described, a man in a blue ball cap approached Marala and said something. Marala nodded. He moved toward her and fervently put his arms around her.

Alyssa gasped loudly and covered her mouth as tears rushed to her eyes.

"Oh no," she cried.

Christian turned around and ran his hand across the small of Lyss's back.

"Are you okay?" he asked with genuine concern appearing shocked.

"Go back," she demanded.

He pressed the button and stopped at the same point she reacted to. Lyss watched, completely horrified as it replayed. Before covering her mouth with a white handkerchief, the man calmly spoke to Marala as if he knew her. Moments later as Marala's body fell lifeless into his strong arms he picked her up and carried her out of an exit door at the far end of the room. Christian pressed a button and played the cd showing the camera view to the exit and it displayed the man putting Marala in a black pickup truck. His face was never exposed.

"That's the new Chevy truck," Christian said, writing it down on a piece of paper. He reversed the tape again. "There! Right there," he announced proudly while pointing at the words on the truck. He pushed a button to zoom in and then picked up his pen and continued writing on the paper. "Hopefully, this will help," he said handing it to her. "It says, Sanders Construction on the side of the truck. That may help you find the guy who has your mother. This looks like a kidnapping! Have you notified the police?" he asked picking up the phone on his desk.

"No," Lyss said shaking her head. She reached for the phone and gently took it out of his hand. "Christian, please, don't involve the police at this stage. I know where she is. If I need any help I'll call them but—"

"You don't understand. I need to report this, Alyssa. If the hotel is responsible for anything happening to your mother—"

"Christian, my friends call me, Lyss."

Lyss's phone rang. She quickly pulled it out of her pocket, but didn't recognize the number. She turned her back to Christian and took a few steps away from him before answering it. A brutal surge of chills swept through her body.

"Mama!"

"No. This isn't. Your mother's safe, for now. I can explain everything. But you'd better keep quiet about this."

Lyss's expression was grave.

"I'm glad she's safe. I'm reviewing all of the security disks from the hotel right now and it looks like something happened to her," Lyss stated.

"I warned you! No police," he shouted angrily.

"There aren't. But you're saying Mama got nauseous and passed out?"

"You have company?"

"Yes."

"Get to a private area and wait for my call. No games and no police."

"Okay. I understand. I'll be right there. Please make sure she's okay. Don't let anything happen to her."

He hung up the phone.

"So that was—" Christian began questioning inquisitively.

"The man who has my mother."

"What?"

"The guy in the State Room when she passed out," she said wiping her eyes before turning to face him.

"You said he *has* your mother?"

"Oh, sorry. I meant he's with her. He'd met her earlier and they'd spoken for a bit. He saw her go into the State Room and followed her so he could tell her how much he enjoyed her speech. He told me she seemed like she wasn't doing too well. Apparently, he covered her mouth so she wouldn't, you know, get sick on the banquet room floor."

Christian's face quickly hosted a momentary look of disgust.

"Is she okay?"

"Evidently, he took her to the hospital since she passed out." Lyss put her hand on Christian's shoulder and said in a soft whisper, "My mother had a serious surgery a few months back. We've been trying to keep it quiet so the media doesn't give it a negative slant. With her book being a *Best Seller* and all, this news wouldn't be good. She wasn't feeling well when we arrived and, well, I should have listened. I think I was pushing her too hard to do these tour dates."

"I'm sorry. To be honest with you Lyss, I thought she looked a little uneasy when she was speaking so I guess it all makes sense." He reached for his clipboard resting on the desk and opened the second drawer, pulling out a form. "I have to fill out a report about the incident to protect the hotel. So I'm going to need to get some information from you. It shouldn't take long."

"The hotel didn't have anything to do with her getting ill. Is there anyway we can keep this quiet?" she asked in a soft and sexy persuasive voice.

"I don't know Lyss—"

"Christian, please. I was worried about my mother and blew it out of proportion. Since the surgery, I didn't know if she passed out somewhere or if something happened. I'm usually with her and I would have been, had she not sent me back to the Imperial Theatre to get her—wrap," she told him, holding it up.

As soon as Lyss heard herself, she knew her mother left the wrap behind on purpose. When she did the walk through, they set the temperature to her specifications. She didn't take it to the meet and greet and never used it during her speech. It was her way, once again, of making sure Lyss was safe. She didn't want her anywhere near the State Room.

"And you're sure she's okay? I mean—you know him, right?"

"No. I don't, but apparently she does. I'm headed to the hospital to check on her now.

Christian wasn't buying her explanation and looked completely unconvinced, so Lyss reached into her purse, took out her wallet and handed him two crisp hundred-dollar bills. If you expect negativity to strike it will.

"Lyss, that's not necessary. I—"

"Christian, I wouldn't want the media to get hold of this given we haven't told anyone about her surgery. It'll hurt her tour schedule and raise a lot of questions."

"Say no more. I totally understand," he conceded. Christian was reluctant to accept the money so Lyss forced it into his hand. "I can't say anything now or I'd get fired for not filling out a report anyway. They're strict about following policy. Don't worry about this getting out," he affirmed sliding the money into his pants pocket.

"Do you mind if I keep the video?"

Christian ejected the cd, handed it to Lyss and said, "It's yours."

"Are there any duplicates?" she asked slipping it into her purse.

"No. You have the only copy," he replied scratching his head. "We haven't had time to backup anything yet."

"Thank you," she said hugging him lightly. "Christian, please keep this between us."

"Oh, for sure Lyss. And I'm glad you know where Ms. Scott is. I hope she feels better."

"Thank you."

"Are you checking out?"

"No. I'll be here until Mama gets out of the hospital."

"I know this isn't the best timing but if you don't mind my asking, are you in a relationship or married?" He glanced down at her ring finger while waiting for a calculated response.

She held up her hand and replied, "No and no."

His eyes lit up as he smiled approvingly. "Let me give you my card, in case you need anything." He took one out of the cardholder on his desk and wrote the number to his cell on the back. "You can call me for anything," he said kindly. "I'd like to take you to dinner while you're here. If you have time and of course, after you know your mom's okay."

"I'll let you know. Thanks, Christian."

The door swung open and a solidly built man walked in. He was six-foot-three with blue eyes and sexy dark blond hair. He was nothing less than jaw-dropping gorgeous. As Lyss turned to leave, she collided with him, hitting his rock hard chest.

"Hey, slow down there beautiful," he said catching her before she fell backwards. "Are you okay?" he asked.

"Yes. I think so," she replied, looking up at him with her mouth open with surprise. She brushed her bangs over to the side and stared at his lustful eyes and warm smile. Although she couldn't place it, he seemed awfully familiar to her. "I, um—Have we met?" she asked, taken aback by his stunning appearance.

He extended his hand and gave her a firm handshake.

"I'm Liam. The Head of Security."

"It's nice to meet you. I'm Alyssa," she said marginally flustered.

"Now we've met," he explained winking at her. "What's going on here, Fish?" he asked with an undeniably, sexy and raspy tone.

"What do you mean?" Christian replied suspiciously.

"Jordan said something about a guest missing. She spoke here tonight," he said pointing to the flyer on his desk.

"Ah, yeah—" Christian began, glancing over at Lyss for help.

"He mentioned her daughter's pretty upset about it."

"I am, I mean, I was. The woman you're asking about is *my* mother. And yes, she was speaking in the theatre adjacent to the hotel tonight."

"Really?"

"Yes."

"So, *your* mother is *Marala Scott*?" he questioned, with raised eyebrows. Lyss nodded. "And?"

"And everything's fine. I guess I overreacted. She was supposed to be doing a book signing and then the fire erupted causing all the chaos. Being her daughter, naturally I was worried."

"Were you able to find her?"

"No. I mean, yes. I haven't seen her yet, but I'm headed over there now."

"Headed where?"

"It appears she became sick before the book signing and was taken to the hospital."

"The hospital? Do you know who took her there? I mean, did she call you?" he asked curiously.

"No. Someone else did."

"Do you know who that might have been?" Liam asked.

"Yes. The man that took her to the hospital was someone who attended her speech. He was headed to the book signing and found her ill so he rushed her over there."

"And you know that how?" he questioned crossing his arms across his broad chest.

"Because he called to notify me," Lyss replied defensively. Liam's questioning was making her feel as if she were on trial.

"Christian, did you check out the security video to get a look at this guy?"

"Ah, no. I told her the police took most of the cd's with them," he said shrugging his shoulders, "At this point I don't think there's much we can do."

"Have you filed a report?" he asked, Christian.

"No. I didn't think it was necessary, Liam. I know I probably should—"

"Well, there you have it. Christian's right. It's been a busy evening around here and the fire added another layer to things. I'd say it was quite a distraction. Hopefully, the guest planning to attend the signing understood and weren't too disappointed."

"I guess we'll never know," she replied, anxious to leave. "Liam, I appreciate your attention to this matter but if you don't mind, I'd like to get to my mother." She turned around and added in a gentle tone, "Thanks again, Christian. And I'm sorry I bothered you unnecessarily."

Christian nodded.

"Do you need a ride to the hospital?" Liam asked.

"No thanks!" Lyss called out behind her as she rushed out the security office. Once she reached the lobby she turned towards the elevators and headed up to her suite.

~~~~~~~~~~

Fourteen

After an hour, he exited the highway and drove down a dark, two-lane road for a few miles before pulling into the lot of an abandoned junkyard. He got out of his truck, slipped his hands into a pair of gray workman gloves and pulled the large magnet that read, *Sanders Construction* off both sides of the truck. Without any consideration, he threw them over a tattered wooden fence. He returned to the truck, removed the gloves and gently covered Marala with a maroon, flannel blanket from his back seat. After staring at the youthful features on her symmetrical face, he took his index finger and dotted the tip of her nose along with her chestnut freckles. Before lifting his finger from her face, he traced the outline of her indulgent lips, adoringly. For a moment, they held him captive.

Tumbling deep into his thoughts he continued driving on the quiet State Route with his kidnapped victim, knowing it was too late to turn back. He pondered what Marala's reaction would be when she woke up to this reality with him. He was certain she'd believe he was unstable and attempt to escape.

However, he made sure it wouldn't be possible. Whatever Marala would think it was likely that this time, she'd be dead wrong.

Nearly forty-five minutes later, he made an easy left turn on another desolate road, which led through the heart of a deep verdant forest serving as a natural habitat for an abundance of wildlife. The trees swayed back and forth with random, angry movements due to the disruption of the violent winds increasing in speed. He put down his window, pitched out one glove at a time, a few miles apart and then put it back up.

The stars turned off their luminous lights and abandoned the sky. It was now painted pitch black in preparation for the heavy storm rolling in with increasing velocity behind them. Within a half mile, the storm covered his path causing him to break his speed as the visibility dissipated. The wipers aggressively scraped the pelting rain off the windshield causing a barely audible, groggy moan to escape from Marala. He ran his hand affectionately through her hair and whispered, "Sleep sweetheart, sleep. You're with me now."

~~~~~~~~~~

Fifteen

Lyss was sitting in the suite with the iPad on her lap and phone charging beside her, impatiently awaiting his call. Every conversation she had with her mother about Minnesota replayed in her cluttered mind. She finally realized her mother's intuition was trying to prevent her from doing that event because she knew something terrible was going to happen. Marala was against speaking in Minnesota from the moment she saw it on the schedule.

The numerous discussions Marala had with her daughter about intuition were deliberate reminders. The premeditated selection of dialogue she shared with Lyss was meant to prepare her for what had befallen. Lyss's guilt saturated her heart and weighed it down so heavily it wanted to crumble.

"Mama!" she cried, "Where are you?"

~~~~~~~~~~

Sixteen

He broke his speed again and made a quick left turn heading into a deep wooded area on a barely visible path. He drove for a half mile before pulling up to a secluded cabin hidden in the dense woods. He parked in front of an old garage. Leaving his headlights on, he lifted Marala from the truck and carried her into the cabin.

He entered a comfortable-sized bedroom and laid her across a bed, freshly made with new linens. There was a soft burgundy throw lying on the rocking chair that he placed carefully across her body after removing her stilettos. He placed them neatly in the closet and went back outside to unlock the garage. To keep his truck out of sight, he pulled it into the garage. He grabbed her bag and then shut and locked the garage before returning to the cabin. The rest of his night was spent in a hand-carved rocking chair beside Marala, watching her closely, as the storm continued its wicked thrashing against the cabin.

Hours later, the sun struggled to ascend upon the cabin. Marala was awake feeling groggy and indolent accompanied by a vicious headache pounding angrily. Her face displayed sheer confusion as she spotted an unfamiliar royal blue mug, with steam escaping from it, sitting on the white oak nightstand beside the bed. She carefully turned her head towards the light sound of the rocking chair moving back and forth.

"How are you feeling?" he asked gruffly, running his fingers backwards through his thick, messy, morning hair.

"I'm sure you already know," she replied holding her head in pain, trying to adjust her blurry eyes to the details of his staid, fearless expression.

"I'm sorry about having to do this but I had no choice."

"We all have choices," she acknowledged sorely, pushing herself up to a sitting position.

"No. I didn't," he alleged.

His serious eyes stayed fixed on Marala, watching her awkward movements.

"Everyone has a choice which involves choosing to do what's right or wrong. Why did you do this? People don't kidnap someone because they don't have a choice," she stated, showing signs of being in pain.

He leaned forward in the chair as though he wanted to get up and help her, except he knew he couldn't.

"I'll tell you when it's time," he stated unemotionally.

"You kidnapped me. You're holding me, only God knows where and you don't think *it's time* I know why?"

He looked directly into her brown her eyes and said, "No."

"Can I at least call my daughter? I know she's worried sick and the police are probably looking for me."

"No. They're not. No one's looking for you. And your daughter—"

"Where is she? Where's Lyss?"

"She's safe. Most likely back at the hotel, waiting to hear from you."

"How do you know this?"

"I spoke with her last night and advised her not to contact the police. She demanded to speak with you, but you were sleeping."

"No, I was knocked out."

He nodded agreeably and replied, "That's fair. But anyway you look at it, you were asleep, so I told Alyssa I'd let you talk with her when you woke up."

"Where am I?"

"It's better for everyone if you don't know."

"Everyone?"

"Let's start with Alyssa for now. It's better *she* doesn't know," he exclaimed suggestively.

Marala slowly swung her legs over the side of the bed and tried unsuccessfully to stand only to fall back on the bed. "I feel sick," she said nauseously.

"You probably need your medicine." He got up and walked over to her nightstand, singled out one of the four bottles of medicine and then handed it to her.

Marala cautiously took the bottle and read the label to make sure it was hers.

"What time is it?"

"It's still early. About 6:45," he replied.

"How long have I been here?"

"Since last night."

She opened the cap on the medicine and took out one of the pills.

"What is that?" she asked glancing up at him.

"Tea," he said offering it to her.

"Is there anything in it that will knock me out again?" she asked prior to reaching for the mug.

"No. And for the record, *if* I were going to hurt you, I could have done it already. And I wouldn't be giving you your medicine, which we both know you need."

She swallowed one of the tablets and washed it down with a sip of tea.

"If you don't want to hurt me then why am I here?"

"Because at the moment, it's where you need to be."

"Can I call my daughter? Please!"

He looked at her merciful eyes and without reluctance warned, "As long as you remember this. Don't give her any clues or it'll be the last time I let you talk with her. Tell her you're safe—"

"Am I?"

"Not yet?"

"Why not?"

"Tell her not to involve the police or anyone. She needs to hear your voice for now. Nothing more."

"Is she safe?"

"If you listen to me."

She nodded agreeably. He dialed Lyss's number and handed her the phone. She answered on the first ring.

"Mama!"

"Yes, baby. It's me."

"Where are you? Who has you? Are you hurt?" she cried out frantically.

"I don't have much time to talk so listen carefully," she said looking directly into his piercing blue eyes. "I don't know where I am. He said I'm safe, but only if you don't involve the police or anyone else. And he hasn't hurt me."

"Mama—"

"Lyss, I promise," she whispered persuasively.

"Okay, Mama, okay. What about your medicine? How are you feeling—And do you know who he is?"

"Lyss, he gave me my medicine, I'm fine and yes. Go home sweetheart and I'll contact you when I can—"

He snatched the phone and heard Lyss ask, "Do you know what this is about?"

"No. For now, it's better this way. Listen to your mother," he cautioned sternly.

"What do you want from her?"

"The same thing you do."

"How can I get her back? Do you know she's not well?"

"You can't, and yes."

He hung up the phone.

Lyss released a loud agonizing scream as she dropped to the floor. She felt helpless.

Marala's heart plummeted as she absorbed every letter of fear in Lyss's words. She didn't know why this was happening. Nevertheless, her intuition warned her it would.

He observed the tears rolling down Marala's cheeks and in a hushed tone said, "I'm sorry." He tussled his hair back appearing genuinely disturbed by her melancholy disposition.

"I believe you are. Yet, it doesn't change that this is happening and you haven't told me why."

"Get some rest and we'll talk later."

"I'm not tired. If you're going to keep me here at least tell me why."

"Marala," he said firmly, "I'll tell you what you need to know for now. If you try to leave here, you'll die and you don't want to involve your daughter. It's too soon to explain anything. Rest for now," he added turning away from her to leave the room. "Your bathroom is through there," he said pointing in its direction. "I'm going to make breakfast."

"I'm not hungry."

"You need it to take the rest of your medicine and it's not good for you to be upset."

"What have I done to hurt you? Please, tell me?" she asked in an entreating whisper.

Without responding he left the room and locked the door.

~~~~~~~~~~

Seventeen

Lyss nervously paced the hotel floor trying to determine what to do. She replayed her mother's words in her head. *Can you believe all of those communications are on my laptop? I keep everything. If you can't find what you need in here, you won't find it.* She grabbed her mother's laptop and turned it on.

"She said, *he* and she knows who *he* is, so he must be in here," she said aloud.

She turned on the laptop and snatched a yellow notepad and pen out of her mother's computer bag while it loaded. Once she logged into her email, she began with the oldest message. She was going to read every single message sent by every male and dissect the contents until things made sense. After reading the first one, she wrote his name down on the tablet. He was now a suspect. In fact, they were all going to be suspects until she ruled them out.

~~~~~~~~~~

Eighteen

Marala opened the small bay window in the bedroom to find an extended flagstone path in the back of the cabin, leading to a breathtaking view of the lake. She watched the raindrops dance gracefully on the lake while the light wind playfully swayed the water beneath them. The lake spanned more than a half-mile to the other side. It was surrounded by a thick layer of trees hosting an assortment of brilliant, colorful autumn leaves falling into nonexistence. The boathouse held a weathered aluminum fishing boat, securely covered and resting on a lift several feet above the lake. The view was so picturesque, not even the bars on the window spoiled it.

After Marala finished taking a hot, steamy shower she returned to the bedroom to search for something to wear. When she opened the closet, she was caught off guard to find it nearly full of clothing. She looked at the tags on several items and discovered the clothing was brand new and sized perfectly to fit her. She opened the top dresser drawer and found it filled with tasteful, yet sexy undergarments. She put on a set and opened the other drawers, which had neatly folded jeans, sweats and t-shirts in them. She pulled out a pair of jeans. After pairing them with a white t-shirt and a charcoal, cashmere cardigan, she got dressed. She thought it was odd that the clothes were items she would have easily purchased for herself.

The bedroom was meticulously equipped with everything he thought she'd need from clothing to personal items. The rustic and comfortable room gave the impression she was being held captive at an intimate and relaxing Bed & Breakfast. Marala viewed the premeditated preparation as evidence that her being kidnapped had been an elaborate plan orchestrated over time. She pulled her wet hair back into a curly ponytail and put on the same hair clip Lyss handed to her the night of the event. Somberly, she returned to her view out the window.

The door swung open and he walked in placing a breakfast tray with a spinach, tomato, mushroom and cheese omelet, along with honey wheat toast, raspberry jam and cranberry juice on the bed.

He turned to leave but added in a mild tone, "Sorry about the bars. They're non-negotiable."

"I hadn't noticed due to the enchanting view."

"I'm no chef but I hope breakfast is satisfactory."

"Are you joining me?"

"I hadn't planned on it."

He disappeared again. Marala sat down on the bed and tried to determine how and why he did it. He managed to make her favorite breakfast. She blessed her meal, picked up the fork and tasted the omelet. She was taken aback by his culinary skills. He prepared it as delectably as possible. Although she didn't want to eat, it was the sensible thing to do. She needed to take her medicine and sustain her strength. The duration of time she'd remain captive or how she'd escape was unknown.

Thirty minutes later, she heard the door being unlocked and he entered the room to remove her tray.

"Thank you."

He pointed towards her prescriptions and instructed authoritatively, "Take it."

She picked up two of the bottles.

"Do you know why I take this medicine?" she asked, opening them and pouring a tablet from each into her hand.

"Yes."

"How do you know?" she asked sipping cranberry juice after both pills.

"Research."

"Obviously, you've done a lot on me. Is there a specific reason why?"

"How was breakfast?" he questioned with a feeble huff.

"Much better than I'd imagine a prisons would be."

"Your bed. Is it comfortable?"

"Yes."

"Do the clothes fit you properly?"

"Surprisingly."

"There's your answer."

"You want me to be comfortable and have what I need, as if I were at home."

"Yes."

"But you've kidnapped me and taken me away from my daughter. This doesn't provide comfort. Can you imagine the discomfort and pain this is causing Lyss?"

"Yes," he said studying her intently. "I can bring her here and lock her up if that's your preference."

"No! Don't go near my daughter!"

"Then don't assume I'm not aware of the consequences of my actions. I took precisely what I needed and nothing more."

"So please explain why you've chosen to do this? Give me a reason or something to help me comprehend your actions. *Why* do you *need* me?"

"*Intuition.*"

Marala observed him with emerging confusion. "I don't understand what my book has to do with this. Is there something in it that's offended you?"

"The book, *no*. It's given me strength to do what's necessary. Before *Intuition*, I would never have done this."

"This? Meaning, kidnap me?"

"Yes."

"You're telling me that's what my book taught you to do, become a criminal?"

"It was you who said, *'people can be taught anything inspiring or encouraging, however you cannot make them practice what they've heard because it doesn't mean they've learned or absorbed it enough to make a change.'* Well, I have."

"Yes, I said that but finish my quote because it concluded with, *'what you can do is focus on practicing the powerful things you've learned and make life-altering changes so others may follow your example.'* Do you want others to follow your example of kidnapping someone because of their book?"

"I'm following your example because I love your book and what you share as inspiration. The message is the message. I've absorbed enough to modifications and your being here is a part of the changes *I* need to make."

"I'm not certain that you're taking from my book what was intended. It's the same way some interpret the Bible, in a manner that is convenient for them, but it's not what was intended by its authors."

"Marala?"

"Yes."

"Are you afraid of me?" he questioned walking towards her.

"No. Should I be?" she asked without recoiling.

"I've kidnapped you," he said in a dangerously seductive tone.

"I'm aware, yet I am not afraid," she admitted boldly.

"Of dying?"

"Of either."

"You're very strong," he said approvingly. "Do you live through your words or do your words live through you?"

"You already know the answer. *'Use and believe in the power of the words, I am to show faith in yourself—'*"

"'*Find yourself and love that person. Be present in this amazing journey of life,*'" he said concluding her words of inspiration.

"How is it that you know my words so well?"

"Research."

"Or is it obsession?"

"You're not afraid of me so *you already know the answer* because you trust your intuition, Marala. Your faith is resolute and so is your heart."

She leaned back against the headboard, gently rubbed her forehead and then let her fingers gently run along the beginning of her scar.

"What's wrong?" he asked moving closer to her bedside.

"I'm—I'm not feeling well," she replied faintly.

The painful throbbing in her head quickly intensified.

"What do you need?"

"To know what you want from me so I can return home to my daughter."

Marala grabbed a pillow from beside her and carefully rested her head on it as though she were in excruciating pain.

"I'm sorry, Marala. This is something that must be done. *'You cannot change history but you can add to the final outcome by changing your future. Share your gift of life with love.'* Those are your beautiful words once again and they've changed me. Now, it appears you don't like it."

"This is not sharing your gift of life with love."

What I don't like is being held against my will and I don't appreciate that you won't tell me why. If I understood—"

"Would you accept this?" he asked genuinely.

"No. But—"

"Then explaining what this is about is futile."

Without further enlightenment he left the room, locking the door behind him.

~~~~~~~~~~

Nineteen

Lyss hadn't slept at all and didn't have any visible signs of exhaustion. She was completely engrossed, avidly searching for clues. The two empty coffee pots were evidence of her conviction to stay focused on finding her mother. Her list had grown to thirty-seven men but a few of them had an asterisk next to their name. Somehow, Robert was one of them. He had communicated with Marala in the past few months, but neglected to inform her that he was the title sponsor of the Minnesota event. His messages weren't alarming, simply out of the ordinary. Lyss matched the business card she received from Robert at the reception and found the email addresses corresponded.

One woman managed to make the list. It was Sharon from Connecticut. The unresolved problems with her ex-husband made him a suspect. There was a guy named Liam, but his comments were extremely positive and he hadn't written in several months. Although similar in appearance to the hotel's Head of Security, he was about ten years older. Regardless, he reminded her of someone but she couldn't place it. Lyss breathed a sigh of relief.

Surprisingly, after reading all of his emails and deliberating, Garrett made the list because she found his last message to be obscure. Lyss poured herself another cup of coffee and continued reading messages. A few minutes later, a new notification alert from Garrett flashed. She opened it.

Good Morning Beautiful,

I hope you're having a great time. I'm sure your speech was as amazing as you are. I don't see anymore of your schedule posted. Is everything okay?

Fondly,
Garrett

Lyss pressed reply.

Garrett,

Last night was great. The crowd was very moved by the speech. It would be nice to finally meet you, especially since we've been emailing each other for quite a while. I'm surprised you've never attended any of my speaking engagements.

The reason my schedule isn't posted is because I've been a little tired lately so I thought I'd take some time off from speaking. How's the weather where you are?

Hugs,
Marala

Lyss pressed send. Within a few minutes, Garrett's reply popped up.

The weather is beautiful, like you. I'm headed to the beach with some friends. I'm in Florida this week. I thought I mentioned that to you? Regardless, I've been following your schedule so I can make one of your speeches soon. Please keep me informed of any changes. By the way, you didn't post your inspirational message today. Don't be a slacker. Have a great day!

Lyss looked out the window and saw the sky covered with murky clouds and blustery rain swirling around heedlessly. She clicked open a tab on the laptop, checked out the weather in Minnesota and all surrounding areas. The storm was widespread. She picked up her yellow notepad, sighed with relief and then crossed Garrett's name off. She opened the next message and read it.

What will happen is going to be above reason.

"I should have read this," she said noticing the date.

It was the last message Marala received in Chicago. Lyss covered her mouth and tears filled her eyes. Her aching sobs grew heavy and her knotted stomach twisted in a violent fit of pain.

~~~~~~~~~~

Twenty

Occupied by impatience, Marala sat at the end of the bed waiting for him to return, exhibiting a drawn out rendition of her tormented captor. All she could think about was the pain he was thrusting into the soul of her innocent daughter through his actions and nothing more. It was beginning to stir emotions in Marala that had long been buried beneath this life. She feared the indescribable thoughts and horror cutting through her daughters mind would make an attempt to mutilate her faith should anything happen to her. Marala closed her eyes and said a prayer that Lyss would circle back to their recent conversations. Only there would she find the outline to this situation already scripted and the solution dangling within her psychological grasp. Possibly, this would be a revelation to Lyss, authenticating intuition's constant presence while revealing its accessibility to follow at will.

Marala's unpolluted faith had mentally prepared her for everything that was being exposed. How this would unfold and at what cost was still unknown but she was certain this was about something far more mysterious than it seemed. She resigned to accept that the situation had to play out. Now wasn't the time to fight, run, or disrupt his plan. It would be a grave mistake to think he hadn't covered all of his bases, especially with how much he appeared to know about her. His captivating calmness was only one layer of many and it was far from his underlying ominous core.

His strong attractive exterior meant nothing to Marala. She was aware he was calculating, had a great deal of restraint and was capable of practically anything without warning. One of the dangerous and volatile components he was comprised of was that he knew how to kill, violently. She had no other recourse except to wait until he allowed her into his head where comprehension of his twisted perception and what he sought to accomplish was locked away.

The persistent scraping of tree branches against the cabin in the harsh and blustery wind caused Marala to climb out of bed and glance out the window. She realized the rain hadn't become weary but instead, picked up fury like her swirling thoughts. A deafening collage of crashing thunder caused her to become unnerved and jump away from the window, carelessly backing into him. When she turned around, she was wrapped securely in his arms staring at the beautiful details of his face, starting with his perfect nose and enticing lips. He was simply gorgeous. This time, she didn't hear him enter the room.

"Are you okay?"

"Yes."

"The storms can get pretty bad up here. After a while you tend to get used to it."

"I guess it caught me off guard. I really didn't mean to—"

"Would you like to get out of this room and sit by the fire? The cabin gets a little drafty at times."

Marala nodded agreeably, pulling her sweater together as she backed away from his affectionate embrace. He stepped aside to follow her into the living room.

To Marala's surprise, the room had a natural warm and inviting feel. The oversized chocolate leather sofa and two matching comfortable leather chairs with throw blankets on them faced a magnificent natural fieldstone fireplace. The fireplace ran from the wooden floor to the cathedral ceiling that had stunning log beams crossing it. The large whitetail deer head with considerable antlers, mounted over the fireplace, appeared to be a trophy.

"Have a seat," he instructed while opening the front door. An unsullied mixture of evergreen and heavy rain blew through the room as he darted outside to gather an armful of wood. When he returned, he kicked the door closed, knelt down and neatly stacked the logs by the fireplace before giving his attention to Marala. She was sitting in a leather chair taking in the details of the cabin. He tossed another log on the blazing fire and clapped his hands together removing the debris from the wood. "How about a hot cup of tea?" he asked, locking the front door.

"Yes. Thank you," she replied with her eyes following him into the kitchen. An attractive characteristic was the natural confidence he exuded. He pulled off his wet sweatshirt, leaving a perfectly chiseled body for display underneath. With blushing embarrassment, Marala dropped her head after eyeing his physique, catching his seductive smile when he noticed.

"If you prefer something other than tea I have—"

"No, um, that's—that's fine. What you've offered is perfect"

"Are you feeling better?" he asked filling the stainless steel teakettle with water.

"Somewhat."

"Do you care to talk about it?"

"Not really," she replied shaking her head reservedly.

He placed the teakettle on the stove and walked over to the living room window.

"It'll be a while before this storm blows over," he said.

"Where are we?"

He walked over to her, cleared his throat and replied, "We need to establish something right now. I'm not going to tell you anything I don't want you to know. The less you know, like I said before, the better it is for everyone, including your daughter. This isn't something I want to do, but regardless of what you think, I didn't have a choice. I don't like being mixed up in this either, but *I am!*"

"So there are others involved," she stated with an outline of fear.

He put his hands on his waist, returned an intense look and adamantly replied, "Yes."

"And—"

"And that's why you need to know as little as possible. Right now, Alyssa doesn't have anything to do with this other than being your daughter. If you want to keep it that way, listen to me."

"And you won't hurt her?"

"No. *I won't.* But understand if she starts interfering or tries to find you, I can't be responsible for what will happen to her," he replied offhandedly.

"I need to tell her this."

"You did. You should pray she listens to you and goes home."

"What do you want from me?"

"Nothing."

"Then why am I here?"

He didn't answer. Instead, he climbed the stairs to the loft and pulled a fitted white t-shirt out of his drawer. He returned to the living room, pulling it over his head exposing his perfectly defined abs one more time before concealing them.

The rain and wind continued pounding savagely on the cabin and the teakettle chimed in with its flamboyant whistle. He went into the kitchen and washed his hands, then reached into a cabinet above the sink and grabbed a mug. After filling it with boiling hot water he removed a teabag from the jar on the counter and dropped it in. He pulled a spoon out of the drawer and added a teaspoon of raw sugar, catching a glimpse of Marala's troubled face. He took the cream out of the refrigerator and added a small amount, stirring it gently.

When he finished, he retuned to the living room and handed the tea to Marala. She took the cup and turned away. He moved in closer and dabbed her tears away.

"I promise you," he whispered, "I have no choice. If I didn't do this, you and your daughter would both die."

Although she tried to abstain from crying, her heartrending tears flushed out. He gently removed the mug from her trembling hand and sat it on an antique leather storage trunk resting on a black bear skin. Marala stared unresponsively out the round arched window into the vast forest of evergreens.

He pulled a blanket over her and tossed another log on the fire before vanishing into his own thoughts in the loft above, attentive to her the entire time.

~~~~~~~~~~

Twenty-One

Hours later, the gusty rain subsided. Lyss was seated in the hotel café sipping on a cup of coffee, reading her notes. When Liam saw her, he made a quick detour and headed her way.

"Hey, you're still here. How's your mom?"

Lyss glanced up from her writing and replied, "Oh, Mama. She's doing much better. Thank you."

"Do you mind if I join you?" he asked already pulling out a chair.

"I was—"

"Thanks," he said cheerfully already seated. "So, was your mom at the hospital?"

Lyss turned her notepad over and nodded agreeably. "Which hospital?"

"Ah, the one near this hotel."

"Canyon Glenn?"

"Are you working today?" she asked avoiding the subject.

"No. I came here to get a workout in; I just finished. If you like to workout this gym is state of the art." Lyss took a sip of her coffee and studied his face along with his infectious smile, "I mean, not that you need to, at all."

"I workout, but lately my time has gone to—other things."

"Do you lift weights? Your arms are pretty tone, along with the rest of you."

"Weights, not exactly. I prefer yoga, for the relaxation."

"Yoga's good. Whatever keeps you looking like that definitely works. So is your mom back here at the hotel or is she still in the hospital?"

"Liam, I'd really rather not talk about Mama right now because I have other things on my mind," she insisted.

"Okay, well I thought—"

"And I appreciate it," Lyss kindly interrupted.

"Will you be staying here a while longer?"

"Right now, that's the plan."

"I guess you're in luck. Since I'm off today, I'll take you and your mom out to dinner.

"Well, unfortunately I'll have to decline. I'm sort of busy trying to solve a major problem and I really don't have time for anything else," she told him, displaying little interest.

"Alyssa, I'm the Head of Security. I solve problems for a living," he acknowledged flashing a gorgeous smile even she couldn't resist.

"What makes you think it's something that needs investigative work from the Head of Security?" she questioned leaning back in her chair.

"Because that beautiful little face of yours looks like whatever's bothering you has been making you cry, unless you have allergies," he added sarcastically. Lyss didn't say anything. She picked up the cup and sipped her coffee. Liam noticed her dejected expression and decided to extend his time with her by bringing up another topic. "You know, when I was a kid I wanted to be an assassin."

She looked at him with a slight frown and said, "Interesting choice of profession. An assassin? Why?"

"To get rid of people that didn't deserve to be here."

"Didn't deserve to be here?"

"Yeah."

"Where'd that come from?"

"I don't know really. Maybe too much television as a kid."

"That's pretty random."

"Perhaps."

"And ruthless."

"Yeah, maybe. But ultimately, I realized I didn't have it in me."

"So what happened?"

"I decided to try and do some good in this world and help people."

"So how'd you end up here? Don't get me wrong, you're still helping people but you could've been a detective, joined the CIA or—"

"Yeah. I tried but I had something in my past that prevented me from qualifying and I ended up here," he said looking around.

"That's too bad," Lyss replied.

"Tell me about it," he shrugged.

"Oh—no. I don't mean working here. This is a beautiful hotel," she explained apologetically. "What I'm referring to is I think it's inconceivable that some people refuse to understand *everyone* has a history."

"But you're aware that some may have quite the unsavory history."

"Yes, and there are negative situations that may have been created or even inherited due to circumstance and environment. However, people can change, if they choose. Whatever was in your past is clearly far removed from who you are today or you wouldn't be here. I'm sure the hotel has background checks they're required to do."

"True, but I had a little help."

"Well, whatever it was, did you do any time?"

"No! I mean, I did emotionally but *no*. I didn't do anything like that. It was something stupid, you know, it happened when I was a kid. To be honest, I've cut out that part of my life and kind of forgotten about it."

"It's not always good to suppress things because they can resurface when you least expect them."

"Really, Doc? You sound fairly convinced about that."

"I am."

"How'd you come to this conclusion?"

"I'm not a doctor yet, but I will be soon," she admitted.

"Really?" he said noticeably impressed.

"Yes, really. Why is that surprising?" she asked with a soft smile.

"I suppose it's not. You are pretty remarkable. So, what type of doctor do you want to be? Wait—hold on, let me guess," he suggested, narrowing his bright blue eyes, examining her carefully. "Kids. Yeah," he said rubbing the light stubble on his chin. "I can see you helping those little guys. I'd say a child psychologist."

"Psychologist. Very good," she admitted. "I thought about it but I wanted to be challenged a bit more. Not that it isn't a challenging area of focus, but I went forensic."

"A forensic psychologist?" he questioned.

"Yes."

"Wow! So you apply psychology to the field of criminal investigation."

"A-huh. But when I really got into it, I realized I didn't want to deal with the minds of criminals and learn to think like they do. Something didn't feel right to me. That's why I settled on Clinical Psychology."

"Well, you can still have the best of both worlds because some of the people you treat will most likely be criminals."

"Yes, but this way I don't have to become them in order to do my job."

"Did you learn much?"

"A little more than I bargained for."

"Why aren't you in school now?"

"Whenever my mother speaks, I usually travel with her during the summer."

"In case you haven't noticed darlin', it's fall."

"I know, but some things came up and I decided to stay with her."

"Was she sick or something?"

"When she released her latest book, *Intuition*, I wanted to learn more about it. It made *The New York Times Best Seller's List* and it's impacting people in an incredible way. Quit honestly, I find the topic fascinating. It wasn't possible for my mother to handle this tour, interviews, book signings and everything that came along with it on her own."

"Doesn't she have an agent?"

"Yes, and Adam is wonderful. But what I do isn't exactly what an agent does."

"Why didn't she hire an assistant?"

"Because, *I* wanted to do it. The way people respond to her is unparalleled and I love being able to share that experience."

"I'd agree. I caught some of her speech last night and I was surprised by the crowd's reaction. Needless to say, I liked what I heard. She seemed a little tired but she did great. I mean the hotel was working on every single detail of this event for weeks. And as you saw, tickets were sold out. The Imperial Theatre where she spoke is adjacent to the hotel. It's the largest in the Twin Cities and your mother had a capacity crowd. The hotel was completely full last night."

"Really?"

"Yeah. The front desk was receiving calls like crazy about your mom. Some guy called claiming he wanted to send flowers and requested her room number."

"Did they tell him?" Lyss asked expressing concern.

"No. It's against policy to give out any information on a guest."

"Good," she said sounding relieved.

"I don't know everything about your mother, but she seems to be quite an inspirational woman."

"Thank you. She's amazing."

"And easy on the eyes like her daughter," he said with a smile. "When she speaks, it appears that her words seep into a cavernous area inside of you whether you want them or not. When they settle, it makes things more lucid. I admit, she's commanding to say the least."

"Did her words get inside you?" Her sensual brown eyes smiled at him.

"They did," he replied with conviction.

"How so?"

"Okay, now you're putting me on the spot?" he asked rubbing his chin again.

"I'm simply checking your memory to see if you pay attention to details, Mr. Assassin," she said challenging him flirtatiously.

"I said I *wanted* to be one, but I'm not," he replied with laughter.

"Oh, but you are the Head of Security here. Your attention to details, I'd say, should be stellar," she advised jokingly.

"Okay, if I can recall a part of her speech—"

"Verbatim." Lyss demanded.

"Verbatim, huh? You're tough," he confessed. "Then you'll have dinner with me?"

Lyss let her eyes travel across his beautifully defined face before meeting his delightful eyes and then replied assuredly, "No. I'm here to—"

"I said dinner, not incredible sex," he said offering his hand.

She observed his unadorned ring finger and then shook his hand.

"Fine. But you have to state her words, *verbatim*. And if you can't, you need to leave me alone for the rest of my stay here."

"Oh. That's harsh coming from such a beautiful woman. Not even a *hello* or *good morning ma'am?*"

"That's exactly why I said it. I'm sure you meet beautiful women every day. And for some reason, I'd guarantee you have absolutely no problem getting what you want." She leaned towards him and clarified, "I'm referring to dinner *and* incredible sex."

He bit down on his bottom lip and then chuckled, "You are something."

"Yes, and that something will be a psychologist soon, remember?"

He laughed and said, "Yeah, how can I forget?" With a light clearing of his throat he said, "Alright. I didn't see all of her speech," he reminded, touching his hands together in prayer form.

"Here come the excuses."

"Make sure you keep your word, Doc," he suggested winking at her.

"Liam, one thing you should know about me is that I always keep my word."

She leaned back and crossed her legs giving him her full attention.

"Let's see," he began conveying pure confidence, "Ms. Scott said, and I'm quoting her verbatim— '*Intuition doesn't work with inference or reason, but it works! Keep intuition in the foreground of your mind instead of in the background because it's a powerful resource and it can save your life. Using it will teach you to have consistency in trusting it. And when I show you how to develop it, you'll find that you're more intuitive in areas or with people that you love.*' Will that do?" he asked arrogantly writing his number on a white napkin. He slid the napkin over to her and stated in his raspy voice, "I'd like to have dinner *tonight* so wear something sexy and I'll pick you up at six," he told her tapping his hand on the table twice before getting up and walking away.

"Liam! Wait!" she called after him, observing the movements of his impeccable body.

"No cancellations," he reminded flashing a winning smile at her.

"How did you remember all of that," she asked completely caught off guard.

He stopped and turned to face her while confessing, "Well, Doc. As I've already shared with you, I wanted to be an assassin," he stated sarcastically, "And they absolutely *must* pay attention to details—as you've made clear."

"So?"

"So, I retrieved the video of your mother's speech last night."

"That's not fair. You said you didn't see all of her speech," she announced slightly nettled.

"And I didn't," he stated offhandedly, "I downloaded it and *listened* while working out this morning." He reached into the pocket of his sweats and pulled out the earpiece attached to his phone.

"'*Use and believe in the power of the words, I am, to show faith in yourself.*'" She said that too," he gloated. "*I am* going to have dinner with you tonight gorgeous— because you always keep your word," he added leaving the café.

~~~~~~~~~~

Twenty-Two

Christian was in the security office watching the surveillance monitor of Lyss and Liam in the café. He frowned angrily as he observed Liam walking away with a victorious smile, as if he'd won a prize. Lyss scribbled something down on her notepad and left the café.

Christian reached into the bottom drawer of a metal file cabinet and pulled out two small disks tucked away in an Employee Benefits file. He smirked mischievously and slipped them into his jacket pocket.

~~~~~~~~~~

Twenty-Three

Hours passed before he left the loft and returned to the living room. Marala was still sitting in a chair watching the blazing fire. He noticed she'd carefully placed a log on the fire and tended to it as needed, refusing to let it burn out. As he observed Marala, he realized she was drawing strength from it by assembling her scattered thoughts. Once the storm subsided and the day became calmer, so did Marala. She was patiently relying on her intuition to convey comprehension.

"It looks like the fire has your full attention." He picked up the poker, shifted the logs around and then added another.

"It does," she affirmed.

"Sounds interesting."

"It is."

"How so?"

"Everything on this earth has at least a dual purpose."

"Really?"

"Pick something."

"Poison ivy," he stated cleverly.

"Well, it's not good for most humans because of the annoying, itchy little rash it causes. But songbirds—they eat the drupe or berries in the winter."

"Nicely done. And your thoughts on the fire," he asked inquisitively.

"Despite the beauty captured in the brilliance and color of the extraordinary lucidity of the flames, it has even more power than its warmth.

"Okay, you have my attention," he remarked putting the poker back in its stand. "Unless you've experienced or witnessed the devastation fire causes, it would be difficult to fully conceive the aftermath left behind from its flames. Think about the wild fires that burn uncontrollably, destroying, land, houses and the lives of those who lived in them. To take it a step further, unfortunately, unstable people are like that too. They use fire to destroy or devastate the lives of others in heinous, criminal acts of setting them on fire, engulfing themselves in a feeling of empowerment and victory."

"So, the implication of doing something like that is an atrocious act which displays how disturbed an individual is," he added ascetically, taking in the intensity of the fire."

"I'd say so," she agreed.

"Do you think those who perform such violent, unthinkable acts should be punished?"

"Of course," she said resolutely. He smiled approvingly. "But, by God," she added.

His look of approval waned. He peered out the window while casually changing the subject.

"It's finally looking better out there," he commented, nodding towards the window. "It was quite a rough night."

"For some reason, I can't remember it."

"At any rate, grab your boots. Let's go for a walk."

"I don't—"

"They're in the closet," he told her pointing towards the bedroom.

He walked over to Marala and removed the flannel throw from her lap and reached for her hand to help her up. She went into the room and grabbed the boots; slipping into them by the time she reached the front door.

"Should I be worried?" she asked derisively.

"Not yet," he retorted.

"That's good to know," she said stepping out on the front porch.

"Let's go by the lake," he said pointing at the path.

He followed her around the back of the cabin, over a slight hill and down the path to the boathouse where the gentle ripples were making their way in unison across the lake. The crisp and refreshing fall air trailed up her nostrils as she made her way down the long dock. She looked out over the lake taking in a deep breath of fresh air, exhaling slowly.

"Be careful," he warned as she crept closer to the water, "The dock's still wet and there's a deep drop off."

She looked down realizing he was right, backed away from the side of the dock and walked to the end, grabbing hold of the heavy metal pole. The boat was hanging four feet above the water. He grabbed the sturdy straps, holding the cover down and gave them a firm tug to make sure it was secure. Reminiscently, he ran his hands along the side of the boat.

"Do you use it for fishing?" she asked observing its age.

"No. I don't use it at all."

"Then why are you keeping such an old boat?"

"I have no choice."

"You do have a choice," she scolded.

He looked at her gravely and repeated decisively, "I have no choice."

"Your choice is that you choose to keep it."

"Not because I want to."

"You must want to or you'd get rid of it. Does it belong to someone else?"

"Something like that," he admitted dolefully.

"Do you go out on the lake much?"

"No. I have no desire to ever go on that lake. In fact, I don't like water."

"I think it's beautiful and rather serene." He didn't respond. "It seems to be pretty isolated out here."

"It is."

"Is there a reason you chose this type of solitude since you don't use the lake or like water?"

"If I had my way, I'd never come up here. But there's something that keeps drawing me back to this place."

He stared across the lake for a brief time, before turning away with notable aversion.

"Is this your cabin?"

"Come on," he said grabbing her hand forcefully.

He led her around to the front of the cabin past the grouping of maple trees, while the falling leaves playfully drifted around the ground rustling at their feet. They followed a barely visible trail into the woods, walking in silence; taking in the surroundings. The playful movement of squirrels and chipmunks reminded Marala of Gods endless presence. When she began to speak, he gently put his finger against her lips instructing her to be quiet and still. Moments later he pointed to a beautiful whitetail doe and her two fawns, thirty feet ahead of them. The movements of the deer were elegant and calculated as they observed their surroundings. When he guided Marala a few steps closer, the deer fled with absolute grace.

"Breathtaking."

"Yes. It is," he agreed.

Marala noticed that with nearly every step taken, he observed the ground around him.

"Are there other animals out here, such as bears or anything?"

"Yes. And like me, they won't attack unless you make them," he warned.

The sun continued to peek through the dense mass of trees while they journeyed deeper into the woods taking in the faint sounds of nature. The smell of pinecones lingered in the forest and the fluttering of birds weaving through the trees connected Marala to a more peaceful state. Marala was drawn to nature the same way she was her intuition.

Cutting the silence between them, she asked candidly, "Do you believe in intuition?"

Without reluctance he replied, "Absolutely."

He was noticeably surprised by her question.

"Why?" she continued pushing for his reason.

"Because once I learned to trust it; I found it to be the truth."

"How?"

"You don't know?" he asked cynically. "You've opened my mind through your faith, words and examples bringing clarity to what intuition is. Looking back to when I was a kid, my father always alleged my mother was intuitive, but I didn't understand what that meant. She seemed more alert to things at times—but I didn't get it. As I grew up, I dismissed intuition and followed my own logic and reason without considering anything else. And in the end, which is now, I realize I should've followed my intuition all along. You brought that to me."

"This isn't the end." He paused and let her words resonate within him without replying. "What are you trying to do, since you understand it?"

In a prudent selection of words he stated with a single breath of honesty, "Return a tremendous amount of retribution."

A streaking dose of trepidation shuddered inside of her.

"Why is it necessary to allow yourself to be baited into vengeance? It's not yours to seek."

"That's what my intuition tells me will happen." He looked back and realized Marala wasn't following. She had stopped and was leaning against a tree. He took her hand and continued walking, somewhat dragging her along. "Now, let me ask you something."

"What do you want to know that you don't already?"

"Are you angry with me?"

"Not really."

"Why not?"

"Do you want me to be?" she asked.

"I want you to understand this is necessary. But no, I don't want you to be angry."

"Although it's a lot to ask of someone who's been kidnapped, I'm not angry with you," she said resisting his steady pace in an effort to slow him down.

"Why not?"

"It takes more energy to be angry than it does to be happy. While I'm not happy with this situation, I understand you have a purpose for doing this. You've made it known you aren't ready to share it. But if—If I knew what it was perhaps I could help."

"You've helped enough," he confessed somberly.

"I don't know what's going on with you, but try to accept this. You can't control other people yet, you can manage your own life."

"And that's what I'm doing. I'm managing my own life."

"Obviously you're a bit misguided because you're in mine," she replied.

"What makes you think you haven't come into mine?"

"Because whomever has you doing this is using you to disrupt my life. This whole kidnapping me, regardless of whatever else you're planning, will send you to prison. That doesn't appear to be the kind of man you are. Is whatever you're doing this for worth your freedom?"

"Prison isn't a threat to my future. I've been imprisoned my entire life. And yes, the reason I'm doing this is worth every bit of what you call freedom."

"You've imprisoned yourself. No one can stop you from moving into a healthier mindset except you. Stop making excuses. Walk out of here and return to your life while you still can. Shut out everything that's not beneficial to you because no one's stopping you. Get away from this self-destructive cycle of hate, anger and revenge because this— whatever *this* is about, if it's not an issue that you have directly with me, you shouldn't be involved."

"I'm sorry to destroy your grand illusion of me, but this *is* regarding an issue I have directly with *you* and whether or not you want to accept it, *I am* involved on my own accord. As I've said before, this is something I'm obligated to do."

"What are you trying to accomplish by holding me here?"

"I told you I—" he began with his nostrils flaring out of anger.

"I'm—I'm not asking that. What *I* want to know is, will you be proud of whatever it is you're trying to achieve by doing this?" She took her sleeve and wiped the perspiration off her forehead.

He rested both hands on the top of his head, locking his fingers together and turned to face her. Carefully, he scanned her body, ending at her eyes as if he were conferring with her spirit for several seconds before replying, with a raw honesty, "No."

"What's being held over you to make you do this?"

He bent down and smoothly ran his hands across the moist ground. Then he picked up a rock the size of his fist and aimed for a tree in the distance, hitting it dead center on its trunk.

"Let's head back," he insisted, observing the cluster of black clouds moving in. "It's going to get dark soon. Besides, you don't look so well and it's time for your medicine."

~~~~~~~~~~

Twenty-Four

Lyss took a cab to meet Liam at the restaurant, insisting she didn't want to be added to his scorecard by the hotel staff. He greeted her as the cab pulled up to the restaurant and opened the door, taking her hand in his. He gave the driver the fare, shut the cab door and stopped to admire his date.

"You look absolutely stunning," he stated while examining every bit of her.

Lyss was wearing a bronze, shape hugging sheath dress gathered slightly at the waist, with a collar of golden jewels. Liam smiled and shook his head as his eyes traveled down her shapely legs to the black and bronze beaded stilettos.

"Thank you."

"I see you went all out for me tonight. Wow! I'm impressed darlin'," he said smiling with his crescent-shaped eyes.

"Don't get too ahead of yourself. This is my customary attire for dinner with arrogant men. I like them to see what they won't get from me," she teased.

He let out a hearty laugh and said, "Note taken, beautiful."

He took her arm in his and escorted her inside.

"Very nice," she said taking in the warmth of the ambience.

"I thought you'd like to see my rugged side. Jeans, dress shirt and a sport coat; I'm still a little rough around the edges, but I tried."

Her eyes narrowed and she flashed a clever smile, "You're not as rough as you think Liam, especially with the designer shirt you're wearing along with those Cavalli boots and matching belt."

"What an eye," he confessed teasingly. "So you really have dated a lot of arrogant men."

"Although you look quite impressive yourself, I was talking about the restaurant."

A tall and slender beautiful brunette walked over to greet them.

"It's been too long," she said hugging Liam excitedly. "I saw your reservation and was looking forward to seeing you tonight. Her eyes turned red and began to water. "Two for dinner?" she asked wiping her eyes with the sleeve of her black dress.

"Yes. Thank you," Liam replied.

"And who's this pretty lady?" she asked flashing a gorgeous and genuine smile at Lyss.

"Beth, this is Alyssa."

They both shook hands, "It's a pleasure to meet you," Lyss replied politely.

"Likewise. You must be doing something right to snag this one," Beth claimed.

"No, no—I'm," Lyss began defensively.

"She's still working on it," Liam interjected. "Alyssa's a bit on the shy side so I thought I'd bring her down here and help her unwind a bit," he said winking at Beth.

"Sweetheart, watch out for this man," she warned thumping him playfully on his solid chest with her hand. "He has every single girl, along with a few married ones, in the Twin Cities chasing him. He's a real catch."

"Really? Well, thank you. That's good to know," Lyss replied winking her eye playfully at Liam.

"Oh, but Liam's not like that. He's a true gentleman and he hasn't been caught yet. You're in the best hands possible and the safest," she insisted picking up two menus.

"Beth, is it possible to get a table that offers a little privacy," he requested courteously. "It's getting busy in here."

"Absolutely. This way gorgeous." She led them to an intimate booth with a dim table lamp near the large windows overlooking the city. "How's this?" Beth asked.

"Perfect," Liam replied.

"You have to try our lobster and blue crab cakes. They're so delicious. Unless, Liam here is planning to order oysters," she said nudging him playfully.

"Slow down, Beth. You're going to make Alyssa start to wonder."

"Well I'm trying to warn the girl," she said winking playfully at Lyss.

Lyss returned a sincere smile and replied, "I appreciate the warning."

"How've you been?" Beth asked as Liam and Lyss sat down.

"Busy. And you, Beth?"

160

"You know me, working my butt off. I'm trying to stay busy too, to um—Well to keep my mind off things."

"How's the family?" he asked changing the subject.

"Everyone's good," she answered unconvincingly.

"Do me a favor and say hello for me."

"Of course I will," she replied placing the menus in front of them. "You did good Liam. There's something special about her," she admitted after stealthily observing Lyss. "Yeah, I like her. She's the smart and sexy type with a good heart. You know how you can just sense it from some people."

Liam said, "I know what you mean."

"Well, I get that from Alyssa here. *Intuition* is what the author Marala Scott calls it. She was just here and I tried to get tickets. Unfortunately, it was sold out. Ugh! Anyways, a few girlfriends of mine went and loved it! I've read all her books. You should pick one up. You'd be surprised what you'd learn about trusting your intuition. It's helped me more than anyone could imagine. If only I'd read it before—well Tony," she said eyeing Liam sadly, "he might still be here."

"Intuition. We'll have to look into it won't we?" he asked Lyss.

"Yeah, Liam's right. For the record Beth, I believe in intuition, too."

"Too bad you didn't make it to the speech," Liam replied. "You deserve to be happy."

"Com'on! Are you kidding me? You of all people," Beth said poking Liam in the side, "deserve to be happy." Beth gazed at Liam adoringly and added, "You two lovebirds enjoy your dinner."

"Thanks, darlin'."

"It was a pleasure meeting you, Beth," Lyss replied softly.

Beth smiled and walked away.

"Aren't you popular."

"Not nearly as much as I used to be."

"Why not?"

"I guess you could say it's because I'm focused on work."

"Or is it that you've gone through the Twin Cities directory of women and you're bored," Lyss suggested mischievously, having set Liam up so she could assess his response.

He smiled and pleasantly corrected her.

"Sorry to disappoint you sweetheart but, it's not in my character."

"Really?"

"Yes, really."

Lyss seductively licked her lips, ran her fingers through her hair and smiled at Liam's attempt to keep a serious face.

His eyes ravenously focused on her lips as she replied again, "*Really*?"

"Oh, I get it now. You're testing me."

"I don't know. Am I?"

"Just because you've grabbed my attention doesn't mean anyone can."

"Beth seems pretty nice."

"She's a great gal."

"She gave me the impression she knows you pretty well."

"She does," he replied candidly before grasping what Lyss was implying. He let out a deep laugh and pointed in Beth's direction and then at himself. "Ah, no, no darlin'. Beth and I, no," he insisted laughing again.

"I thought the two of you were—"

"I've known Beth for years. Her husband, Tony, was a close buddy of mine."

"You said, *was.* May I ask what happened?" she asked guardedly.

"Unfortunately, a few years ago Tony took his life. Said, he couldn't handle the stress of his job and quite frankly, life anymore."

Lyss dropped her head with embarrassment and said, "I'm sorry. I truly didn't mean to—"

"Don't beat yourself up about it. You couldn't have known. Beth's a tough girl. She's always smiling and taking things on the chin but losing Tony was hard on all of us." He leaned back reflecting on his friendship.

"Did you notice any signs of depression or anything?"

"At the time, I was working and traveling so much I hadn't seen him in practically a year. Not that I didn't try, but he grew distant for some reason. We'd spoken briefly once or twice before it happened, but Tony never mentioned anything specific to me. He was always trying to hold it together. In our last conversation, I suspected there was something wrong. I didn't really know what it was. Maybe it was the way he sounded or the manner he said things. I don't know. He was just different. I knew he wasn't himself."

"What happened?"

"He was talking about being tired of everything. I told Beth I'd be over to check on Tony that week and for her to keep an eye on him. That was the last time I spoke with him." Lyss covered her mouth. "Tony was a great guy. Everybody loved him, except the people he put away."

"Was he a police officer or something?"

"Yeah, something like that."

Lyss could tell it was difficult for both Beth and Liam to discuss Tony. They both tried to manage the friendly conversation, but Tony was the link to their bond and quite frankly, all they really had to talk about. Their communication and expressions revealed they weren't over his death.

"I'm sorry," she said sounding remorseful.

"We all are."

"And Beth, she really seems like a wonderful person."

"Yeah, Beth is one of the good ones. I was a little surprised to see her take to you so fast."

"Why?"

"Beth, never approved of anyone she saw me with and she never bit her tongue about it either. And for the record, I'm extremely selective. I don't settle for just anyone."

The waiter came over to the table and politely interrupted.

"Excuse me." Liam and Lyss stopped talking and gave him their full attention.

"Welcome to The Twin Flame. My name's Kent and I'll be your server this evening. May I start you off with something from the bar?"

"The lady will start with a cranberry juice because she's not ready to cut lose yet and I'll have the same."

Liam glanced at Lyss and she smiled approvingly.

"Yes, sir. I'll be right back with your drinks."

"So this is one of those *take charge* type of dates?" Lyss asked lightly shifting her position to a more comfortable one.

"That's a good start."

"What's a good start?"

"You called it a date," he replied affectionately. "Does it bother you that I'm a *take charge type of guy*?"

"Not in the least bit. I've been making a lot of decisions lately and it's nice for someone else to make them for a change."

"Then I think you'll like the rest of our *date*," Liam assured her.

Lyss allowed her alluring eyes to observe him.

"So, have you had many serious relationships?"

"You really want to talk about this, Doc?"

"Well, I'd like to know a little about the guy I'm on a date with," she said glancing down at her phone.

"Are you planning to use it against me later?"

"Are you going to give me a reason to?"

He hung his head for brief moment and then returned his attention to her with a gentle stare.

"A while back there was this girl."

"Okay. And—"

"Her name was Callie. We dated for a few years."

"What happened?"

"I let her go after I found out she was cheating," he admitted, matter-of-factly.

"I'm sorry to hear that," she replied sounding embarrassed by her intrusive questioning.

"Yeah. Well, I'm not."

"Really?"

"Absolutely."

"Why's that?"

"Sometimes things happen to protect you from yourself. I happen to think that was one of them. I knew Callie wasn't the one but I kept trying to hang in there. I guess I was hopeful she'd change and I didn't want to hurt her. Eventually, it all worked out for the best."

"Did she break your heart?"

"If someone doesn't break your heart, I don't think it was ever love."

"So she did?"

"No."

A brief moment of silence flirted between them. Liam glanced at the fire realizing he'd never truly committed to being in love.

"You said that was a while back. Are you seeing anyone now?"

"I wouldn't be on this date with you if I were," he said. Lyss tried to hide her smile but he spotted it. "I've dated occasionally, but there's no one special yet."

"That's hard to believe," she said lightly blushing. "What's holding you back?"

"The right one; someone that doesn't have the morals of Callie and—Well, I guess you could say I'm waiting for my twin flame."

"Hmm. Twin flame huh? You're an interesting one."

"You think so?"

"Well, yeah. I never would've considered you to be into the whole soulmate thing."

"Then you've misjudged me, Doc."

"Have I?"

"Am I on trial now or what?"

"No. You're not. I think your desire for a more committed and intimate type of relationship is impressive. You want someone who shares the other half of your soul. I've heard that you just *know* when you've met the one you're meant to be with."

"That you do. What about you?"

"Oh goodness. Um, well—I started dating a guy my freshman year of college. It was kind of serious for a while, but we casually drifted apart once I began working on my Masters. School seemed to take precedence over everything and we kind of let things go from there. Although that was a few years ago and we don't see each other anymore, we keep in touch here and there."

"What about your mom, did she like him?"

"Oh yeah! Mama still loves him because he has a wonderful personality and he's really driven. He's intelligent, compassionate and a lot of fun. We were able to talk about anything for hours on end. He was close to my heart."

"Okay."

"Okay what?"

"I think I get it."

"Get what?"

"He was close to your heart but not in it."

"Actually, he was. It was his family that kept things from materializing further, not him. I didn't like having to make him choose between his family and me."

"Why wouldn't he have. Was he crazy?"

"No. He chose me, but I didn't want to take him away from everything he was familiar with and loved."

"Wow," he replied, startled by her consideration. "Why not?"

"Because I loved him. Sometimes love means you're willing to sacrifice your own happiness for someone else's. He was worth it."

"That's strong."

"Yes, we were."

"What was the problem with his family?"

"Another story," she replied dismissively.

"Speaking of your mom, how's she doing?" Lyss took another glance at her phone hoping it would ring before looking across the room, attempting to force her tears back. "Hey there. What's wrong? Did I say something to upset you?"

"No. It's not you," she said with quivering lips. "I was thinking about, Mama."

"Is there something you want to talk about?" Lyss was silent. "Look," he began, hesitantly. "Let's be honest here. I like you and if there's something wrong with your mother, tell me what's happened so I can help. I already know there's more to your being here then you've let on. Her speech is over and we both know she's not at Canyon Glenn Hospital."

Lyss returned an incredulous gaze and in an alarmed, yet, composed manner asked, "How do you know that?"

"Because there isn't a hospital by that name in the entire state of Minnesota darlin'. And as much as you love your mother, *you* of all people, would know exactly what hospital she was in." He leaned across the table and spoke in a hushed voice, "You can tell me now and let me help or we can keep playing games and accomplish nothing beneficial to you or your mother."

"Liam, I can't. I'm sorry."

Lyss swiftly slid out of the booth and quickly exited the restaurant to hail a cab. Seconds later a yellow cab pulled over to the curb and Lyss opened the back door to climb inside.

"Good evening ma'am," the driver said, politely greeting her.

Liam walked up behind her and slammed the door, sending the cab away. He removed his jacket and protectively wrapped it around Lyss's trembling shoulders as large raindrops began to invade the evening.

He drew her closely against his raw masculinity, allowing his lips to barely graze her right ear. Whispering in his mild raspy voice he confessed, "As much as I'd like to think you came here to have dinner with me, I'm well aware you need help with whatever's going on with your mother. You're smart and brave. Follow your intuition because it's right. I'll help you and you *can* trust me." He handed the valet his ticket and held Lyss tightly. She rested her head on his muscular chest, sobbing. When the valet pulled up in his truck, he stated firmly, "I'm taking you to my house so we can talk." He backed up to wipe her tears, locking eyes with Lyss until she conceded.

~~~~~~~~~~

Twenty-Five

By the time they returned to the cabin, the fire had gone out. He turned on the lights and leaned against the granite countertop watching a fatigued Marala struggle to take off her boots.

"Can I call my daughter," she muttered.

"Not yet. I'll allow you to call her when it's time."

"But, I need to make sure—I need to make sure she's safe."

"Right now, she is safe."

"How can you be sure?"

"I'm sure because I don't have her."

"I need—I just need to hear her voice—" she said weakly.

"You should shower and take your medicine while I make you something to eat. Okay?"

Marala slowly disappeared into the bedroom shutting the door behind her.

~~~~~~~~~~

Twenty-Six

Liam turned on the lights and tossed his keys on the granite countertop. He took his wet jacket off Alyssa's dainty shoulders and went into his bedroom to grab a flannel blanket. When Alyssa sat down, he draped the blanket across her and lifted her legs on the sofa after slipping off her stilettos.

"You have a nice place."

"Thanks. It's not the hotel, but it works for me."

"It's extremely comfortable and would work well for anyone. It's open, bright, fresh and has beautiful lines. And your kitchen's impressive."

"Thank you. Can I get you something to drink? Wine, water, cranberry juice?"

"Water will be great. Thank you."

He grabbed a bottle of water from the refrigerator and a tall glass from the cabinet.

"Ice?"

"No thanks."

He returned to the living room, opened the bottle of water, poured it into the glass and handed it to her.

"Thank you."

He picked up the lighter and lit all three candles on his sofa table. Then he walked across the room, dimmed the recessed lighting and sat down at the opposite end of the sofa. He elevated her feet to his lap and with his strong hands, began massaging them.

"Are you okay?"

"Yes, better, thanks to you."

"That's good."

"Liam, I'm really sorry about tonight. I know you went through a lot to make things special for me but I can't stop thinking about, Mama."

"I want to help you but I can't if you don't tell me what's going on."

"I believe you want to help, but I don't know you well enough to—"

"Trust me?"

"Something like that."

"With a mother like yours, I think you do or you wouldn't be here."

"What I'm trying to say is I don't know the whole situation or even have a clue what this is about. Liam, I don't know what I'd be involving you in and I can't do that to you."

"Are you saying your mother's been kidnapped?" Lyss's eyes welled with tears and she said, "Yes."

"Have you contacted the police?"

"No. Because he warned me not to involve the police or he said, she'd die."

Lyss started crying. Liam put her feet down and scooted closer, wrapping his muscular arms around her. "I'm sorry," she said choking on her words.

Liam hugged her tightly and then kissed her forehead before decisively stating, "I'm not asking for your permission to help because I'm not going to let you handle this on your own."

"Liam, please. You have to stay out of this."

"Why?"

"I spoke to my mother and *she* told me to go home."

"Did you tell anyone about this?"

"No."

"Family, friends, anyone—"

"No! He told me not to say anything. Not even to the police. I didn't tell her agent, Adam, or anyone. No one knows."

"Do you know who has her?"

There was a long silence before she replied, "No."

"Did he give any indication of what he wants or what this is about?"

"No, he didn't."

"Did he ask for ransom?"

"No."

"Do you have any idea where she may be?"

"I've been trying to figure that out since she's been missing. I have a feeling she's been taken to Wisconsin."

"Why?"

"I can't say exactly. Something is telling me she's there—I don't know what or why really. I just feel it. I don't think she's here anymore."

"Was she hurt?"

"She said he hadn't hurt her."

"How did she sound?"

"She—she didn't sound like she was afraid. But if she were she wouldn't let me know."

"Why not?"

"Because she doesn't want me to be more upset than I already am."

"Alyssa are you sure she didn't say who has her?"

"I told you, *no,* she didn't say."

"Did she give any clues or hints to anything?"

"Not exactly. But for some reason, I think she knows who he is."

"Do *you* have any idea who he is?" Lyss didn't answer. "You do don't you?" She remained silent. "Alyssa, if you don't tell me everything you know I can't help you as quickly as you need me to. It's not helping your mother either because you don't know why he took her. And neither of us know how much time we have to get her back."

Lyss sat up, clasped her hands together and slipped them between her thighs. She studied Liam's eyes, holding on to a slow response.

"I don't know anything about you or your family. So how can I trust a stranger with my mother's life? How do I know you're not a part of all this? I don't know who took her or why, so that means everyone's a suspect to me."

"Ask me whatever you need to in order to believe you can trust me. After seeing your mother speak, I know intuition's a significant part of her life and yours. Trust it the way she does and you'll find all the answers you need. We can sit here and talk about my family all you want, but knowing about them isn't going to help you get your mother back. On the other hand, if it makes you feel better and you have time to waste, I'll open a fine bottle of wine and we can sit here and talk as long as you'd like.

"You don't understand. I don't–"

I don't know anything about you either, other than you had some guy who couldn't keep you long enough to see how amazingly beautiful and intelligent you are. I think you let him off easy and used his family as an excuse because you knew he couldn't handle the pressure. You're not with him because he wasn't your soulmate." He pulled her warm hand from between her thigh, placed it in his and continued, "I want to get to know you better, regardless of the distance between us because I've never met anyone that's captivated me the way you have. And *I am* certain that you need my help," he told her sweeping her hair off her shoulders, "And I—I need to help you." He lifted her chin and lightly embraced her beautiful face with both hands, indulging in the most passionate kiss to her supple lips either of them ever had. Lyss was speechless as her encumbered heart melted like falling snow into a flowing river. Without warning, her tense body collapsed affectionately and safely into his strong arms.

"The only thing that matters to me is–"

"We'll find your mother. Just let me help you. Listening to her speak made me aware that she's dedicated to trusting her God given intuition. Even now, her intuition's protecting you because you're not with her. Trust me, so I can do the same."

The exotic candle fragrance blended with crystallized ginger, golden amber and accented with sandalwood filled the room. It alleviated some of the tension overwhelming Lyss.

"It's Lyss. You can call me, Lyss," she said surrendering freely to him. Liam leaned forward and blew out each of the candles. He began kissing her soft lips, parting slowly in between each one. He set Lyss's soul on fire with every passionate touch, warm kiss and affectionate word as he pressed his hard body against hers.

~~~~~~~~~~

Twenty-Seven

By the time he entered the room, Marala had showered and curled up on the queen-sized bed.

"Dinner's ready. Would you like to eat out here? I can build another fire if you'd prefer."

"I'm really not hungry," she responded faintly.

"It's not an option. You need to eat something."

"I need to rest for awhile. I'm not feeling well."

He went over to the side of the bed where Marala was resting and gently placed his hand on her forehead. He dropped his hand down to the side of her neck and confessed, "You're running a fever."

"I know," she replied edgily. "That's why I need to rest."

"Have you taken your medicine?"

"Yes."

He left the room for several minutes and returned with a damp washcloth and a tall glass of water. "Here," he said after helping her sit up. "Drink this. You need to stay hydrated." She took the glass from him and had a few small sips before setting it on the nightstand. When she leaned back, he folded the blue washcloth into thirds and placed it across her forehead. "How long have you been feeling like this?"

"Since the morning of my last speech."

"It's been that long?"

"I was beginning to feel a little worse prior to our walk. While we were out, I guess it hit me harder," she moaned sluggishly.

"Why didn't you tell me?"

"I needed some fresh air and the walk gave us an opportunity to talk."

"You should've told me."

"I did, in my own way. I felt weak and thought I was running a fever so I leaned against the tree to rest, but you took my hand and—"

"I get it. I apologize, I didn't know."

"Do you have any Tylenol or Ibuprofen?" she asked, trying to shift into a comfortable position.

"I checked but didn't find any," he admitted. "If I went into town it wouldn't do any good," he stated looking out the window at the falling darkness. "The stores are closed at this hour. I'll head out first thing in the morning. In the meantime, you need to eat."

He left the room and returned carrying a tray with a plate of pan seared walleye and sautéed asparagus. He positioned a goose down pillow behind her back, laid a napkin across her lap and sat next to her with the tray. Breaking off small pieces of walleye, he slowly fed her.

"Is it edible?" he asked.

"Very. Were you—a chef at some point?" she asked, slightly stumbling over her words.

"No," he replied picking up another forkful of walleye.

"This—is one of—of my favorite dishes. Prepared exactly like this. How did—"

176

"I didn't, but I'm glad you like it. Here," he said putting the glass up to her mouth, "You need to drink this."

After she took another small sip, he sat the glass down and picked the fork up again.

"No—no more," she mumbled. "I really need to rest." Her exhausted body slumped over and she placed her head on her hands. In seconds, her heavy eyelids fluttered shut. She used what little energy she had to curl her shivering body up into a fetal position. "I'm co—cold," she stuttered with her teeth clattering together. He pulled the blanket up to her shoulders, tucking it lightly around her body. After removing the cloth, he put his hand against her forehead. Without saying anything, he left the bedroom and returned with a bowl of cool water.

"Your temperature seems to be getting worse." He soaked the cloth in water and then squeezed it out in the bowl.

"It can't. It can't get—higher," she insisted becoming lethargic.

"Can you try to eat a little more?"

She was barely able to shake her head, no. "I need—my temperature down," she mumbled inaudibly. "I want to go home. I want my daughter."

Discernably concerned by Marala becoming ill, he went into the living room and opened the front door. When he exhaled the crisp night air, he was able to see his own billow of breath. He stepped outside on the porch unable to view the familiar forest now blanketed with dense fog that crept in with the black of night. He couldn't risk leaving her like that. Only someone vastly familiar with the drive could navigate in and out of the woods in that weather. He was beyond worried but refused to let Marala sense it.

Quietly, he returned to the bedroom where Marala was drifting asleep. He rested his hand on her clammy neck, cautiously monitoring her temperature. It had dangerously escalated. Returning the warm washcloth to the bowl of water he squeezed it out and placed it back on her forehead. He had to find a way to get her what she needed. He snatched the tray off the bed and took it into the kitchen. He couldn't contain his troubled emotions as he scraped the remainder of her dinner down the disposal and turned it on. He rinsed the plate, sat it in the dishwasher and slammed it shut. His body filled with rage and in a furious movement, he pounded his fists on the counter yelling, "No," followed by an angry grunt.

It was clear what he needed to do. He pulled out his phone and sent a text. By the time he returned to Marala she was asleep in a fragile state. He climbed in bed and sat next to her, laying her head in his lap. He wrapped his arms around her and spent the balance of the night, attentively caring for her.

~~~~~~~~~~

Twenty-Eight

Morning broke with bright rays of sunshine slipping through the edges of the bedroom blinds. A chorus of birds chirping cheerfully outside the window made its way to Lyss's ears. The comfort of

Liam's Egyptian cotton sheets made her peek under the blankets to make sure she was still dressed. The other side didn't appear to have been occupied. She sat up and called out to him. He didn't answer. She tossed back the blanket and found a note sitting on the nightstand. The handwriting was very neat.

Beautiful Lyss,

I had to run out. Please don't leave. There is a pair of sweats and a t-shirt for you to change into on top of the dresser. Everything you need to shower is in the bathroom and coffee's ready. I'll be back soon. Make yourself comfortable.

Liam

Lyss grabbed her phone from the nightstand only to find there weren't any messages from her mother or the kidnapper. Faithfully, her knees fell to the dark brown calamander flooring with orange and gold streaks. Beginning her day by consulting with God was the alpha. She prayed for the longest time unyielding in dedication until her soul was replenished with strength by drawing nearer to God. She believed her mother was safe, for now.

After putting her faith in God's hands, she went into the living room to find that Liam was still gone. She followed the irresistible aroma of Kona coffee into the Euro styled kitchen where she found a cup next to the pot with a teaspoon resting beside it. Being thoughtful, Liam left it out for her. She dropped two cubes of sugar into her cup, filled it half-full of coffee and then looked in the refrigerator for milk. He had cream. She smiled and filled the other half of the cup with it. After giving it a few quick stirs, she returned the cream to the refrigerator and went into the living room sipping the delicious blend.

Lyss lifted a panel on the wooden blinds and peeked out the window sighting nothing but nature at its best. The nearly bare, tall shade trees were gracefully dropping leaves with bright hues of orange, red and yellow after overtaking its original balance of green. The grass had a sheer covering of frost lacing each blade while the rays of sun made them sparkle elegantly before the warmth would melt it. It appeared to be a picturesque late autumn day. The only thing missing was her mother.

Lyss didn't see Liam's truck in the driveway so she returned to the bedroom locking the door behind her. Lyss looked at her phone again, but still there was nothing. When she entered the lavished bathroom she was engulfed in the relaxation of a spa. Letting her clothes drop carelessly to the floor she undressed. Lyss got into the large steam bath in an attempt to relieve the unwelcomed tense sensation that hadn't left the taut muscles aching throughout her body.

~~~~~~~~~~

Twenty-Nine

Marala lethargically opened her eyes as if they'd been taped shut realizing she was laying on his lap. His strong arms were wrapped securely around her in an affectionate embrace. When she moved, his eyes opened and he lightly ran his fingers through her hair and massaged her scalp.

"You're okay," he whispered soothingly. "I'm here sweetheart."

"What—What happened? Why are you—" she began sounding completely befuddled.

"You had a rough night. You became very ill. And—Do you remember anything?"

"We went for a walk. Everything was like a potpourri of magnificent colors and then—I don't remember anything after that."

"Are you feeling any better?" he asked laying the back of his hand on her neck to check her temperature. It was still marginally warm.

"I think so," she replied in a whisper.

Using what little energy she had, Marala shifted upward into a sitting position while letting a few low moans escape.

"Sorry about the clothing. I didn't have any other choice."

"Again with the no choice," she said before noticing her clothes had been changed. "Oh no. Please explain—" she began tugging at her shirt. "I wasn't wearing this, or—Oh my goodness—How could I? Did we? Please tell me nothing happened," she exclaimed unleashing a load of embarrassment.

"Actually sweetheart, a lot happened," he said with a clever grin climbing out of bed. She covered her face with both hands and dropped her head shamefully. "Your fever shot up to 105.1. I couldn't get it down so I carried you upstairs to the loft and put you in a tub of lukewarm water. I couldn't leave you in wet clothing, so I dried you off and dressed you in what you're wearing. You did a lot of talking and rambling throughout the night."

"But did—"

"No," he said gently shaking his head. "You can call me a kidnapper, but I'm not a rapist."

"I wasn't saying you—"

"Forget it. What's important is that your temperature's finally going down, although I wouldn't exactly say you're out of the woods yet." He reached over to the nightstand, opened the bottle of ibuprofen and a prescription. "Here, take these," he said dropping them into her hand.

When she reached for the glass he picked it up and placed it against her lips. Marala put the pills in her mouth followed by a slow drink of water. Her face tingled with humiliation. The fact that she suspected something might have happened gave him something else to ponder.

"Thank you."

He sat the glass down.

"I'm going to make you some toast and pour a glass of juice. You can shower if you're feeling up to it."

"Okay," she said in a low whisper.

"Are you alright?"

"I will be."

He turned and left the room. Marala noticed the small box to the ibuprofen and bottle of antibiotics sitting by the lamp. When she picked up the bottle of antibiotics, she noticed the name had been peeled off.

~~~~~~~~~~

Thirty

Lyss was sitting Indian style on the sofa checking text messages on her phone when Liam leisurely walked through the door. He had a Louis Vuitton carryall with her personal items, along with a box of pastries and a bouquet of Calla Lilies wrapped in a stream of sheer green ribbon.

"Sleeping beauty's finally awake," he commented with an irresistible grin.

"What's all this?" she asked taking the carryall from him.

"Some of your personal belongings. I grabbed the notes you were working on, your iPad and some of your clothing. I wasn't exactly sure what belonged to you or your mother; it seems that both of you are about the same size."

"How did you get into my suite?" she asked inquiringly.

"I'm the Head of Security. Remember?"

"What about work? Is helping me find my mother going to cause problems for you?"

"While I was there, I changed the schedule. Christian has my hours covered."

"Does he know about this—us?" she asked sounding embarrassed.

"I like the sound of that, *us*," he repeated, "But *no*. Of course not."

"It would have been easier for me to go back to the hotel you know."

"Call it selfish, but I wanted you all to myself today," he replied handing her the flowers as his sexy eyes traveled her body.

"Liam these are—" she began blushing.

"Beautiful, like you," he said assuredly placing the box of pastries on the counter. "I take it you found the note I left?"

"I did. That was really sweet." Lyss went into the kitchen and glanced around the room before asking, "Do you have a vase for these?"

"Not exactly," he replied walking up behind her. He kissed her on the cheek and pulled a glass pitcher out of a cabinet above the refrigerator. "Will this do?"

"Absolutely, Mr. Bachelor."

He filled the pitcher a third of the way up with cool water and sat it on the counter. She placed and arranged the flowers in it and then sat them on the sofa table.

"You look exhausted. What time did you leave?"

"A couple hours ago."

"I would have gone with you, Liam."

"Darlin', you were up most of the night talking about your mom and when you finally fell asleep, you looked so peaceful I didn't have the heart to awaken you."

"Why'd you leave so early?"

"I had a few errands to run. I stopped by the hotel, grabbed some of your things, went by the florist and then the pastry shop. I know you want to keep things private and I thought we could work on finding your mother without interruptions. Speaking of your mom, any calls?"

"No. I'm worried about her and to be honest I don't know how much longer I should keep this from the police. I'm going to get my mother back and if I need them to help do it, then—"

"Then, I suggest we start piecing things together before we put her life in further jeopardy by involving the police."

Lyss sat down, opened her iPad and pulled out her notepad while Liam poured himself a cup of coffee.

"Would you like more?" he asked holding up the pot after noticing her cup on the table.

"No thanks. I'm good for now."

He returned to the living room and sat next to Lyss. "It looks like you were developing a list of people as potential suspects," he said picking up her notepad.

"Yeah, I was. I went back through my mother's emails and read messages from the people she'd been communicating with. The list I compiled is comprised of those whose communications I considered to be strange or persistent."

"You've already crossed off someone by the name of Garrett. He was one of your suspects for some reason or another, correct?" Liam's phone vibrated. He read the text and slipped it back in his pocket, seemingly irritated.

"Yes, but not any longer. He's written my mother since she was taken and he asked how her speech went."

"Lyss, how can you be sure he doesn't have anything to do with this?"

"Garrett said he was in Florida with friends and I asked him about the weather there. He told me and I checked it out. He was right."

"Any other reasons?" he asked suspiciously.

"It doesn't seem like Garrett's character. He and my mother were very close and he's shared a lot of personal information about his life with her. In my opinion, he sounds grateful for what she's helped him accomplish. It's clear they've become friends."

"Really? Friends? Hmm. That's funny. With your mother's life at risk you didn't hesitate to rule him out. Have you met him?"

"Not yet."

"What do you mean, *not yet*?" he asked casting a line of irritation towards her.

"He was planning to attend one of my mother's speeches but he hasn't as of yet," she said sounding uncertain as her words came out. "I thought we'd meet him when he does."

"Why's that?"

She shrugged and replied, "There are some people you look forward to meeting after you've been communicating with them for a while. For some reason, Garrett's definitely one of them."

"Is that so?"

"Absolutely. In the last three dates alone we've met several people who've written my mother. Typically, we don't have time to meet many of them. And it's nice to put a face with the person we're communicating with on such a personal level."

"What else do you know about him?" he asked sipping his coffee while analyzing her expression associated with each response.

"I know a lot about him because I've been helping keep up with the business end of things for my mother over the past few months."

"That's interesting. How so?"

"I've been returning her email messages, overseeing schedules and reviewing contracts for

186

her. Although Garrett doesn't know it, he's been communicating with me instead of her and truthfully, I've grown quite fond of him."

"Excuse me. Did you say, *fond* of him? Are you joking?" he asked forcing a contemptuous laugh.

"Yeah. There's something special about Garrett and I'm certain he wouldn't do anything to hurt my mother," she replied affectionately.

His brooding eyes looked directly into Lyss's and he asked, "I'm sorry. Are you— Are you attracted to this guy?"

"Seriously? Liam, come on. I told you I haven't met him. I mean he's attractive and all but it takes more than looks for me. He's just different in the way he expresses himself with my mother. There's always this underlying tone of affection in his words and they genuinely seem to understand one another. Spoken or unspoken, they have a connection."

"So now that you've been writing him, are you affectionate in your replies with this guy?"

"Really? How is this type of questioning going to help me find my mother?"

"I need to know that you aren't biased with any of the people we should be looking at as a suspect. Except, it sounds to me like you're the one interested in Garrett and I don't think I'm off base."

Lyss sat up straight and shook her head disappointed by his negativity and false accusations.

"I really don't want to believe what I'm hearing. Are you serious? Please tell me you're kidding Liam? You must be."

He shrugged condescendingly and replied, "I wish I were, but I'm not."

"What's this about?" she asked defensively. "This isn't you. You're doing this for some other reason because this doesn't make sense. I'm absolutely positive you aren't worried about Garret having my interest because I'm here with you."

He ignored her and continued with his incandescent anger.

"If I'm hearing you correctly, all I had to do to get your attention was have a few email sessions with you. Sorry. I mean email your mother and I'd get *you* instead. Maybe that's why I'm single," he admitted with unconcealed sarcasm. "I don't know how to build a solid relationship through email. I suppose I'm the hopeless idiot waiting for a soulmate the regular way, huh?"

"Liam, you're being ridiculous."

"What's ridiculous is that you haven't met the guy, yet there's something *special* about him. And let me get this straight. *You're* the one writing these people back?"

"Yes, but—"

Liam put his hand up interrupting her response.

"Instead of Marala?"

Lyss studied Liam reeling in disbelief. They were supposed to be having an honest conversation to help find her mother, but Liam was thrusting it completely out of control. He sounded more like a jealous boyfriend.

"Let me explain why," she said rubbing her hand across his back in an attempt to calm him.

"So, all these people," he said picking up the yellow notepad in front of him, "like *Garrett*, think they're talking or confiding in your mother, but what they're really doing is spilling their guts to you," he stated shaking his head. "I actually feel sorry for the poor—"

"Hold on, Liam! It's really not what you're thinking," she scolded.

"Then what is it? Some kind of twisted game between you and your sick mother to screw with their lives or better yet, their trust? These people have probably been through more than they've told you and here you are explaining that they're being subjected to this pathetic method of helping them," he retorted angrily slamming the notepad on the table.

"How could you allow something like that to escape your mouth? This is how you've judged me? No! Forget about me! How dare you say that about my mother! You have no idea how much effort she puts into people who need inspiration. She's dedicated—"

"To what? Having you do her work? Her ego's too inflated to do it herself because of *The Best Seller* status! You don't care about these people. Neither of you do!"

"Liam. That's enough!"

"You know, perhaps the both of you are getting exactly what you deserve," he confessed angrily.

He lowered his head and put his hands on his waist, immediately regretting his words; knowing he couldn't take them back.

Lyss clutched her hand over her mouth, shocked by Liam's reckless comments. She turned off her iPad, slid it into its black case and packed it into her carryall lying on the floor next to the sofa. Without a word, she got up and went into the bedroom. Lyss sent a text, folded her clothing and put it inside her shoulder bag. Twenty minutes later, she returned to the living room, picked up her carryall and headed for the door.

"What's this? Why are you leaving?" he questioned sternly, quickly stepping in front of her.

"Really, Liam? You need to ask?"

Her typically stoic and assured demeanor was beginning to wane as the worry over her mother continued to rise.

"We're having *this* conversation because *I* need answers. Let's calm down and finish it."

"Finish? I don't converse in the manner you choose to Liam," she said shaking her head in disappointment. "But I am sorry."

"Sorry? Sorry for what?"

"Apparently, I've completely misjudged you. Your perspective on things is distorted because for some unknown reason, you're emotionally tied to what's going on and it's impaired your judgment."

"What are you talking about?"

"How can you possibly help someone you don't trust? You haven't heard my reasons as to why I respond to those people."

"You're right. I don't know your motives."

"Motives?" Lyss repeated.

"Whatever they are, you shouldn't meddle in other peoples lives!"

"And you'd be correct if I were meddling, which I'm not. At my mother's request, I'm communicating what she can't do as coherently as she'd like."

"You're kidding, right?" he sneered. "Your mother can give a brilliant speech but she can't return her own confidential emails to people who trust they're communicating with her. These people actually believe they're getting help from some kind of intuitive guru and she has her—wannabe psychologist daughter playing doctor with them," he spewed out crossly, throwing his hands into the air.

"Do people actually know who they're trusting? Let's face it Lyss—Marala Scott doesn't give a damn about them, but they'd put themselves on the front line for her!"

"Since you think this is *exactly what we deserve*, I want you to know something. A few months ago, my mother had a craniotomy also known as, brain surgery. And I, Liam—*I* was the one shoving her back on tour before she was ready! I can't tell you how many times she warned me about not wanting to come to this place! But again, *I* insisted she needed to promote *Intuition's* powerful message to these people."

"Why? Why did you push her to come here?"

"Because she had numerous requests. That's why this happened, because of me! She had emails from Sharon and—"

"Sharon?" he repeated in a whisper.

"It doesn't matter who wanted her here, I should have listened to my mother's intuition! Don't think for one second it's not killing me that my mother's been kidnapped!" she screeched, letting out a painful cry. "The only way to undo this damage is for *me* to find her and bring her back. Sitting here defending myself to you is a waste of time!"

Liam's face transitioned to a warm shade of crimson.

"Lyss," he began, wading in a bottomless well of uncomfortable humiliation.

"You wanted to finish this so let me speak," she insisted. "*I* wrote them back because my mother has trouble with her memory. She's not as fluent in her communication or as healthy as people think with the *titanium plate* screwed into her head. Nevertheless, her passion for helping people is the reason she came back on tour this soon. You said she appeared tired on stage. Not that it matters to you, but she was fatigued because she was becoming ill and I overlooked that, too. My mother doesn't have any room for error with her health. The only reason she asked me to return her messages was so the people she cared about most wouldn't feel abandoned by her. And for the record, *Garrett* was on the top of her list. Liam—she was healing from having her skull sawed open so they could clip multiple aneurysms! Barely anyone knew about the surgery because she didn't want anyone to feel sorry for her. *That's* who she is! These people have given their permission for her to write about their lives on her blog. Had they not, she'd never allow me to read their messages. Perhaps you should read their stories so you can learn something."

"My God! Lyss, I'm—I'm sorry. I didn't know," he said completely deflated by his unwarranted outburst.

"That's okay, because we're getting exactly what we deserve for caring so much about others."

Lyss brushed past Liam and swung open the heavy front door. He grabbed her arm to prevent her from leaving.

"Darlin', please," he said trying to ease some of the tension he crafted. "I've had a *really* long night and okay, I'll admit, I was completely out of line. But there's something you don't understand."

Although his face was covered with a surge of shame, she whispered to him sweetly, "No, Liam. There's something that you don't understand. I'm more than disgusted with myself for thinking *you* might have been that someone. I thought you cared about the truth, let alone, helping get my mother back. I didn't peg you for someone that would eject spiteful and unfounded allegations with such vehemence without taking into consideration something known as, facts. And as for Garrett, not that it's any of your business, but I think he's in love with my mother. She had another guy named Liam writing her too, I just pray that he was nothing like you." She pulled her arm away from his grip adding, "There's nothing more between us."

Interrupting Liam's opportunity for a rebuttal was a horn blowing a couple of pitchy notes in his driveway. She shook her head and walked away without looking back before climbing into the yellow cab. Liam pulled out his phone and sent a text that read.

It's done.

~~~~~~~~~~

Thirty-One

Taking careful and gradual steps, Marala emerged from the bedroom into the dining room to join him for breakfast. He was sitting at an imposing table made of redwood and juniper sipping on a cup of coffee with a swirl of steam escaping. Bright sunlight was streaming into the house from the three skylights, leaving a floating trail of tiny dust particles drifting carelessly in its beam.

"It's good to see you moving around. Are you feeling better?"

"I am."

"Have a seat," he said standing to pull out a chair for her. "Are you ready to eat?"

"If you don't mind, I think I'll—"

"Have some toast and a glass of juice. Good," he said suggestively finishing her sentence.

He went into the kitchen and dropped two pieces of wheat bread into the toaster and poured a tall glass of orange juice, placing it in front of her. She took a drink and sat the glass down.

"I don't know if this makes sense to you, given that I'm being held here, but thank you for taking care of me last night. It could have been much worse," she said with sincerity.

"There's no need to thank me," he replied modestly. "If I didn't have you isolated up here, you could have gone to the hospital."

"Well, that isn't the case and you did whatever was necessary to get my fever down. For that, I'm grateful. I don't remember much about last night, but I didn't think you had any ibuprofen or antibiotics here," she said squinting at him reminiscently.

"No. I didn't." He turned around to the sound of the toast popping up. He placed the toast on a plate and offered, "Butter or jam?"

"Neither. Thank you." He placed the plate in front of her and sat down. "May I ask you something?"

Carefully, he studied her brown eyes. Sounding sedated from his typical brash tone he replied, "Yes."

She took a sip of juice and then asked, "I'm aware you have your own reasons for doing this but how long are you going to keep me away from my life? Every bit of my intuition tells me you aren't going to hurt me, especially after the way you took care of me last night. All I'd appreciate knowing is, how long will this—whatever it is, take to resolve?"

He got up and stood behind her gently placing his hands on her slouching shoulders. He leaned over and whispered in her ear, as if someone would overhear his reply, "Do you know what your fate is?"

"No, I don't," she replied. "Only God knows."

"You're right. And now, so do I, because He told me. Until I can change that, I will keep you here. A lot has to change before I can let you return. I need you to accept that it may be a few more days, weeks or as long as it takes until I accomplish what I need to. Don't become a disruption." Marala nodded her head, agreeably. "Is there anything else?" he asked.

"Will you call my daughter and let her know I'm okay. If you hadn't taken care of me last night, it's possible I might not be here."

He reached in his back pocket and handed Marala the phone; she noticed it was different. She was speechless as he placed it in her warm hands. A thick layer of tears formed in her eyes. She wiped them with her sleeve and dialed Lyss's number.

"Mama?"

"Yes love. It's me. How are you holding up?" she asked with her voice slightly trembling.

"How can you ask about me? I'm worried sick about you! How are you feeling? You don't sound well. Has he hurt you in any way?"

"I'm fine, baby. I'm fine. You may not believe this, but he's taking very good care of me."

"Then what's this about? Where are you? And what does he want?"

Marala turned around and looked at her captor, interpreting what his blue eyes were revealing. The truth resided in them. Confidently, she assured Lyss,

"Sweetheart, I promise that I don't know where I am. But I can tell you that he doesn't want to do anything other than protect me from someone."

"Who?" she asked, sounding puzzled. "And why didn't he call the police if that's the case?"

"I don't know. But he won't harm me."

"Can you tell me who *he* is?"

"No, sweetheart. I don't want you searching for me either. I'll be home," she said unconvincingly. "I don't know when, but I'll be home one way or another."

"One way or another? Mama! I need you home now and I need you to be safe! Please," she begged. "Find out who he's protecting you from and why. You haven't done anything to anyone."

"Lyss trust your intuition. Trust it," she whispered into the phone, gripping it tightly as if she were holding her daughter. "I have to go, but like I told you when you were a little girl, keep these words with you. I'm thinking of you fondly, even when I sleep, there's nothing in this world that can separate you from me. I love you beautiful daughter."

"Mama! I love you!" Lyss yelled into the phone.

Marala ended the call and handed him the phone, expressing gratitude through the widespread sadness covering her face. She got up from the table and carried her dishes into the kitchen; he watched her rinse and then load them into the dishwasher. He was certain her strength was challenged every time she spoke with her daughter and imagined it was ripping Alyssa apart one piece at a time.

Without uttering a word, she went into the bedroom holding her stomach and rested in the rocking chair. She tried desperately to focus on the scenic autumn view instead of what she had no control over. He followed behind her and leaned against the wall for a few minutes collecting his thoughts. He realized she was compromising his plan.

Completely confounded by her disposition, he finally broke the silence by asking, "Do you actually believe I'm trying to protect you from someone?"

"Yes," she replied without turning to face him.

"As you say, I have a choice, so I choose to do this. Everyone has their obsession and this is mine."

"This or me?" she questioned. He didn't reply. Instead, he moved to face her and studied her features. "Don't let anything happen to my daughter. I'm not concerned about my fate."

"I know. That's why I'm here," he replied modestly.

Tears clouded her eyes again allowing him to absorb some of her pain; he dropped down on one knee in front of her and folded his hands together as if he were going to repent to God through prayer.

"Don't cry," he insisted chivalrously.

"My heart's heavy," she confessed, clutching her hand against her breasts. It aches," she acknowledged, weeping softly. "I can hardly breathe."

"But, you said you're not worried about your fate," he restated.

"I'm not. I miss my daughter and I know what this is doing to her. That's what's hurting me. She's been learning to completely embrace her intuition and this is her final test. Yet, I understand her burden because it's with me. I'm her mother but she has to trust her intuition regardless of that. Although her journey's difficult, I'm certain she will."

"I'm not what you think," he proclaimed with an emanating sadness.

"You have no idea what I think."

"I believe you try to see the good in people and help them make it back to that good character when they're lost or weak. But I'm nothing more than an assemblage of negative things. It's all I really know."

"Don't boast as if you're unique. All of us contain something that causes question to our moral fiber? It's up to us to change it."

"Then I'll put it this way, I have more than most. Marala, don't trust me, because I don't trust myself and I don't know what I'm capable of doing. Whatever compassion you have for me, you'd better release it because I guarantee I won't be deserving of it when this is over."

"At the moment I felt compassion for you, I prayed for God to guide you through this. I won't loose that faith in you. It's who I am."

"How can you pray for someone that's deliberately stripped you away from your daughter and life?"

"I know better, even if you don't. You're forgetting that my intuition has allowed me to see the truth about you and yes, it rises above reason."

He stood up and left the room. Marala sat placidly in the chair waiting, wondering and then praying. The cabin fell quiet. Marala closed her eyes and unwillingly drifted off into a deep sleep.

Several hours later, she found herself lying comfortably across the bed covered with a blanket. He was standing in the doorway watching her like a prized possession. No matter how hard he tried, his complicated mind couldn't shake her out of it. Marala consumed him in a way he hadn't expected, causing his thoughts to run rampant with intensity and heat. When she looked up and saw him standing there, her heart began beating faster.

"I have to go out," he said.

"Where?"

"There are a few things I need to handle."

"May I go with you?"

He looked at her oddly and replied, "That's not a good idea. If there's something you need—"

"No. You've already given it to me," she said speaking softly in an unflustered manner. "Are you going to lock me in this bedroom again?"

He gave her a serious gaze and asked, "Do I need to?"

She slowly shook her head, *no*. Without another word, he left the bedroom and climbed the stairs to the loft. He opened the bottom drawer of his dresser, pulled out a handgun and slipped it into the back waist of his pants. The black Tumi backpack sitting on his bed was where he kept his laptop, wallet and a roll of cash. He zipped it shut and tossed it over his left shoulder. Minutes later, Marala heard the door shut. She got up and went into the living room. By the time she opened the front door and stepped outside, he was pulling away from the cabin.

"Why would he leave me alone?" she said out loud.

Marala went back inside, returning to the bedroom where she opened the closet, grabbed her boots and put them on. She glanced out the bedroom window and saw the boat was still there. She reached into the second dresser drawer and grabbed a heavy sweatshirt, pulled it over her head and slipped her arms into the sleeves. Without delay she went into the kitchen and pulled open the silverware drawer. There were spoons and forks, but there weren't any knives in it. She opened another drawer and removed a pair of sharp culinary scissors and tucked them into the pocket on her sweatshirt.

She was certain the driveway trail would lead her out of the woods to whatever road there was, from there she could try to hitch a ride to safety. She realized that she didn't know where the road led and how frequently it was traveled. The boat looked so old; she wasn't convinced it even worked. But if it did, she could take it to the other side of the lake and try to find help.

Marala didn't know when he'd return and had little time to determine whether or not to run or stay and accept her *fate,* as he'd put it. She had to make the right decision and the only source that could give it to her was God. Without further contemplation, she dropped to her knees and prayed with every bit of unwavering faith she had. Shortly after her consultation Marala gathered her strength, rose to her feet and left the cabin.

~~~~~~~~~~

Thirty-Two

Lyss respected her mother's decision and came to the resolution that she wouldn't search for her; instead she'd track down her mother's kidnapper. She thought it was necessary to begin communicating with the suspects on her list so she could rule them out one at a time. Her objective was to find the person most likely to have done this. Her phone rang, disrupting her thoughts. Again, the call was blocked. She answered immediately.

"Mama!"

There was a slight pause before she heard, "Lyss. This is Liam. I need to see you. I want to apologize for what I said."

"You just did. Apology's accepted. Now please leave me alone so I can find my mother," she instructed heatedly and hung up the phone. She hit, new message on the laptop and began writing Sharon.

Sharon,

The trip to the Twin Cities was exciting and my speech went well. You've been on my mind since your last communication. I'm truly sorry to hear you went through such pain. I agree it's difficult to trust someone with a history such as your ex-husband's and I pray you're enjoying your newfound freedom in Connecticut. Make sure to protect it.

I don't know if you have any children with him, but it's unfortunate his children witnessed what he did to his wife. Do they keep in touch with him? It's disappointing (I'm sorry to keep saying your ex-husband but I don't know his name) to hear he wasn't brought to justice. The children's lives can be devastated if not overrun by painful memories because of what they've gone through. All I know is; it took a great deal of courage to leave him. Is he still in Wisconsin?

Keep in touch and know I'm praying for you to embrace love, peace and a beautiful life without the sorrow you've experienced. Breathe deeply and enjoy life.

Love,
Marala <3

Lyss clicked on an email from a man by the name of Kevin. After reading it again, she began writing him back. Kevin wrote Marala about everything. He made the list because he communicated his attraction to her although Marala's responses were careful not to solicit any intimate interest. She replied solely to his questions about forgiveness and intuition. Once Lyss began tapping on her keys a loud pounding on the door broke her concentration. She slid the computer off her lap, onto the sofa and went to look out the peephole. Christian was waiting nervously, with his hands in his pockets. She yanked the door open.

"Christian."

"Lyss."

"What can I help you with?"

"I'm sorry to bother you, but do you have time to talk?"

"Christian," she began, letting out a disinterested sigh, "I'm really tied up right now. I'm trying to work on a few things that are extremely pressing," she replied, exhaling heavily. She caught his anxious expression and followed up with, "Is it important?"

"I think so, but I'd rather you make that decision. Do you mind?"

"Why not?" Lyss questioned stepping aside so he could enter the suite. She pushed the door shut and then motioned for him to have a seat.

"You were pretty worried about your mom the other night."

"Yeah, I am. I mean, I was worried, but what's this about?" she asked sounding confused as she sat down.

"How's Ms. Scott doing? Is she here?" he asked looking around.

"No. She's fine, Christian. Can you tell me why you're here?"

"When you left the security office the other night I was really worried about you."

"I know, I was pretty upset, thinking something happened to my mother. But you Christian—you were a tremendous help."

"Thank you, but that's because I didn't like seeing you upset over your mom, especially after she'd given such a moving speech to inspire all those people. *Intuition* made a great impression, so you guys should've been celebrating. The guests were talking about her speech the rest of the evening, even with the fire and all."

"That's always good to hear. Christian, why are you here?"

"When I left work that night, I kept reflecting on the expression you had on your face when that guy wrapped his arms around your mother and put a cloth over her mouth. I keep replaying what happened in my head. Lyss, I'd swear she was being kidnapped."

"Yeah, I know and she's fine, Christian," Lyss said, nervously pinching the center of her bottom lip.

"I hear what you're saying, only my intuition won't release that thought." Lyss looked away from Christian. "I couldn't shake your initial reaction and frankly, it bothered me the rest of the night. It still does. That's why I'm here."

"Naturally, I'd be upset."

"For some reason, I think the thought of it is upsetting you now. Lyss, when the phone rang, you weren't relieved like you should have been after finding out where your mom was. To the contrary, you were more distraught after the call."

"I didn't know who that guy was. I had to trust he was telling the truth until I saw her for myself."

"And did you?"

"Christian, she's fine."

"You haven't told me anything about your mother. Where is she?"

"I don't think I need to discuss that with you. Are you forgetting some random stranger took my mother to a hospital without my knowledge or consent? I didn't know who *he* was or what was wrong with her. And to top it off, I didn't know how serious the situation was. Are you forgetting her health? This is pointless. There's no need for you to worry about either of us."

His eyebrows scrunched together. Christian didn't buy it. He was deliberating on whether or not he should share his concerns or stay out of it. After taking a deep breath he spoke up, cautiously asking, "How well do you know Liam?"

"Okay. We're done. I don't think we need to have this conversation," she said clearly agitated. Christian didn't move. Instead, he waited for an answer. "Just to stop your prying, the first time I met Liam was in your office. I've only been here a few days."

"I thought you recognized him from somewhere. When you bumped into him—"

"Well, I don't. He looked like this guy that used to write my mother, but it wasn't him. That was the first time we'd ever met."

"I know you didn't come here to interrogate me about Liam," she warned. Lyss stood up and placed her hands on her waist in a confrontational pose. "I don't know what I need to do to make you understand I don't have time to play charades with you. Just leave, Christian."

"Lyss please sit down and let me explain."

"Christian, out!"

"I'm concerned for your safety and I don't think you should be around that guy. In my opinion, there's a few things about Liam that aren't connecting."

"I'm sorry but I really think this conversation's unwarranted. There's no reason for you to discuss Liam with me. If you think there's something wrong with him then take it up with your General Manager."

"Lyss," he began pleading with her, "He's involved in something that's dangerous for both you and your mom. I haven't been able to put my finger on it and I know this sounds extreme, but stay away from him. I can feel it," he insisted passionately.

Christian locked his hands together and snapped his fingers back causing his knuckles to crack. Lyss looked into his eyes finding them as precious and transparent as the emerald they resembled; he wasn't lying. Although she didn't agree with his logic, she was certain his intentions were genuine.

"My mother calls that, *intuition*," she explained, relaxing her tone.

"I know and I'm pretty sure I'm tuned into mine," he said nervously rocking his right leg up and down. He reached inside his shirt and pulled out a silver cross, revealing his faith to Lyss and then carefully tucked it back in.

"Okay," she told him, "You have my attention. What's your intuition telling you?"

He scooted to the edge of his seat and began, "The night of the incident, Liam knew I should've written a report about what happened, but I didn't and he was okay with it."

"So."

"Our policy states, once he found out that I didn't follow company procedures, he should've fired me or at least written me up, but he didn't. Liam fired a guy two days ago for smoking on the job."

"Okay, so he plays favorites."

"When the fire started, he wasn't with the police while they were reviewing the tapes, I was. Liam's the Head of Security; he was supposed to handle that situation."

"He may have been handling something else at the time. Come on Christian, you have to do better than that."

"I was working the overnight shift last night and well—"

"Christian, please. Say whatever it is you came here to say."

"Alright," he replied staring directly into her analytical eyes. "Liam was in your room, early this morning."

"And you know this how?" she asked awkwardly.

"The surveillance cameras in the hallway," he replied defensively.

"What makes you think I wasn't here? He may have stopped by to talk to me or check on Mama, which is the same thing you're doing now."

"I'd buy that except *I* didn't walk in here using my own key. Besides, the time he entered your suite didn't make sense."

"I'm sure you're trying to look out for me but—"

"I already know you weren't here, because I watched you leave last night. At first, I figured you might be going to the hospital to be with your mom. Then, I wasn't sure because you were wearing such a—a beautiful dress," he said slipping in a compliment. "I thought you were going on a date."

"Christian—"

"It's okay, wherever you went isn't my business. That's not what this is about. All I'm saying is you didn't get back here until this morning," he admitted dejectedly as if she cheated on him. "And Liam was in your room while you were out. At least, you weren't with him," he said letting a suggestion of jealously escape his thoughts in a cutting whisper.

"I don't know what the problem is between you and Liam, but it doesn't have anything to do with me. I'd like to keep it that way. This isn't something you should be concerned with."

"I know I asked you out but that has *nothing* to do with this," he confessed. He nervously tapped on his right knee. He descended into a calm disposition trying to be persuasive through self-control. He cracked his neck on one side and then the other before asking, "Can I use your laptop?"

Lyss dropped her head and replied, "Look, Christian, as much as you think you know what's going on with Mama or Liam—you're off base on this one."

"Liam's not the only one with an investigative background. I came here because I have evidence to prove he's involved in your mother's disappearance somehow."

"What are you talking about? Why are you targeting Liam this way?"

"I'm not targeting the guy. All I'm trying to do is inform you of the facts," he said holding up a flash drive. "Now you can make that determination yourself before it's too late. Your mother is the one missing. I know where mine is." He saw Lyss's expression and knew his comment was unnecessary. "Lyss I'm sorry about—"

"Please finish," she stated firmly.

"Liam erased all of the surveillance video from that evening."

"Why is that an issue?"

"Because the hotel policy is that they're stored for two years before discarding them."

"What makes you think Liam erased them? Couldn't it have been someone else that works security?"

"I would've thought the same thing if I hadn't walked into the office as he finished watching the video of your mom speaking. When Liam left that night, I tried to pull up the surveillance he was viewing and everything was wiped out. He was the last person to view them."

"You told me the police took the videos."

"Yes, but remember I told you, they didn't take everything. That's how you were able to see that guy take your mom. They took the disk showing the area the fire was in."

"Christian, I'm merely a guest in this hotel. Do you worry about everyone this much?" she asked.

"If I thought they were in jeopardy, *yes* I'd be concerned the same way. It's my job to make sure our guests are safe and for some reason I think both you and your mother are in danger. You can stand there and act like I don't know what I'm talking about but we both know your mom was never at the hospital. I checked. Unless, she's here—I think something's terribly wrong and I have an idea Liam knows exactly what's going on. The guy hasn't even been—"

There was a loud pounding on the door interrupting their conversation.

"Are you expecting someone?"

"No," she replied.

Lyss walked over to the door and looked out the peephole. Liam was standing there in a pair of black sweatpants and a faded Badgers sweatshirt looking ruggedly handsome with his unshaven face. She barely cracked the door open to keep him from entering.

"Lyss, I know what you said but I need to explain my comments. I admit I was completely out of line and I need you to understand I made a mistake."

"Liam, so did I and this really isn't a good time. There's nothing else we need to say to one another. Besides," she said moving aside so he could see into the room, "I'm having a conversation with, Christian."

Christian threw his hand up giving Liam a disingenuous wave and slipped the flash drive back in his pocket.

"You're kidding me," Christian mumbled to himself.

Liam shed an intentional appearance as though Christian's presence completely baffled him. He adjusted his stance and questioned in an accusatory tone, "Am I—" he began sarcastically placing his right hand on the center of his chest, "Am I interrupting something here?"

"Yes, you definitely are," she retorted defiantly, irritated by another one of his underhanded insinuations. "Christian was *genuinely* concerned about my mother so he stopped by to see how she's doing. I didn't realize I hadn't given him an update since the night of the incident. Now, if you don't mind, I'd like to finish our conversation."

"Well, if you don't mind, I'd prefer to join you," he said adamantly, pushing the door open so he could enter the suite without an invite. "You don't mind do you, Christian?" he asked plopping down on the sofa. "I'd like to hear the update on Ms. Scott as well. So where's Ms. Scott today? Is she here now?" he asked mockingly.

"Christian, I'm sorry. Would you mind if we finished this later? Your Head of Security is quite discourteous."

"Sure," he replied apprehensively. Christian got up and headed for the door with Lyss following closely behind him. "If you need anything, call me," he whispered.

"I will. Thank you," she replied patting him on the back.

"Do me a favor," he said entering the hallway.

"Christian," she sighed.

"Please, don't trust him. I need to show you what's on this flash drive."

210

"I can handle, Liam. I appreciate your concern because I'm certain you mean well. If it makes you feel better, I don't trust *anyone* right now," she confessed.

Once Christian left, she returned to address Liam's abrasiveness.

"Lyss, sit down for a minute and hear me out," he asked pensively, tracking her every move with his subdued eyes. He was seeking an opportunity where Lyss would offer forgiveness and reconcile his misrepresentation of the facts.

"I don't know why you feel you have the right to disregard anything I have to say. You're so out of control I can't understand where you're coming from and what it is that you really want. I told you there's nothing more between us. As if it's entertaining, you arrogantly show up here like nothing happened. You behave as though an apology makes it all better. We're not kids Liam. I don't play games. I really need you to leave me alone because this situation is troubling to me." Lyss sat in a chair across from him and responded with a sharp tongue, "I'm not one to deliberately breathe in toxins. I need to keep my head focused on finding my mother since we both know she's missing. Right now, I'm politely asking you to leave since I didn't invite you here."

"All I'm asking is for you to hear me out."

"Do me a favor and let yourself out the same way you let yourself in this morning. I don't want you meddling in my life so let *this* and whatever *it* may have become, go. I'll be checking out tomorrow morning so your game's over."

"What about your mother? Are you going to involve the police?"

Liam hadn't moved so Lyss got up and went to open the door. She held it wide open and stated firmly, "I don't have any more time to waste."

"Look. Your mother gives speeches about forgiveness and you can't forgive one mistake I've made?"

"I don't get what it is that you're not understanding. You're forgiven for your *mistake* as you call it. I don't hold grudges Liam. Life's too short and precious to spend being upset about something in the past. And now, you're history. Like I said, forgiving you isn't a problem."

"Then what is?"

"Now that I've forgiven you, I'm done with you because you have no control over me. I'm going to find my mother. I don't have time for anything or anyone else but her. I won't allow you to be a distraction."

"Let me help. Nothing will come between us."

"Liam, please. What I need is for you to leave and stay out of my life. My attention can't be diverted. You had an opportunity to show me who you were and you did that very well. One of many things I learned from my mother is when someone shows you who they are; accept it as their true character. People like you try to conceal their character in order to get what they want. However, there are warning signs to help differentiate between real and not so real. You, Liam, were way too good to be so right."

"Right for you?"

"Right for anything."

Lyss took a step back, motioning for him to leave. Finally, Liam stood up and walked towards her moving as though every step was painful. He put his hands on the wall with Lyss lodged in between, nearly pinning her against it. His words were suspended in his mind while his eyes traveled across every detail of her slender, beautiful face.

"I'm sorry," he said. "I have an agonizing history. For whatever reason, I unintentionally blended it with your mother's situation. It morphed into my own reality and before I realized it, I was belligerent and casting inappropriate accusations," he admitted clenching his teeth together. "The things I said were in defense of the history I've carried. I never should've reacted that way. You didn't deserve it nor did your mother. Especially at a time like this."

"As I said, your apology's accepted but it doesn't mean I'll forget what I've learned about you. Liam, my mother had a horrific childhood, but she doesn't go hurling sharp insults at people or passing judgment as a result of what she lived through. You can't morph or blend every small connection together and prejudge it. When you went back to wherever your pain came from, you weren't the same man I was getting to know. It's like you have another side to you that quite honestly, I don't care to encounter again."

"Lyss, I buried those memories a long time ago. I guess I thought they were gone, as in having disintegrated from my memory all together. But, somehow they flooded back when I realized so many people trust your mother without ever having met her. I thought both of you were misusing their trust. There are people willing to—"

"*I* was willing to trust you, without actually knowing much about you. I guess that's okay. Or do you feel entitled, as if everyone should automatically trust you?"

"I didn't see this coming."

"Neither did I. You have significant trust issues, like a lot of people. But trust is a vital part of any relationship. Unresolved issues about something that happened in your life should be addressed. If you don't handle them, they'll handle you and interfere with your ability to have a healthy life. Liam, you're a nice guy, but every second I waste is critical."

"Then let me help!"

"I tried to. Goodbye, Liam," she stated without a single drop of remorse. She pushed his arm aside and stepped away from his reach.

"Lyss."

"Goodbye."

He left the suite and she let the door swing shut behind him. Without another thought of Liam, Lyss returned to her laptop without any emotional change and picked up where she left off; writing messages to everyone on her suspect list. She was confident that some indication of what happened to her mother would manifest as communications were returned.

She finished her message to Kevin and started to write Robert, but changed her mind deciding to call instead. She sat the laptop on the sofa and reached for her purse removing his business card from her wallet. It was necessary for her to use every minute wisely. She thought Liam could have been of help, but he proved to be more of an unnecessary distraction. She picked up her phone and dialed Robert's number. It was time to find out more about him.

A pleasant voice on the other end of the phone answered and recited kindly, "Thank you for calling the Nerual Corporation, Robert Rankin's office how may I help you?"

"Good morning, I'm trying to reach Mr. Rankin. Is he available?"

"I'm sorry Mr. Rankin's out of the office this week. If you'd like, I'll send you to his voicemail and you can leave a message there," she suggested politely.

"No, thank you. I was asked to schedule lunch with Robert this week. We met at the event for Ms. Scott the other night."

"Oh, yes. What a wonderful speech. I had a chance to attend with a few of my girlfriends and we loved it. Anyways, I'm sorry to tell you Mr. Rankin hasn't been in since the event. Like I said, I can send you to his voicemail. He checks his messages throughout the day."

"That's not necessary. I'll try back next week. Have a beautiful day." Lyss hung up the phone and mumbled, "Okay, Mr. Grimm Reaper, what's your story?"

She dropped back into deep thought wondering what or who was keeping Robert away from his corporation this week. Lyss pulled the laptop back in front of her and followed up with an email to see if he'd respond.

Robert,

It was a distinct pleasure having Nerual sponsor my event. The reception was absolutely amazing. Before I leave Minnesota, I would appreciate having the opportunity to thank you properly by taking

you to dinner this evening. I look forward
to hearing from you.

Marala

~~~~~~~~~~

Thirty-Three

He followed the road around to the opposite side
of the lake driving routinely past an area where only
a few homes were snuggly tucked away in the heart
of the evergreens only visible to the lake. He turned
down a barely discernable driveway covered with
tall wilting grass revealing the remnants of an
abandoned house. Large bushes growing unevenly
against the weathered white house surrounded it.
The porch and roof yielded ungracefully to its age.

He parked in the driveway and reached into his
duffle bag pulling out a pair of black binoculars.
When he stepped out of the truck his feet were met
by high weeds, mud and grass. The force of the wind
rattling the tattered screen door against the house
broke the uncomfortable silence. He paused to allow
a skunk to make its way from underneath the front
porch making certain not to cross its path. Once it
scampered away, he made his own trail around to
the rear where the lake was serenely resting. He slid
his sunglasses on top of his head squinting copiously
to shield his eyes from the blinding rays of the sun.
He squatted in the tall grass and peered through the
binoculars observing the cabin where Marala was

now free to escape. The boat was still on the lift and there was no sign of Marala. He waited several minutes before jumping into his truck and pulling away from the house.

The long desolate winding road was lined with deep woods of evergreens that were home to an abundance of deer and other wildlife. The thirty-five minute drive to the nearest town gave him plenty of time to contemplate his actions. His kidnapping wasn't going exactly the way he planned because he didn't think Marala would be amenable. It would have been easier for him to do what he deemed necessary if she were challenging. Although it was becoming more difficult for him to continue, there was no chance he'd alter his plans at this stage. He knew if Marala tried to escape it would be nothing more than a fruitless effort because the solitary road belonged to him. He intentionally left the cabin to give her time to try and escape so he could get his head aligned with his objectives.

He parked around the side of the building and got out. He was at the only grocery store in town. He pulled open the doors and went inside observant of his surroundings. The blue handcarts were stacked from the ground up to his waist. He grabbed one and walked to the back of the store to pick up a few meats and other items needed at the cabin. Before he began shopping, he saw a familiar face leaving. He pulled his sunglasses over his eyes and went to the opposite side of the store.

Minutes later, he approached the checkout and set his cart on the counter.

The cashier, a young woman in her twenties, began scanning his groceries and asked, "Paper or plastic?"

"It doesn't matter," he said, in a hushed voice.

"Sure it does, paper destroys trees."

"Then why offer it?"

"You're not from around here are you?"

"No."

"Where you from?"

"I'm visiting."

"There's not much up here to see. You got family here?"

"No."

"Then if you don't mind, who are you visiting?"

"I do mind. How much?" he asked cutting off her conversation as she scanned the last item.

"$57.80," she announced dryly.

The young woman filled four plastic bags with his groceries and took the three twenties he handed her.

"Keep the change."

He wasn't interested in conversation. His mind was on his problem, which included making another stop. Abruptly picking up the plastic bags, he left the store, placed them in the front seat and headed down the street to the hardware store. When he pulled along the side of the curb to park, he saw the same familiar person coming out of the store with a paper bag full of supplies. He turned his head the other way and sped off, driving past him as he headed back to the cabin.

~~~~~~~~~~

Thirty-Four

Another disruptive knock rattled the door. Lyss headed to answer it and she looked out the peephole finding Christian, once more. Reluctant to let him in, she began to back away until he knocked again, pounding harder.

"Lyss, it's me Christian. Please this is important!" he shouted.

"Not again," she said furiously yanking the door open. "Look Christian. I'm out of here tomorrow so you and Liam can find someone else to fight over! I don't play games with egotistical boys that masquerade as men. I really don't have time for this nonsense. I've had it with the both of you!"

"I'm not here because of Liam. This is about your mother," he objected annoyed with her persistent dismissal of his intentions. He reached into his jacket pocket and said, "Here, load this. It'll help you find her if you're interested. If not, I can take this evidence and leave you right where you are in finding your mom, which is nowhere," he added, making a casual about-face away from her door.

Lyss grabbed his arm and seized the flash drive. Christian spun back around and followed her into the suite. She sat down on the sofa and loaded it onto the laptop.

Christian stood behind her.

"Okay. What am I looking for?" she asked sighing heavily.

"The night of the event, right around the time of the reception. Both you and your mother exited the elevator and there was a man swiftly walking away from your door?"

"Yeah. Mama grabbed my hand when we got off the elevator like she was concerned about something."

Well this shows a man walking down the hall toward your suite. Pause it—right there!" he announced. "See? Do you recognize him?"

"No."

He reached over her shoulder and pressed play.

When the video displayed a clear facial shot, he pressed pause and asked, "How about now?"

She looked at it completely startled and replied, "Yes! That's Robert—Rankin!"

"He was your title sponsor, right?"

"Yes. But—"

"Keep watching."

He pressed play and it continued. Robert pulled out a keycard and entered the room with a black duffle bag. As the tape continued, a several minutes later he left the room and headed down the hallway, walking away from Marala and Lyss.

"What was he doing in our room? Better yet, what does Robert have to do with this?" she bellowed heatedly.

Christian selected the second video file, hit fast forward and then pressed play. It showed Liam walking briskly down the hotel corridor. The same man in the video carrying Marala out of the banquet room stopped to talk with Liam right before the fire. They shook hands and embraced as if they were friends that hadn't seen one another in a long time.

"Can you tell who he is by this angle?" Christian asked impatiently. Lyss's eyes stayed firmly fixed to the screen while her mind attempted to process what she was viewing. She paused the video and fell back on the sofa wrestling with whether or not to trust Christian.

"How do they know each other?" she mumbled.

"Do you know him?"

Her voice quivered with her response, "It's a long story. Christian, why didn't you tell me you had this?"

"I've been trying, but for some reason Liam keeps showing up as if he knows I suspect he has something to do with this, and I do. I think this evidence associates Liam with the guy that took your mom."

"Wow. This is a lot to process. Christian, I don't see Liam wanting to hurt anyone, let alone my mother. As arrogant as he is, I don't get that from him."

"Lyss, that's not all."

"What else is there?"

"Liam hasn't been here very long and for some reason he was mysteriously made Head of Security about the time your mother's event hit our schedule, which was a couple of months ago. I'm not going to sit here and say I was happy about it because I was first in line for the position. The General Manager already promised it to me and I didn't give him any reason to change his mind. But Lyss, I swear to you, that isn't why I brought this to your attention. It's been more than vague as to how Liam even got the job here anyway. He doesn't fit."

"How do you know?"

"I have keys to every room in this hotel and yes, *after* I watched this video, I went into the H.R. office and looked for his file. Guess what I found?"

"What?"

"Nothing, because he doesn't have a file here? What he does have is all the elements of an anonymity."

"Christian, what's Liam's last name?"

"Christianson. Why?"

"I was wondering if he had any connection to Robert."

"It doesn't look like it but you never know. I need to run a check on Robert and find out more about him, but I can't do it from here."

"Why not?"

"It'll show up. I've got a buddy with the department downtown. I'll call him and find out everything I can get on him. What about the other guy? Do you have an address or last name?"

"No. I don't believe he ever gave one."

"Well, I'm going to need an address or something to do a background on him. Try to find something I can work with."

"Okay."

"You have a good heart Lyss. I can tell," he said confidently. "Don't beat yourself up for trying to see the good in people. What's important is now that we know Liam didn't tell you the truth, we need to find out what else he's lying about. The man on the video abducted your mother and we still don't know why?"

"Mama told me she knew who he was."

"You've spoken to her?"

"Yes, twice."

"Did she say it was the same guy you recognized with Liam in the video?"

Lyss began trudging through her memories. Dumbfounded, she dropped her head.

"Yes. When I spoke to her earlier today. She told me something."

"What'd she say?" he questioned eagerly.

"She said, '*like I told you when you were a little girl, keep these words with you. I'm thinking of you fondly, even when I sleep, there's nothing in this world that can separate you from me. I love you beautiful daughter.*'"

"So what's strange about it? That's beautiful."

"Yes, but other than, I love you beautiful daughter, Mama never said the rest of it. It was a clue. She must have been talking in code because he was close to her." Lyss picked up her iPad, opened her mother's email and scrolled through the inbox. She pulled up one of his messages and read it. She clicked on three more of them and they all said the same thing. The clue was there. Like her mother said, everything was in her laptop. Without showing Christian, she closed it.

"Let me make a few calls and I'll get back with you as soon as I get what we need. Don't check out of this hotel," he said picking up Lyss's phone. He dialed his number.

"I'm not staying here. Robert has a key to this room. He could be spying on us right now for all we know. I'm out of here tomorrow morning."

His phone vibrated, he locked in the number and typed her name in as the contact.

"Lyss, right now this suite is the safest place for you to be. Liam's out there somewhere and we don't know his involvement in all of this. The problem with him is that we have evidence validating he knows the man who kidnapped your mother. And Robert's another issue in itself. He can get into your room but only when you're gone. At least I'm here where I can keep a close eye on you. If you leave this hotel, I can't guarantee you'll be safe."

"Why is all this happening?"

"That I don't know," he confessed. "But one thing I'm certain of is your mother's trying to tell you exactly where to look and what's going on. We have to listen. Run every conversation you've had with her over the past several days through your head and get back to the truth," he exclaimed, handing Lyss her phone.

"The truth?" she questioned.

"Yeah, your intuition. It'll produce more answers than you can. Didn't you read her book?"

"Christian, she's been warning me about this engagement since I added it to the schedule. I thought she was nervous about speaking because of her surgery. How could I have missed this? I heard everything she said but I didn't think she was implying I'd have to use it this soon. I dismissed everything she was warning me about. She did it as delicately as possible so I wouldn't worry. Mama always tried to keep me from worrying about anything."

"My mom was the opposite," he acknowledged sadly. "She complained about everything; even things I shouldn't have known about. Some people prefer to have company wallowing in the bowels of their misery. My mom was one of those people."

"I'm sorry. That had to be difficult."

"It was back then. Nowadays, it's nothing but history. I made the decision to move far away from that stress."

"Good for you," she acknowledged, sounding happy for him.

"Thanks. Is there anything else I should know?" he asked.

"Several of our conversations circled back to discussing intuition. Right before her surgery she began pushing me to trust it."

"From where we're standing I'd tend to think that's a good idea. I think you should know I've read all your mother's books long before this event was scheduled. They've helped me in many ways. I got the latest book the day it came out and I agree with her. There were times I should've trusted my intuition but naturally, I'd change my mind to support whatever it was I wanted to do."

"What were the results of not trusting it?"

"I always regretted my decision. With hindsight, I guess it's easier to see."

"She told me to use my faith to move past the fear because she knew I'd be afraid to do anything if I thought it would cause her any degree of harm."

"I can tell you're not afraid, but you're worried sick. I know you're doing everything you can to find her."

"Yeah but even though Mama's been kidnapped when I spoke with her she told me he wouldn't hurt her and I believe her."

"Why?"

"Because she sounded convincing. I think I wanted to believe her so I could handle this better. But after I let it settle, I can tell she trust him for whatever reason."

"We need to concentrate on recalling everything she's told you because the answer to what's going on is concealed in her words and she's confident you'll figure it out. Let's not disappoint her. When you talk to her again, write down everything she says.

Everything! It took a lot of planning for him or them to do this and we need to find out why so we can uncover a solution to get her back. She's an author and inspirational speaker. I don't understand why anyone would want to hurt someone like her."

"Perhaps they don't want someone to follow their intuition because they might become cognizant of the truth about something they're trying to conceal. People go through a lot to cover up the truth."

"That's very possible," Christian agreed.

"She told me he doesn't want to do anything other than protect her from someone."

"Protect her from who and why would he feel it's his responsibility? Why wouldn't he let the police handle the situation?"

"She didn't say."

"All I know is we may not have much time. I did a search on the company name on the truck that pulled off with your mother."

"Did you find anything?"

"There was no record of a Sanders Construction in this state. They've obviously planted seeds to distract you or anyone that's involved in trying to find her. I'm going to find out everything I can about Liam from my buddy and I believe it's going to be a complicated task. I'll scrape together whatever there is on Robert too. In the meantime, I don't want you to leave this suite. Lock the door and keep it locked unless you confirm that it's me."

She nodded agreeably.

"Don't open this door for anyone, not even room service. If you need something, text me and I'll bring it to you."

"Christian."

"Lyss, this is something I'm convinced I need to do. I was out of line hitting on you the other night. You were worried sick because your mom was missing and—I can't even believe I crossed the line. All I want to do is help. I don't have any other agenda. I promise."

"What about Liam?" she asked.

"Stay away from him until we figure out his role in all of this. Give me some time to check things out. I'll return in a couple of hours."

"I don't know how to thank you for bringing this to my attention, especially after the way I treated you. I thought this was something personal, you know, some male rivalry between you and Liam to see who gets to do the girl first."

"That's easy," he began, causing Lyss to drop her head with embarrassment. "He would. But as much as I'd like to say he's narcissistic, it doesn't seem to be his style. He's had plenty of opportunities, but even when the other guys nudge him to go for it, he's made it very clear he's not here for that. In my opinion, it really seems to annoy him when people assume he does. I'll get back to you as soon as I have something relevant."

"Thanks again, Christian."

When Christian left, Lyss secured both locks. She paced the floor a few times deliberating before perching in front of the window overlooking the city. Lyss had to regroup and figure out Liam's role. Christian gave her plenty to think about.

"Liam, what's your involvement?" she murmured.

Lyss returned to her typical spot on the sofa and picked up the laptop. Underneath it was the money she had given to Christian. She returned it to her wallet and clicked on her email. There were several messages. She skipped down a few to one from Sharon.

Marala,

I feel privileged to have you writing me. You make me feel like I matter to you. I'm beginning to breathe again here in Connecticut being away from my ex-husband, Robert. Although, initially I wanted children, he didn't so things worked out for the better. He already had two children. After he killed his wife he continued to raise his son until he was old enough to leave. Once he left, he didn't have much contact with him. I met his son in passing one time and he tried to warn me about his father but I can't say I listened. He was a nice-looking young man. I remember the pain in his face when he spoke about his mother.

I do believe Robert has a dual residency in Minnesota and Wisconsin. He owns a hotel near the Twin Cities along with his Nerual Corporation. He's a real dangerous charmer. Thank you for keeping up with me and I look forward to reading more of your inspiration. Sending you lots of hugs! <3
Sharon

Lyss covered her mouth in shock. Then she hit "reply" and began typing.

Sharon,

228

Although I hear several tragic stories along with inspirational ones, for some strange reason this story sounds somewhat familiar to me as if I've heard it before. Do you remember any of the kid's names?

Marala

There was a quick response.

I'm sorry. I don't remember his daughter's name because he didn't' talk about her. I think his son's name was Gary but it's been awhile since I saw him last. I sincerely pray these aren't people you know. xoxo

Sharon

~~~~~~~~~

Thirty-Five

When he returned to the cabin, he dropped the bags on the counter and then placed the groceries in the refrigerator. The cabin had a deserted feel with a steep silence dwelling inside of it.

"Marala!" he called, placing a box of green tea in the cabinet above the sink. There was no response. He went into the bedroom finding no sign of her. He jogged up the stairs to the loft and looked around. She was gone.

"Ahhh!" he shouted, angrily as he fled down the stairs. Once he reached the bottom of the steps the front door swung open. He reached behind him and drew his gun with his hand firmly on the trigger leaving it pointed straight at Marala's head.

"No—Garrett!" she screamed, thoughtlessly releasing her handful of assorted and colorful wildflowers. As they inaudibly dropped to the floor she tightly clenched her hand over her heart as if barely catching it dangling off a cliff.

He placed the gun on the counter and rushed to take a visibly frightened and trembling Marala, securely in his arms.

"I'm sorry sweetheart. I thought," he whispered.

"I know," she said softly with tears streaming down her flushed cheeks.

"Where'd you go?"

"I stepped outside after you left. It was really strange."

"What was strange? Did you see someone?"

"No, nothing like that. I was trying to shut out everything so I could think."

"About what?"

"You. The swaying trees and—and rustling of the leaves swirling around pulled me out there. I know it doesn't make sense but I felt—" she paused trying to explain her staggering thought.

"You felt what?"

"Like I was destined to go out there and explore the surroundings in order to better understand you. Garrett, it felt like a part of you is buried here and part of your life has been scattered throughout these woods and around this place. Even in that lake for some reason." He was completely caught off guard, speechless by her eerie revelation. "I'm sorry I left the cabin, but I needed to get closer to you," she explained after the truth sifted out of her.

"Why? Why would you want to do that? There's no benefit."

"I'm—I'm not going to make this easy for you," she said unable to stop her cascading tears. "I know you better than you think. I've paid close attention to our communications over the past few years and I've watched you progress in a way that's affected me profoundly. Not once did I write you because I felt obligated. I was writing because I was proud of every step you took to rise above your challenges. I loved what I learned about you and I respected what you changed in yourself. I still don't have any idea as to what this is about, but like I told my daughter, you're trying to keep me safe. I've accepted that because I love—"

He quickly interrupted her thought.

"Marala don't," he insisted, uncertain and afraid of what she might confess.

"If you don't want me to judge you for whatever it is you have to do, then let me do what's necessary to protect *you* from harm?"

With sullen words he questioned, "Why would it matter what happens to me?"

"I'm disappointed you don't know. It matters because *you* matter to me," she whispered convincingly. "Please trust me the way I trust you. I won't run. I promise."

In a sweeping and thoughtless movement he tightened his temperate embrace drawing her closer to his muscular body. He lowered his head allowing a tender wave of genuine passion to move him to kiss the top of her head. His guarded heart was miraculously unlocked, freeing his soul. His eyes softened with shame as if he were a man that had frightened the woman he was clandestinely in love with. It was apparent his internal scales were tilting in the opposite direction as his lips deliberately journeyed to her forehead and longingly ventured down her nose to meet the erogenous zone where he tasted her sweet lips, searching for a small suggestion of approval. He encountered a brief pause as their lips scarcely touched only to the sensation of remorse enveloping his opposing logic. Surrendering to his truth, he kissed her tenderly until a deep thrust of passion from his heart overcame him and physically intervened. Garrett indulged in what he felt and she didn't force him away. Her arms wrapped around him in a captivating embrace. For the first time, this was as real as he imagined. This single, tender kiss quickly traveled to his emotional core and gave him a furious jolt. He backed away appearing upset that he'd given into his hidden attraction. Without uttering a word he snatched his gun off the counter and climbed the stairs, two at a time, to retreat in the loft. This wasn't part of his plan; it was a part of his dream. Now wasn't the time to become emotionally confused anymore than he already was.

Marala bent down and picked up the flowers one at a time understanding his unresolved turmoil coupled with her own. She went into the kitchen, put the scissors in the sink and found a tall glass. She turned on the faucet and filled it half full of water. Without glancing up at him, she arranged the flowers, set them on the counter and then voluntarily returned to her room.

Garrett was leaning back in his leather chair. He was loaded with explosive emotions speeding recklessly throughout him, setting his veins ablaze along the way. He didn't understand how this happened. In another place and time it may have been possible, but not now. Having kidnapped her, he couldn't consider she'd ever think to have any degree of personal attraction or trust towards him. He shuddered when his mind returned to their passionate kiss derailed by his own plunging guilt. His disillusioned mind was inundated with cutting thoughts of mass confusion. Never had he kissed anyone with so much unbound passion. No one mattered that much to him, until now. Marala had breached his wall and was closer to him than she imagined. Garrett understood what Marala was experiencing being away from her daughter. He was given his own IV drip of fear and pain. As ugly as it was, he wasn't ready for her to know his truth. However, the inescapable reality was already forcing its way to the surface.

Even though she was beginning to make unconscious connections to some of the pieces, he thought Marala's heart was too optimistic and she'd be devastated when proven to be wrong about him. All Garrett desperately sought for the past few years was to be the man Marala deserved. Unfortunately, Marala didn't have the faintest idea that it was too late to stop or save him. He understood a kiss like that could never happen again, although his heart already belonged to her.

Reality broke into his surge of convoluted thoughts as his phone vibrated. Heatedly, Garrett snatched it off his desk and read the message.

My intuition says its time. Tonight, my house and bring her to me!

Thirty-Six

Liam paced his living room floor with beams of anger rushing through him like a deadly tsunami. There was nothing that could keep him away from Lyss, regardless of what she told him. He took a great degree of satisfaction in not losing to anyone and he wasn't about to let it happen now. He had a job to do and it was going to get done with or without her consent.

Lyss and Christian were wrong about him; he didn't know Garrett personally, but he knew Robert, very well. Unfortunately for Lyss, Liam needed her in order to accomplish his goal. No one really knew the truth and time was running out.

Liam left his apartment with a small black duffle bag, jumped into his truck and headed over to the hotel. When he pulled up, he sat out front, blocked his number then called Lyss. The phone rang once and she picked up.

"Mama!"

Before she could hang up the phone, his voice authoritatively streamed into her ear.

"Lyss don't hang up! I'm out front of the hotel and I need to see you."

"That's too bad. I don't have a reason to communicate with you, Liam. I trusted you and we both know that was a mistake."

"Get down here so I can take you to mother before it's too late. Trust your intuition or I'm leaving without you."

"You know where she is?" she questioned eagerly.

"I have a strong suspicion."

"Where?"

"Lyss, I don't care what Fish has shown you or what he thinks he knows—"

"Fish? Why do you call Christian that? It's not his name."

"I don't call him Fish for any other reason than he's an excellent swimmer. He's a Division One champ in the men's freestyle so I nicknamed him Fish. See how words can be misconstrued? It's all a matter of perspective."

"Note taken."

"He's a good kid, but completely mistaken. I don't blame him for having concerns; he works in security and should. Look, I'm in a bit of a hurry so I'll make this easy for you. I have one question."

"What's that?"

"Do you trust me?" There was a long silence and she gave no response. "Fine, you have five minutes to make that decision and get down here or I'm gone for good. And whatever happens to your mother is no fault of mine," he said warning her.

"Liam!"

He hung up the phone.

Lyss collected her purse, sweater and iPad as she slipped into a pair of flat shoes.

She wrote a quick note, shoved it into an envelope, rushed down to the hotel lobby and handed it to the woman at the front desk.

"Can you please give this to Christian in security. It's extremely important."

"He just returned. I think he's in his office. Would you like me to get him for you?" she asked politely.

"No thank you. But can you let him know I was in a hurry?"

In a few quick steps Lyss swiftly vanished through the revolving doors to find Liam holding the door to his truck open for her.

"What made you so sure I was coming?" she questioned, sounding slightly aggravated by his elevated arrogance as she climbed inside.

"I know you well. And you know me much better than you'd care to admit," he affirmed closing her door. He gave a quick nod to the valet and then jumped into the driver side and sped off.

"Where are we headed?"

"Up north," he replied. "You're in for a long drive so make yourself comfortable while I fill you in."

Lyss tossed her bag on the seat behind her and responded, "I'm ready."

"Where do I begin?" he huffed affably.

"With my mother. Where is she? And how is it that you know?"

"It's a long story so I want you to hear me out before passing judgment."

"Like you did with me?"

"The only objective I have is to get your mother back safely."

"Are you sure about that?"

"Yes, I'm sure," he responded, notably offended by her sour insinuation.

"You said it was a long drive so, let's talk. And Liam—" she began. He gave her a quick glance and then returned his attention to the road. "Getting my mother back is the only reason I'm here."

Liam hit his turn signal and picked up speed as he entered the ramp heading east towards Interstate 35.

"Lyss," he said taking a deep breath. "There's a reason I've been vague about things."

"Oh, you think?"

"I don't work for the hotel itself."

"That's obvious Liam."

"Why?"

"When we went out for dinner the other night, I could tell by Beth's reaction and communication about you that there was a lot more to who you are then you let on."

"Really? You think you know me?"

"I'm not claiming to. But what I do know is you're working undercover as Head of Security at that hotel. It has something to do with my mother and the person trying to harm her. I don't know why or how you're connected but you know who has her. That much I'm certain of."

"Alright, Doc. Since you don't think I work for the hotel, what is it that I do?"

"I'd say, some type of investigative work. If you want me to be more specific, knowing your skill level and that you wanted to be an assassin, you probably went for the Bureau and I don't think your little childhood situation would have interfered. And that's if it happened at all."

"Wow, you think that highly of me?"

"Things don't connect where you're concerned but my intuition keeps telling me to trust you irrespective of what I've observed or been told. Beth obviously does. When you told me about Tony, I started to consider he might have been your partner or someone you worked with. For some reason, like my mother, I believe you knew this kidnapping was going to happen, but not because of your intuition."

"You think I knew?" he asked with a terrible poker face.

"She's not afraid of her kidnapper and evidently neither are you."

"What makes you think that?"

"I don't work for the Bureau but I have my own sources," she disclosed in a clever tone.

"We both know Fish is one of them," he said cutting his eyes at her.

"I don't reveal my sources either. You should know that being in the Bureau. So think what you want," she said waiting for a reply. He didn't give one so she continued. "What's the real story?"

Liam gripped the stirring wheel tightly and exhaled heavily.

"A few months ago when your mother's book, *Intuition* came out, my superior dropped a thick green file on my desk. When I reviewed the case I was caught off guard because it involved Marala Scott. At that point, I wasn't familiar with her work so I read her books and did as much research as I could possibly find on her. I know everything about her and yes, it's quite impressive. I can see why people are so taken by her. And about the other night, I had to throw you off and I'm sorry. We were getting too—"

"What does your case have to do with my mother?"

"There was a man who killed his wife decades ago. Unfortunately, he managed to get away with it even though his children allegedly witnessed the murder."

"This sounds like a woman that recently wrote my mother. She even went to see her speak. She was married to a man named—"

"Robert," Liam answered.

"Yes."

"That's Rankin."

"Do you have any idea what he has to do with this?

"Apparently, Robert's steep arrogance caused him to confess the murder to Sharon. Maybe that was his way of threatening that she'd be next. She did the right thing and got out of there. Most likely afraid he'd come after her, she reported it to the police. The bureau took over the case and it ended up on my desk."

"Why are you investigating it now if they weren't able to catch him years ago?"

He glanced over at her and said, "Because she had a recorded confession and knows what he did with the body."

"Uh! Do you know anything about Robert?" Lyss asked.

"Actually Doc, I know a lot about him."

"Because of your investigation?"

"No, not at all. Lyss, you're not going to like this but Robert Rankin—He's my stepfather and Sharon happens to be his *second* wife."

"But your last name is—"

"Christianson. I know that's confusing. My mother had two kids with Robert and I wasn't one of them."

"Why not?"

"I lived with my adoptive parents since birth."

"You don't have to answer if you don't want to, but do you know why your mother gave you up for adoption?" she asked gently, trying not to cause Liam any pain in thinking about it.

He released a heavy sigh and responded defensively, "Mom. She was young and from what I understand, it was her parents that forced her to give me away. They were rather affluent and having a kid at sixteen wasn't a good thing."

"How'd you find out who your mother was and about Robert?"

"I think it hit me when I was around fifteen. I wanted to know more about the people I shared my DNA with," he said.

"Okay, so you wanted to know more. Like what?"

"Typical things any adopted kid would be curious about at some point in their life," he said veering right onto a two-lane state route. "I was trying to figure out who I was. Did I have any siblings? If so, were they put up for adoption? Who did I laugh like? I never looked like anyone or fit anywhere and I didn't know anything about my family. I had a lot of questions that needed to be answered so when I was old enough, I went looking for Mom."

"Was it difficult to find her?"

"Very. By then she married Robert, her last name changed, they had a couple kids, moved away and all that good stuff. He actually turned out to be a pretty successful businessman. He came from old money and turned it into more."

"How did your mom feel when you found her?"

"Mom," he repeated reflectively, "That didn't work out too well for her. I didn't think it would be a big deal because I didn't want anything other than to know who she was and a little about her. But Robert, boy, he didn't like it. I guess she'd never told him about me because he looked like he wanted to kill her for having a son out of wedlock."

"What was Robert like?"

"He happened to be there the first time I showed up at their house. I didn't think about it causing problems for Mom because I just wanted to meet her. But Robert, he was nothing more than the devil in a suit. You could feel his torrential energy. To this day, I'd never felt anything so intense and negative in my life. This man had a patent on evil."

Lyss shuddered.

"What's wrong?" he asked.

"That gave me chills."

"Why?"

"I got the same upsetting feeling from Robert when I met him at the reception. There was something disconcerting about him and I wasn't mistaken. Did he see you in the hotel?"

"No, and even if he did, he wouldn't have recognized me. When Robert and I met, it was brief and I was in college. I had the crazy scruffy beard, long scraggly hair and boy was I skinny," he laughed.

"But what about the hotel?"

"So you're aware that Robert owns it?"

"I suspected it."

"How?"

"Like you, he was in our suite. How did you get the position as Head of Security?"

"To my knowledge, Robert never knew my last name or anything about me. Oddly, my mother didn't ask either. Besides, the Bureau made sure the connection wouldn't happen."

"For clarity, is your real name Liam Christianson or is that your undercover name?" Liam let out a hardy laugh.

"What's so funny? I think I have a right to know who kissed me."

"He replied with more laughter, "*For clarity*, as you like to call it, that's my real name. Other than the Bureau, most people don't know my last name. But you do," he confessed, glancing at Lyss. "And I'm pretty sure you kissed me back, Doc."

Lyss turned her head looking out the window to conceal her smile.

"Did you ever meet your step-siblings?"

"Yeah," he admitted shaking his head pitifully. "That would have torn anyone up. Those kids were abused. And the way he spoke to them, I'd *never* seen a father with such rage. They were terrified of the man and unfortunately, so was Mom. After meeting them, it didn't take a second thought for me to realize everything worked out for the better. I mean, my being adopted. But not for those kids. I'll never forget the looks on their little faces," he added sadly. "No kid should ever look that way."

"Did you spend much time with your mom or ever find what you were searching for?"

"Not initially, but I kept sneaking back when Robert wasn't around. At one point I asked her to leave him and come live with me but she wouldn't leave her kids. I told her to bring them."

"Really?"

"Yeah."

"How did she respond?"

"She told me Robert would never let any of them leave there alive. It wasn't long after that when she asked me to stop coming to see her. She said she wanted me to enjoy the life I had and let whatever fantasy I created of having her as a mother wither away."

242

"Liam, I'm sorry. Sometimes parents do things to protect us and we may not understand it at the time. The way things tend to go is that when we're older our perspective changes, making things clearer. The perception we had may not always have been the true reality."

"I can't say I disagree with you. Looking back on things, it sure felt as though she was in a rush to get me out of her life, but in hindsight, I realized she was protecting me from Robert's grasp. Although I didn't get much time with Mom, I got what I went looking for."

"What's that?"

"To see her face. Her beautiful blue eyes and angelic voice was enough for me to carry the rest of my life."

"That's an extraordinary memory, Liam."

"Yeah well, there's something that never settled with me."

"What?"

"The last time I saw her, she grabbed both of my hands and looked at me as lovingly as a mother could. She was about to tell me something. I felt it. She opened her mouth but never got the chance to say it."

"Why not?"

"Robert came home and she had to shove me out the back door before he saw me."

"Did the kids know when you were there?"

"Sometimes, but Mom said they'd never say a word to their father. I guess they didn't like him much either."

"What do you mean either?"

"Mom didn't like Robert. She just happened to be stuck with him."

"How do you know that?"

Trying to hide the irritation in his voice he cleared his dry throat and replied, "He killed her."

They continued driving for several miles on the State Route without a single word being spoken. Liam skillfully mastered the sharp curves and winding turns with increasing speed to coincide with his ascending suppressed thoughts. Lyss knew she shouldn't have asked her last question, but was still focused on connecting his case to her mother. It was time she pulled out every detail she could.

Liam drove as though he were in a slight trance, simply following the lines on the road. Lyss appeared to be gazing out the window but she was organizing her questions. They slowed down as they passed through a small town that appeared partially abandoned.

"We're coming up on a gas station, do you need to stop for anything? It'll be a while before the next one," he said with a keen sense of familiarity.

"No, I'm fine."

He drove past a little shack vaguely representing a store and gas station. It was as dead as the undisturbed road they were on, leading them into the unsounded forest ahead.

"Did you guys talk about anything meaningful?"

"Who?" he asked as if he'd forgotten the conversation.

"You and your mom."

"Not really. She was soft spoken and careful with her words. I think I wanted to observe her beauty more than anything. I could sit and stare at her for hours but I never got more than thirty minutes at a time. One day she handed me a note as I was leaving."

"What did it say?"

"She asked me to do her a favor."

"Really? What was it?"

"It said if either of the kids ever reached out to me, not to turn them away."

"What an odd request. It's as if she expected they would. Whatever happened to them?"

He took another long heartfelt breath and answered, "It wasn't good."

"Why? What happened?"

"His daughter Tess killed herself shortly after our mother was murdered. I could only imagine what she was going through, especially if she witnessed it. Whatever she saw must have been too much for her to deal with," he said shaking his head disparagingly.

"So that left—"

"Her brother."

"This is incredibly heartbreaking. Liam, I had no idea you carried all of this with you. No wonder you have an issue with trust. It makes sense."

"Darlin', I'm sorry you found out in the manner you did. I was way out of line the way I spoke to you about your mother. I didn't want you to have any feelings towards me in case—"

"That's forgiven. At least I understand where it came from. I thought—"

"I know what you thought, that I was crazy. Right, Doc?" He cut his eyes at her while following the snaky road nestled through the woods.

"Not exactly. What I saw in you was such a confident and compassionate man. Your emotional outburst completely contradicted my intuition; which was telling me I could trust you. I didn't think you were crazy but like I said, I thought you had issues with trust and allowed your fear to take over."

"That's what I was going for," he boasted patting her thigh.

"Liam, you jumped to the belief that we were deceptive and malevolent people, without having any tangible evidence. It didn't make sense and yes, it hurt."

"Lyss, I had to. I'd rather you hate me than—"

"What Liam? Than trust you?"

"No Darlin',"

"Then what?" Lyss paused before admitting, "Liam, although we both know this situation is extremely confusing, I don't completely understand all of the dynamics yet. When you kept me from falling after I bumped into you in the security office, intuitively, I knew you were a good man. After things revealed themselves and became complicated, I wanted to stay away from you because I didn't understand everything. There were so many uncertainties where you were concerned that I questioned my intuition, which is something my mother told me *never* to do. I felt there was a lot of mystery surrounding you and it made me uncomfortable."

"The way we met and the reason behind it isn't a typical case or situation for me either. Of all people, what are the odds of this being placed in my lap? The mechanics behind it hit me so quickly that even with my expertise I didn't know how to react. And you hit me fast and hard too. I didn't see this coming because I've never felt—this."

"Liam," she said reaching over to delicately touch his hand, "We let ourselves get completely unbound and caught up in something we shouldn't have allowed to happen. I think we're both running on high octane right now; especially with everything we're trying to figure out. I think we simply—"

"No, Lyss. Go ahead and validate it any way you need to, but for me that was *no accident.* What happened between us is our reality, not work and not a moment. I wanted you then and I still do. Darlin', you're that one; that soulmate most people never find."

Lyss turned her head and stared pensively out her side of the window for a few minutes before responding. She was trying to reject his words and her feelings for him. Until her mother was safely returned, there was no room for a soulmate or anyone.

"I think you have a lot of confusion because of this case and everything attached to it. What I can say is you're a man that's been through a lot. I'm basing that on what I know about your friend taking his life, Callie and what happened to your mother and siblings. Liam, that's a lot for anyone to handle. And I do mean *anyone.*"

"I thought I'd put it behind me," he said sounding frustrated. "I thought I was handling it."

"I can barely accept what's going on with my mother right now, which leaves no room for us. One day, life is great and then out of nowhere, everything's out of control. Believe me when I tell you I didn't see this happening either. This is so painful—and what you're dealing with—" she cried, "I can't even gauge how deep it runs."

Lyss wiped her tears as Liam rubbed her arm and then let his hand drop down to hers, holding it tightly.

"We all have something or another that opens our Pandora's box. I'm sorry to say I was never able to lock mine."

"Suppressing pain, anger or secrets is never a good thing because at some point, it returns. When it does, it can bring about more devastation than you'd ever imagine. I see a glimpse of that in you and it hurts my heart. Everyone and everything isn't good for you and God can save you from yourself if you trust in Him. That's what intuition is about, *trust in God*."

"I know," he replied without looking at her. "I know."

"When I was a teenager, my mother taught me the perception versus the true reality of people's lives is usually two very different things. Now that I'm in the field of psychology, it gives more credence to that and it's nothing but the truth. People let you see what they want you to see when their reality is generally something different."

"Well, your mother was right. Theirs certainly was. Mom and the kids appeared to have everything anyone would want but nothing they needed or deserved."

"Have you figured out what Robert has to do with my mother missing?"

"It started back when your mother wrote *In Our House*. It appeared she was opening up doors across the country where people were talking more openly about what went on behind them."

"I'd agree that it helped create more dialogue about what goes on behind closed doors. My mother received so many emails from people confessing a variety of situations that were disturbing and some I'd say, unspeakable. She shared her life with me and she exposed her soul in that book. People trust her because they can identify with her on some level or another, even those who aren't abused."

"And trust is what brought people closer to her."

"Yes. I watch it happen time after time."

"Robert was no different. The problem with him was that he didn't like what she had to say because it tore through his soul, twisting at three hundred miles an hour, disrupting everything in it, like a tornado. She reminded him of the kind of man he really was. All the money and notoriety didn't erase the murderous blood on his hands and his conscious wouldn't let it drip away."

"I wonder what caused him to be so filled with evil?"

"Who knows? He killed my mother, Lauren. His bloody actions caused his only daughter to take her life and the only family he had left was his son, Garrett."

"Garrett? The same Garrett that writes my mother?"

"Yeah, that's him."

"You knew Garrett was Robert's son all this time? Why didn't you tell me?"

"I didn't get the sense that's what you wanted to believe."

"This isn't about whether I *want* to believe something or not. It's about my mother! What if I'd said something to Garrett I shouldn't have?"

"Did you?"

"I—I don't know."

"I tried to warn you but—"

"That's why you reacted the way you did. You thought we were causing harm to your brother, after everything his father had done. You knew how much he was beginning to trust someone, probably for the first time in his life and you felt we were deceiving him. Oh jeez!" Lyss groaned loudly. "You were protecting your brother. How could I not see this?"

"Lyss I knew you nor your mother would ever cause anyone harm. Darlin' that was my way of protecting you from—us."

"I know, but still, he's your brother. I thought you looked familiar for some reason. I wouldn't say you look *exactly* like him but you have what I'd consider to be comparable features."

"Really?"

"The first time I laid eyes on you, I actually thought you resembled this other guy that was writing my mother because I'd seen his picture. But he was much older than you are. For a moment I was—"

"Afraid of me? Is that the reason you left the office so quickly?"

She shrugged and then replied, "I didn't know what to think. You startled me."

"Now it makes sense."

"My intuition keeps connecting you and that guy. And oddly, his name is Liam too. But in another sense, you seem to be protective of Garret. I felt I could trust the both of you even when the evidence said I shouldn't. It's strange."

"Interesting."

"Anyways, back to Robert. Do you know why he's so angry or what caused his explosive rage to recur? At this point in his life, one would think he has too much to lose trying to kill again. On the other hand, I suppose once you do it, that thirst doesn't always go away."

"He's angry because he didn't want Marala to awaken Garrett's conscious or teach him how to follow his intuition like she'd done so many other people."

"What you're saying is Robert didn't want Garrett to stop carrying his hatred and anger so he'd remain loyal to him."

"Well, from what I've read in the file, Robert had an extremely toxic hold on Garrett and it caused them to have quite a history together. Trust me when I say it's a history that *you,* darlin' know nothing about. Robert became obsessed with your mother because of what she's able to do. She's helped inspire a lot of people; both men and women."

"She's not the only person out there doing this. There are people just like her changing lives and making a difference every single day."

"True. No one's disputing that. The problem is your mother happens to be the person doing it in *Robert's* life. Somehow she's unknowingly invaded his sick little world and he wants her out of it, permanently."

Lyss turned to look out the window noticing the scenery hadn't changed in miles. Her thoughts veered off to a question that she wanted an answer to but wasn't sure if this was the right time. It kept gnawing at her so she decided to ask.

"Tony. You said you guys were close but you hadn't seen him much in the past year."

"Yeah that's right."

"How close were you guys?"

"Like brothers, I thought," he added with an odd expression.

"You thought?"

"Yeah."

"Liam, give me the unvarnished version of the truth?"

"As far as?"

"Did you ever find out what caused Tony to take his life?" Liam didn't make eye contact with her. Instead, he tightened his grip on the steering wheel and replied, "Actually, I did."

"What happened?"

"Tony was the one that had the affair with Callie. I guess he couldn't handle the guilt," he added dryly.

"Did Beth know?"

"No. I couldn't tell her. As much as I wanted to, I couldn't do that to her. She was in love with Tony."

Lyss looked at him somberly. She retreated back into a quiet state for a few minutes until she noticed Liam picking up speed like he was running out of time.

"Exactly, where are we headed?" she asked.

"To Robert, before he gets to your mother. The thought of what he might do sickens me."

~~~~~~~~~~

Thirty-Seven

Christian impatiently waited for his reports on Robert and Liam to come through. When the white pages began rolling off the printer, he pulled off each one and read the report. His mouth dropped open and he exclaimed. "My God! This can't be right! This is insane!"

Hurriedly, Christian left the security office heading to Lyss's suite when the young lady at the front desk stopped him.

"Hey Chris! Hold on a sec. I almost forgot. A woman stopped by and asked me to give this to you," she said handing him the envelope. Christian opened it and read the contents.

"How long ago?" he asked frantically.

"Oh, that was about forty-five minutes ago. Maybe an hour." Christian turned to leave and she added, "She said to tell you she was in a hurry."

"Did she leave?"

"Yeah. I'm sorry, I hope it wasn't important."

"Actually, it was." He reached into the front pocket of his pants, grabbed his keys and mumbled, "It could cost Lyss her life."

Nearly knocking a few people over, he raced down to the hotel's parking garage and jumped into his black mustang. He started his car, glanced at the address and entered it into his navigation. Christian sped out the garage heading for the same highway Liam took with Lyss. "This was all a setup! God, please let me get to her in time!"

~~~~~~~~~~

Thirty-Eight

There was a soft tapping on the bedroom door but Marala didn't respond. Garrett turned the knob, slowly pushed it open and entered the room. He observed her staring out of the window before disrupting her thoughts. He was conflicted over what he had to do and how he was going to tell her. At this point, he couldn't prevent the situation from happening and he knew better than to try because it wouldn't matter.

"Would you mind coming out and sitting with me? I need to talk with you about something." Without saying a word Marala got up and followed him into the living room and sat quietly on the sofa. "Would you like me to make a fire?" he asked, already beginning to stack a few logs." She didn't reply. Garrett knelt on one knee by the fireplace, crumpled up a piece of newspaper, lit it and then shoved it beneath the logs. Once he manipulated the wood into a warm and inviting fire, he picked up the throw blanket, rested it across her lap and sat beside her.

"I'm sorry about earlier today."

"I think I understand. There's—" she started, slightly choking up, "no need to explain."

"I think I should," he insisted warmly.

She gazed at him despondently and acknowledged, "I know whatever you want to talk about isn't what I need to hear. I've been praying you learn to accept all the amazing things I see in you as who you are; yet it doesn't appear that it matters." She felt his eyes inspect every inch of her troubled face. "Do I—Do I mean anything at all to you? Is it easy for you to be laden with so much passion one moment and callously hurl it off a cliff the next?" Garrett didn't say anything. Instead, he turned his head away. She grabbed his jaw forcing him to look at her. "That's why you kissed me—because I'm nothing more than a diversion to you? You're going to stand by and allow me to be used for bait to satisfy your own revenge!"

"Stop it! I would never hurt you! Never!"

The tone and sincerity in his voice was irrefutable. Involuntarily, his chorus of words quickly resonated in her soul.

"I know you won't hurt me but this game has to end before it's too late."

His guilt for leaving Marala with this painful insinuation soaked through to his deepest center, abrasively upsetting it. He put his right hand on the nape of her neck and wrapped the other around her lower back. Garrett drew her close to him in a forceful embrace and kissed her the same way he had earlier, adding another layer of intensity neither of them believed possible. Before he let go of her slender body, he left his tender imprint of kisses down her neck ending at her collarbone before he ventured out-of-control. She turned away, embarrassed that she couldn't govern her own jagged emotions that were already intertwined with this man.

"There is *nothing* about *you* that's a game!" he announced stanchly in his sexy, raspy voice. "Since you have this all figured out, tell me, did that *feel* like a diversion?"

She couldn't address the impassioned kiss any other way than honestly. Marala said, "No," under her breath because she felt it again. Even more than Garrett, she didn't expect this emotion to surface.

"Then what is this? What are you after? This life is a beautiful gift from God and how you see it depends upon how you've decided to live it."

"I didn't decide to live this way!" he argued.

"Don't blame others for the choices you make. You have an amazing amount of passion and—"

"Love?" he questioned condescendingly.

"Yes, love," she replied placing both hands over her heart.

"Tell me who? Who's lucky enough to be the recipient of what I have to offer?"

"You don't think I'm deserving of it?" she asked dropping her head.

He looked at her perplexed and replied, "No. Not what I have to offer. If things were different, but they're not."

"Then change them!"

"I can't. It's too late."

"I don't believe you and that's a problem because I don't view you as a liar."

"You want to see the good in me when *I'm* telling you it's not who I am."

"I've seen the good in you. When you're running with people that are unlike your true core, you may end up like them. Don't allow negativity to take root in you or the branches that grow will bare spoiled fruit. You're allowing others to burden you with layers of resentment and doubt so that you no longer see or remember who God intended you to be. You can't tell me I'm wrong. I know what I feel and I know who you are!" she said pleading with him to believe her.

Garrett got up and walked over to the fireplace, attempting to block out her piercing words. He couldn't allow himself to be distracted.

"I am who I am."

"Then tell me. Who is that Garrett? Do you really know?"

"I know I'm not right for you."

"Then why kiss me that way? Why be so cruel and start something only to walk away?"

"It wasn't my intention; it happened. It's who you are Marala. Do you really know who you are?"

"Yes, I do."

"If this is it, I suggest you learn to make more prudent choices because I'm not good for you. Your intuition should tell you that."

"You can dress up your exterior but God is always viewing your interior. He knew who you were to be before you were conceived. My intuition tells me what God wants me to know, not man. You can't change that Garrett; no matter how hard you try."

"I need to tell you what's going on. It's time you know because—" he said pausing to find a way to say what he needed.

"Because what?"

"Time has run out."

"Run out, how?"

"Marala, you've brought a major disruption to someone's life and he wants to end it. You've been asking what this is about and—you're right, it's about revenge. He wants me to take you to him tonight."

"But why? Why are you doing this? Why would you hand me over to someone that wants to hurt me? Is this who you're working for?"

"Marala, this needs to be done in order for me to make things right with him."

"You owe him? So doing this is going to make things right? What, Garrett? What have I done to hurt you?"

"Nothing."

"When someone close to you is angry or going through something that has nothing to do with you; yet you're the target of their negativity, don't engage or retaliate. Rise above their insecurities, pain, anger or whatever it is and pray with passion for them. If you stay in their pool of problems they'll become yours. It's like wadding in quicksand. *This* is not your problem!"

"Once again, I'm sorry to disappoint you but I've been fighting quicksand for a long time. It's time for change. What else is there to do?"

"Have you thought about inspiring, encouraging and loving him?"

"This man can't be inspired. He can't be encouraged and certainly not loved."

"Of course he can. Obviously I've inspired him to want to hurt me. He's encouraged enough by my words to feel threatened and although he seems to be some kind of monster, he's still capable of being loved by God if he repents. Please, stop with the excuses!"

"They're not excuses. This is who he is and there is nothing good about him."

"So you're afraid of him?"

"I was."

"Then rise above him so he doesn't destroy what you've worked so hard for. God can renew and repair anything; talk to Him about this. Rising above something can sometimes mean you have to walk away, but trust in God because He doesn't leave you!"

"It was you that said, *'there are many things we can accomplish if we don't waste precious time complaining about things and people.'*"

"Yes, but why is it that you only take from my words what benefits you? I'm sure you know the rest of them. What are they?"

"It's too late," he insisted.

"For what? You told me you're doing what I said. You're acting out my encouraging words. Don't you dare give me credit for doing that because you're not acting them out as written. *'Walk past the barriers that are there to keep you from reaching your hand to God and accomplishing your personal goals. Life is meant for living so don't remain in a situation that makes you unhappy when the opportunities to live with passion and happiness exist for all. Stop complaining about whatever is holding you emotionally hostage and begin rebuilding or progressing. Life is beautiful and so are you. Find your inner peace and dwell in it.'* That's what I said."

"Marala, what I want isn't possible. I feel something for you that I haven't felt before. It didn't develop out of lust, but out of love. The problem I have is that I am very loyal. In this situation, I'm loyal to someone else. Unfortunately, that someone isn't you."

"How can you say you have feelings of love for me? That isn't the kind of love I want Garrett. Don't hide behind meaningless words."

"I understand what they sound like and I'm sorry. That's what I'm trying to tell you. I'm not right for you and I know you aren't my reality regardless of what I feel. Let me explain who I am and why you're here. Then we'll see how you feel after knowing my truth."

Marala took a deep breath and replied, "Garrett, I know who you are and who you're trying to convince me of being—you aren't that person."

"No sweetheart, the man you're trying to convince yourself that I am was never here."

Marala looked at him but her spirit wouldn't accept what he was saying. Garrett was so poised and committed to helping this man; Marala couldn't bring to focus the bond. The picture wasn't vivid enough.

She stood up and walked over to the fireplace. "No Garrett! This isn't right. I trusted you."

"I didn't ask you to."

"But you didn't stop me either," she snapped.

Garrett pulled her back over to the sofa with slight resistance.

"Sit down," he instructed firmly. Marala complied in silence. "I need you to do something for me." She looked at him and remained quiet. "Listen to me without judging, defending or trying to change my mind. *'When someone shows you their true core, whether or not you like it, accept what they're showing you.'*" Garrett sat next to her and said, "Those are your words so know I'm showing you my true core. This must happen."

Marala let her eyes fall shut and leaned her head back against the sofa. As Garrett began talking, she took in his strong tone and energy. There was more to this story. He was right. She needed to hear it.

"We've been communicating for two years, nine months and twenty seven days up until the point that—"

"You kidnapped me," she added without opening her eyes.

"When I was first introduced to you, it was by someone that sent me a copy of your very first book, *In Our House*. One day, it came in the mail without a return address, letter, card or anything. I didn't have a clue who could've sent it. I guess it didn't matter because I dug into it and finished it two days later. What I remember most was how I felt after reading it. I was ashamed that you'd been through so much suffering as a little girl. Marala, I couldn't wrap my mind around the possibility that you evolved from a tiny caterpillar inching her way through a horrible life into this beautiful, elegant butterfly that was able to overcome it all. Through your writings, you offered forgiveness to the very person that hurt you the most. You moved through that life crafting a new one full of inspiration and love. I was mystified. I wanted to know how you defeated every dagger thrown at you by the devil himself."

"Forgiveness is powerful and hate is too Garrett, but one heals and the other destroys. Determine what end you want to be on because they both affect your life and that of others. I had to lessen the burden on my spirit by carrying less anger and more love instead. I had to stop being the victim and holding myself hostage to what was impeding my growth. It happened and it's over. That wasn't what my life was destined to be. When I made the determination to trust God, I watched Him block those daggers. Not me."

"I know and I get that. That's why I wanted to learn as much about you as I could. When I found you online, I began to read your inspirational post and like everyone else, I needed the air you were breathing into this world. You'd throw me a harsh blow of reality and then kiss the same wound. I kept reading and learning."

"What?"

"About forgiveness. He reached into his back pocket and pulled out two folded pieces of paper. When he opened them, both pages were worn. "This is what you wrote." Marala sat up and opened her eyes as he handed them to her. It was her poem. Marala looked at him in disbelief and then back at the papers. It had been years ago she'd written it. Although every word was embedded in her heart, she began reading.

A few minutes later, Marala folded the papers and handed them back to Garrett. She closed her eyes and leaned her head against the sofa again, listening as though peacefully surrendering to his commanding voice.

"This poem of yours began my life the right way. Marala, I had a lot of mistrust, doubt and anger because of the things I experienced. It left me no good for a relationship or anyone, let alone myself. I was empty inside. Going through life without emotion is what I was doing. My childhood was horrific and I didn't think I could get over it until I read your memoir. Then I read the rest of them. I appreciated your acknowledgement that the pain others suffer was no less than the pain you went through. And the pain you spoke of ran straight into my adult life like a freight train. Our lives," he said pointing at her and then back at himself, "were created from similar circumstances that flowed into the same raging river of hatred and destruction. Unlike you, I didn't stop hating my father for what he did. The insane part of this was that he wouldn't let go of me even after I'd let go of him so I became more like him; packed with hatred. No matter how hard I tried, I—I couldn't find a way to escape any part of my life until I surrendered to your words of inspiration. Your words were the cure for my pain."

Marala opened her eyes and sat up, turning to face Garrett.

"What exactly was the root of your pain?" she asked with emerging sympathy.

"When I was a kid—like you, I had a mother."

262

"What was her name?"

"Her name was—um, Lauren," he replied choking up as he spoke her name in a breaking whisper.

"I'm sure she was beautiful."

"She was as beautiful as anyone could ever imagine a woman to be and rare, like the Ghost Orchid."

Marala nodded, acknowledging her awareness that the Ghost Orchid was rare in addition to being the most mysterious Orchid of them all.

"Can you tell me about her?"

His eyes shifted up and to his left.

"Mom was lighthearted, loving and she cared about everyone around her. Much like you Marala, Mom believed in intuition and everything connected to her was tied to it. She loved God more than anything and even an earthquake couldn't vibrate her faith in Him."

"She sounds amazing."

Garrett lowered his head and replied, "She was." After a short pause, he casually continued and acknowledged, "I had a little sister too, Tess. She was only four years younger than me. Boy, talk about a feisty little girl," he shared with a light chuckle. "Just like Mom, Tess was beautiful. She never hesitated to speak her mind and it didn't matter what anyone was talking about, Tess would jump in. She was quick to give her opinion on things. Unfortunately, that was another reason my father despised her."

"Were the two of you close?"

"Oh yeah! She'd tag along with me almost everywhere I went. Tess was kind, loving and she was really smart. Yeah," he said reminiscently, "she was the smart one, but she always tried to convince me I was," he said leaning his head back in an attempt to keep his tears from falling. "Mom and I were protective over Tess. It's strange that neither of them are here."

"Garrett, what happened?" she asked noticing his grievous expression.

He took a deep breath of air and let out a hard exhale, "My father threatened to kill my mother." He clenched his teeth together and added, "He didn't like her faith in God, her dedication to church, or anything she loved, including us. He wanted her as a possession and she was just *one* of his many things."

"So he was controlling?"

"In more ways than anyone knew. My mother tried relentlessly to convince my father that he was a good man and nothing like his own father. That was a lie because both of them were abusive. I guess she had a hard time accepting he was *exactly* like his father in between the threats to gut her like an animal and the random beatings he gave her! Right up to the moment he killed her, regardless of what he did, my mother loved him. She kept feeling sorry for him because of his past." Garrett leaned closer to Marala and looked directly into her eyes and whispered in a cacophonous manner, "You remind me of her."

Marala leaned back growing uncomfortable.

"Why?"

"Because you have to acknowledge a person for whom and what they are when you see it. Mom wouldn't give up on him because she refused to accept who he was. She remained focused on what good she thought he had buried inside of him. She said he was intelligent, handsome and hardworking, but there were words like loving, caring and compassionate that didn't go into his description.

She wouldn't accept the fact that he wasn't willing to change. And as you believe, he had the ability to change it, but he wouldn't. It wasn't him," he added coldly.

"How did your father carry himself around others?"

"Just like an actor. He was warm and charming on the outside, but evil, destructive and angry inside."

"Is there anything in particular that may have triggered his emotions or set him off?"

"Nearly anything would accomplish that. One day, there was this young, scraggly guy showed up claiming that Mom was also his mother. Apparently, she'd given him up for adoption years prior. Until that point, my father didn't know anything about it. None of us did."

"Do you know his name?"

He took another deep breath and replied, "My stepbrother's name is Liam. He came to see her on a day my father happened to be there. My father was the type of man that knew everything that went on. It didn't matter where we were, he knew."

"I hate to say this, but he sounds obsessive."

"He was. There was nothing she could do to escape his watch. When my father found out, he just wouldn't let it go. He saw how happy Mom was the last time Liam visited and it must have killed him. He realized she wasn't the pure innocent woman he thought he married and claimed she deceived him."

"Why didn't Liam live with you?"

"He lived with his adoptive parents. Liam was the result of my mother being raped when she was younger. Her parents made her give him up for adoption and some random day, he found her."

"How did you and Tess feel about Liam coming to see her?"

"As far as Tess and I were concerned, we were happy to see Mom smile whenever possible. He didn't spend much time with us because his time with Mom was limited. But once he knew about us, he always bought us something. Candy, books, toys—it didn't matter, he thought about us and we were nobody to him, or to anyone except Mom. He was a different kind of person. He was one of the good guys."

"How did your mom handle it when he left?"

"When he returned to his home, part of Mom seemed to escape with him."

"How old were you and Tess when Liam came into the picture?"

"I was seventeen, Tess was thirteen and he must've been about nineteen or so.

When he came by, all he wanted to do was talk with Mom."

"Your father. Tell me more about him?"

"Well, he used his intellect to build a successful business and continued to grow from there. He came from old money and appeared to own everyone and everything around him. But make no mistake; the man is dark, deceptive and filled with pure unfaltering hatred. All he did with Mom was argue and beat her. That's why your book had such an affect on me. Like your house, the perception versus the reality in our house was something unsuspecting. My father was quite the charmer and Mom was his trophy. On the outside they looked perfect and there wasn't a woman in town that didn't seem to envy Mom."

"What makes you believe that?"

266

"Because my father cheated on my mother with plenty of them and didn't bother to hide it. I used to wish one of them would take him from her just to get him out of our lives. But after what happened to Mom, I wouldn't want that for anyone."

"What happened? And did you or your sister witness it?"

"You mean my father pulling out his hunting knife and slitting her throat because of Liam's visits to her. I lost my mother because some kid she gave up years ago wandered back into her life. The sick part about it was that my father wanted us to see it. His eyes had a burning look only the devil could furnish when he dragged that knife across her throat! You know why?"

"No."

"Because Mom asked to spend a little more time with Liam. Liam's need to be in my mothers life cost me everything I loved!"

Marala took his hand and carefully began to ask, "What do you mean, *everything*?"

"After my father ended my mothers life, he made Tess and I clean up the puddle of blood she was lying in and then help carry her out to the boat."

"That boat?" Marala questioned pointing to the back of the house.

"Yes."

"That's the reason you keep it?"

Garrett nodded as he used the palm of his hands to wipe the painful tears escaping the corner of his eyes.

"He doused her body with gasoline and lit it on fire, inside the boat. After she burned into ashes and the smoke cleared, he towed the boat back in, like nothing ever happened. The next day, he made Tess and I get a metal bucket and scoop her ashes into it."

"To do what?" she exclaimed.

"He made us take them across the lake and scatter them like rose pedals throughout these woods." Marala covered her mouth and gasped loudly. She was rendered speechless. "Remember how you explained that you felt part of me was in the woods and even in the lake?" Marala nodded. "He made us get in the boat and bring it to this side to wash the residue out in the lake. The following day he made us cover up the burn marks on the inside of the boat with gray paint."

"Oh no! Garrett, I—"

"You couldn't have. No one knew. Jeez! Poor Tess, she didn't last after that. For days she kept crying and saying she loved me, but Mom needed her and she had to go find her. It was like she lost her mind. She'd wander into the woods looking for Mom, picking up specks of dirt, talking to it until I'd bring her back to the house. There were a few occasions she took the boat out on the lake and sat calling Mom for hours. Tess wasn't mentally there anymore."

"Garrett, what did your father do about it? What happened to Tess?"

"One morning I woke up and she was dead. Her wrists were slashed. It was ruled a suicide but Tess—I never believed she killed herself. There wasn't a knife or anything near her body. I didn't buy it then and I still don't."

"How did your father get away with what happened to your Mom?"

"He said she ran off with another man. The police came out and never even spoke to Tess or I. The

268

chief was a friend of my fathers. I'd seen him around a lot. My father's power and money kept him in office. The case was closed and that was it."

"Her parents, what about your mother's family? Did she have anyone asking about her?"

"No. Her parents died in a suspicious fire a few months before my parents married. She didn't have any siblings. As you can see, my life's been shrouded with mystery. There were always unanswered questions where my father was concerned."

"Where is he now?"

"My father?"

"Yes."

Garrett grabbed Marala's hand and led her upstairs to the loft. Marala looked around trying to figure out why he brought her up there. He motioned towards the black telescope, pointed out the window and unceremoniously suggested, "Take a look across the lake. That house you see, it's his."

Marala peeked through the lens and said, "Is that where you're taking me?"

"Yes."

"Who—who is he?" she asked slowly backing away from the telescope.

"I didn't tell you, yet? It's the title sponsor of your engagement, Robert Rankin."

"That man's your father?" she asked gasping.

"Yes."

"What? How?"

"The night you spoke at the hotel, my father went to your suite."

"Why?"

"To kill you."

"That's why you took me from the hotel, to protect me from him?"

"Something like that."

"Why didn't you just tell me?"

"Would you have come?"

"No."

"Why not?" he asked.

"Because look what you're doing. You're willing to hand me over to a murderer?"

"I thought I'd try to reason with him about a few things first."

"And if it doesn't work we both know he won't let me go."

Marala's face turned pale and her body tensed. She leaned against the wall to keep her trembling body standing. Her mind raced back to Lyss.

"I know. But if I don't, he'll keep chasing you until he kills you or your daughter."

"Lyss! I need to make sure she's safe. Please, Garrett," she requested holding out her hand.

He reached into his pocket and handed her his phone. She dialed the number and it rang eight times. There was no response. She hung up and called again but still, no answer. Marala's worry for her daughter manifested quickly.

"What's wrong?"

"She didn't answer."

"Perhaps she's on the other line."

"No, Garrett. Lyss answers on the first ring because she's waiting every chance she has to hear from me."

"Try again. Ring the hotel and ask for your suite. It's number two on speed dial."

Marala pressed the number and it rang the hotel. A woman with a pleasant voice answered the phone on the second ring.

"Good afternoon. Thank you for—" she began.

"I'm sorry," Marala said abruptly cutting her off. "Can you ring room 2643 please?"

"And the name?"

"Scott. Marala Scott."

"Please hold."

"Thank you."

The phone rang ten times before Marala hung up. She closed her eyes and began praying. Her body filled with an abundance of unbreakable faith. When she opened her eyes her apprehension had disintegrated. She handed the phone back to Garrett and went downstairs to the kitchen to make a hot cup of tea. Garrett followed her. He took two cups out of the cabinet and dropped a teabag into each from the green box sitting on the counter. While she was adding the sugar, he studied the serenity sweeping through her body. A few minutes of silence filtered between them before he spoke.

"Lyss—"

"Is fine, Garrett. She's fine," she insisted calmly while dropping the sugar into her cup. She paused and looked at Garrett and said, "I'm sorry, do you take sugar?"

"Just one."

"So your father is across the lake. Is that where you grew up?"

"No. We had a cabin on the same property but you can barely see it from this view. My father fished and hunted so we went there often. Our main house was in town."

"Do you fish or hunt?"

"I didn't have a choice when I was a kid, but ever since I left there, I had no desire."

"Would you kill someone if you deemed it necessary?" she asked handing him a cup of tea.

Garrett didn't respond.

~~~~~~~~~~

Thirty-Nine

The cabin was warm and toasty. The wood paneled office was filled with a rich selection of furniture, mounted trophies and collectibles. One of the walls displayed mountings of three prized animals. There was a rocky mountain big horn sheep, a mountain lion and bison. A nine and a half foot grizzly bear was mounted and standing in the corner towering next to the leather sofa. Displayed on another wall was an assortment of guns.

Oddly, a third wall had nothing except seven printed pictures tacked into it. The first was a young man in his early twenties with thick black hair parted and combed to the side. Next, was a fairly attractive and clean-shaven man in his early forties with sprouting gray hair and a neatly trimmed mustache. An attractive woman about the same age was next to him. She had dirty blond hair styled in an upward flip just above her shoulders and a radiant smile. Barely in her middle thirties, the stunning facial features and bright blue eyes stood out on the younger woman in the following picture. Her beauty would cause anyone to look twice as she walked by. Her long blond hair, holding loose curled ends, added a soft touch to her elegant look. There was a photo of a little girl about thirteen, hosting the same beautiful features as the woman with the long blonde hair. Her innocence, coupled with pain, rested in her eyes. The next picture was of a gorgeous man in his late thirties. He had a very polished and gentle demeanor. His hair was light brown and his striking eyes were peaceful. The last picture was a headshot of Marala.

Robert Rankin was sitting comfortably at his overly impressive cherry desk with a hunting knife in his hand. He was admiring the razor sharp blade made of high quality carbon steel. He placed the gleaming knife in front of him on the desk and grinned proudly. Then, he closed the elegant cherry wood display case of his other valued knives and moved it top and center on his desk, next to Marala's books.

"You'll do fine," he said taking gratification in his thoughtful carving selection.

He opened his right desk drawer and pulled out a cranberry sheath and slid the small knife majestically into it like the sword of a king. After placing it inside his back pocket, he very carefully zipped the black duffle bag resting on the floor beside his desk, trying not to disturb its contents.

Robert opened his laptop and logged in, typing the password, INTUITION while mockingly saying the word. When he opened his email, his eyes darted to the inbox and scanned the contents. He had thirty-two messages and one of them was from Marala Scott. He clicked on the message and then read it. With a visible outburst of anger, he slammed his fist on his desk, rattling the contents and began tapping on his keyboard in a heated fit.

Marala,

You're more than welcome. Your speech was magnificent and your conclusion, a spectacular finale! I'm sorry; I'm out of town this week. If you don't mind, I'd like to get back with you regarding dinner when I return. I'll call to see if you're still available.

Regards,
Robert

Robert released a bloodcurdling grin and spewed out crossly, "Your mother's right where I want her and you're next!"

He typed Alyssa's full name in the address bar and without difficulty, found a close-up picture of Lyss with her mother. After cropping Marala out of the photo he pressed print, pulled a tack out of his desk drawer and then got up from his chair to remove the page off the printer. He hung Lyss's photo right next to Marala's.

"I may as well keep the pattern going. Like mother, like daughter," he snared releasing a sadistic laugh. He walked over to his sliding patio door and took in the panoramic view across the lake like a madman.

~~~~~~~~~~

Forty

Lyss grabbed her phone out of her purse to check for messages. Liam observed her expression transition to a taut uneasiness and decided to warn her.

"Don't waste your time. For about—I'd say, the next twenty minutes."

"Why not?"

"You won't get any service. It's where we are. Look around."

Liam was right, all she could see were intermittent deserted trails that led to a few random cabins, most of which were abandoned for the season. There was a half-mile or more between each house. Liam was driving so fast that the barely discernable glimpses of white-tailed deer were sometimes questionable. The isolation was prevalent and what should have been beautiful emitted an eerie sensation.

"I can't miss any calls from my mother. Due to the situation, they're indiscriminate. I've been praying he'll allow her to call soon. I just need to hear her voice."

"I understand how you must feel. If it helps, we don't have far to go," he said reading the green and white road sign.

"Once we get to Robert, have you devised a plan or are we going to wing it?"

"Lyss, I'm with the Bureau. I'm way ahead of you."

"I'm aware. But out of curiosity, do you have your federal identification with you?"

"After everything I've explained, you still don't believe me?"

"Actually, to some degree I do."

"So, you still have doubts?"

"Shouldn't I? You've been evasive about a lot of things, Liam. I've heard what you've said, but it doesn't mean I believe *everything* the way you've chosen to convey it. I admit that you have similarities to Garrett and supposedly detailed knowledge about his family but something isn't adding up."

"Such as?"

"Oh jeez. Liam, have you forgotten that you went from being Head of Security at the hotel to working with the Bureau. I was wrong about you before and I'd like to make sure that I'm not this time. If I hadn't figured it out, you wouldn't have told me anything. So back to your Federal Identification?"

"It's here somewhere."

"Somewhere? Really? Then do you have a gun? Have you called for backup?"

"Lyss, I know what I'm doing."

"Okay, so let's talk about your plan. Do you have one?"

"Yes. I have one," he said with his eyes narrowing.

"Well this is about my mother so would you mind sharing it with me?"

He glanced at Lyss and said firmly, "All I need you to do is stay close to me. Are we clear?"

"Why?"

"Robert won't hesitate to kill you too."

"Is that why you're here, to protect me?"

"No. Don't get off focus beautiful; I'm not here for you. I'm here to close a case on a murderer. You were never supposed to be a part of this. They said you'd be in school, something about your PH.D and Stanford University. You were scarcely mentioned in the report."

"Really?"

"Yeah. Every case has a twist and I guess you're mine."

"That's what I am, your twist?"

"Don't go down that road because it's not meant for you to travel. We've already been there and we both know there's no outlet. You're not a game, twist, challenge, anything other than—"

"Okay, stop. I get it. Let's get back to my mother. All I want to know is how are we going to get her home safely?"

"We're going to Robert's because I have a feeling that's where she'll be. He wants her dead and he's the type of man who gets exactly what he wants."

"What about you?"

"I haven't gotten it yet," he replied demurely, taking a quick glance at her striking features.

"Do you think Garrett will hurt my mother? She sounded certain that he wouldn't. But the fact that Garrett took her the way he did is what concerns me. Why didn't he just tell her what was going on?"

"She's right about Garrett. He won't intentionally hurt her because he wants revenge. He's doing what he thinks is best."

~~~~~~~~~~

Forty-One

Garrett was preoccupied with his thoughts while Marala placidly sipped her lukewarm tea and watched the crackling fire melt the logs into ash. She was thinking about her daughter. When his phone vibrated, he reached into his back pocket, pulled it out and read the message.

> Don't keep me waiting. We have work to do.

He pressed reply.

> On our way.

"Garrett, what is it?"

He slid his phone back into his pocket and turned to face her.

"It's my father. It's time to get this over with." He walked over to Marala, reached for her hand, pulling her up. She took it and was left standing face-to-face with him. "We're at the point where—"

"I'm going to trust you," she stated confidently.

"Don't you get it?"

"The problem you're having is that I do."

"My mother refused to accept what type of man my father was and she's dead because of it."

"That's what Robert meant when he told me your mother's God given intuition cost Lauren her life," she admitted sadly. "And now you're trying to convince yourself that I'm making the same mistake."

"You are! You're able to help people, which is something I came to love about you. There were lessons you unknowingly took me through that shaped me in some ways. But as I told you before, the forgiving part, I'm still working on. You weren't able to penetrate that damaged part of me yet. What I lost somehow destroyed the person I was meant to be. It's because of you I've been trying to get it back, but can't."

"Don't use the word can't, say *won't* but you can do anything you want. You don't want to forgive your father."

"I'm sorry, I didn't realize we were talking about my father. No, sweetheart. There's someone else I can't forgive. That's what I have to deal with."

Marala's face fell blank.

"I'd swear on my life that you aren't capable of doing or being anything like your father."

"My mother's death—*I* kept it a secret—Tess—I never told anyone until now. I'm just like my father. Listen to me. You made a difference. You changed a lot about me but you couldn't quite finish the job."

"So what happens now?"

"My father wants me to take you to his house."

"And that's it. We're going there to talk?"

"Actually Marala, I'm going alone. I need you to take this and keep it with you," he said pulling his gun from the back of his waist and placing it in her hand.

"No," she said sharply, dropping it back into his grip. "I don't support violence."

"Would you, if Robert had a gun aimed at your daughter's head? Take the gun for protection. Please!"

"I'm sorry, I won't. I'm prepared. That's my faith and evidence of how much you've changed me."

"You're making a mistake."

"For trusting in God? With God, mistake's never happen and never will," Marala stated powerfully.

He knew he couldn't change her mind, so he tucked the gun into the waist of his pants and grabbed his jacket from the closet.

"Lock the door behind me and don't open it for anyone."

Marala clutched his arm to stop him and said, "Never engage in a battle with hate; it'll destroy you. This isn't your destiny because you're not like him. Are you willing to allow everything we've discussed to become nothing more than empty conversation?"

"At the time you were writing me I thought I was breaking free of the pain and him. The fact that he was able to disrupt my life so easily is when I realized that I had to take in more of your inspiration. You helped me as much as you could and believe me when I say that I took everything you gave me to heart. I waited for your inspirational and encouraging words to work in me and they did. Finally, I had something to look forward to instead of the agonizing memories of what happened. I couldn't sleep without having nightmares of Mom and Tess. I couldn't breathe at the thought of Liam being the reason my father murdered Mom. I thought of my father carving Mom and Tess up like animals and I needed to—"

"As difficult as this may seem to understand, that happened years ago and it's history. You have to let what's past go. It's hurting you too much. You were just a child then."

"Yes, that's all history and I had resigned to letting that go, but then came you and you are what's now. You were going to be my future and he wants to take you from me. I'm not that kid anymore."

Marala took in his pain and leaned her head back to keep the tears from falling. Now she understood.

"This isn't you. You're not a killer."

Marala let go of his arm, grabbed her aching head then stumbled backwards but he caught her and swept her off her feet before she hit the floor. He laid her back on the sofa.

"What's wrong sweetheart?"

"I don't know," she replied.

"What do you need?"

"To understand why you're doing this. You're a good man. I can feel it."

"I was working towards being that but I didn't get to finish," he said placing his hand on her forehead. "I had you to myself for a few years until my father forced his way back into my life. He saw the changes in me and didn't like them. Your books gave him a reason to target you and that confrontation was the beginning of this."

"The beginning of what Garrett?"

"*Reality*. It's when I became conscious that I was nothing more than a coward who needed to stop hiding, running and suppressing my past." He bent down to kiss Marala on her forehead. "Once I leave, don't open this door."

"Garrett, I—"

"I know. Me too." he said, steadily walking away. He locked the door and was gone.

~~~~~~~~~~

Forty-Two

Garrett pulled into his father's long, paved driveway and rested his head on the steering wheel as thunder began to crash and light raindrops fell. "*I am* obedient, Father. You can count on me," he whispered in his raspy tone. He got out the truck and slowly walked up to the front door and knocked loudly. Within seconds Robert answered.

"It's about time. I was beginning to question your obedience and loyalty towards me," he spewed out in an accusatory tone. "Come in," he ordered, stepping aside for Garrett to enter the dimly lit living room. As Garrett stepped inside, Robert looked out the front door and replied angrily, "Where is she?"

"I know you said to bring her here, but I wanted to talk with you alone."

"You mean, question me alone. You've failed again!"

"No. She's here. Bringing her all this way should tell you that I'm obedient or I wouldn't have gone through the trouble."

"She's across the lake?"

"Yes."

"Alone?" he questioned with a steely smile.

"Yes," Garrett replied.

"What do you have to talk to me about you ungrateful little—"

"I'm asking you to leave her alone. She has nothing to do with any of this."

"Please tell me you haven't fallen for this—this—"

"No! I just don't want this to end the way things did for Mom and Tess. I can't go through it again."

"You didn't go through it the first time you coward! Your mother did! Don't ever let a woman come between you and your own mind, if you still have one left. This woman's changed you. I've watched you turn into someone moved by inspiration, intuition and God! You're becoming dangerous, Garrett. I can't let you run around with this woman. We have too much to lose. You don't even realize I've been protecting you, son. You helped bury your mother."

"I don't need to be protected. I'm trying to find some sense of peace so I can stop—"

"Stop what? Whining about your mother and sister!" he snapped coldly. "Wait here. I have to make a call. Sit down!"

"We need to talk!" Garret said beginning to follow him.

"Give me a minute!"

Garrett stood by the sofa while Robert went into his office, slamming the door behind him.

"I have to end this tonight," Garrett mumbled.

A few minutes later, Garret saw headlights flash through the window. No one was supposed to be there except his father. Two doors slammed and then there was a loud banging on the door.

Liam put his index finger to his lips and motioned for Lyss to stay on the porch, against the house, while he entered. Before she could comprehend what was going on, he turned the doorknob and went inside. By the time the door swung open Garrett and Liam were in a confrontational stance with their guns pointed securely at each other's head.

"Where's Robert?" Liam whispered. Garrett took his aim off Liam and pointed towards Robert's office. "Is he alone?" Liam asked walking briskly towards the office with his gun drawn.

"As far as I know," Garrett responded.

Lyss stepped inside the house catching Garrett's immediate attention. He stared at her recognizable face without saying a word. She looked just like her mother. Liam kicked open the door to find Robert's office empty and a boat pulling away from the dock.

"He's gone!" Liam shouted. "And let me guess, you left Marala at your cabin by herself?"

"Where's your cabin?" Lyss shrieked.

"Across the lake," he said pointing at the only lit cabin. He took the short cut. It's longer driving around the lake."

"Take me there now," Lyss yelled at Liam.

"Is there another boat out back?" Liam questioned sharply.

"No," Garrett replied.

Liam saw the seven photos on the wall and a black duffle bag on the floor by the desk. Before he took another step he heard a slight clicking and shouted as loud as he could, "Out! Everybody! Out! Now!"

Garrett grabbed Lyss's hand and ran out of the house, headed for his truck followed closely by Liam. They backed out of the driveway full speed and reached the road just before the violent explosion shook the ground, leaving the house engulfed in flames.

~~~~~~~~~

Forty-Three

Marala was sitting on the sofa when two gunshots destroyed the front doorknob followed by a forceful kick opening the door. Marala didn't move. Drenched from the heavy rain, Robert stepped out of the shadow. Deafening thunder continued marking its territory, pursued by steady raindrops underneath the blackening sky.

"There's the little inspirational speaker, Ms. *Intuition* herself. I can't tell you how anxious I was to see you again. Like I said before, *some things God can't foresee* and so, here I am!"

"Where's Garrett?" she asked.

"He was at the house waiting to help me get rid of you like he did his mother. He's real good at hiding a body, but he never had much of a stomach for killing. Regrettably, I don't think he realized it was time for him to join his family. I guess you didn't see my impressive explosion across the lake."

"It doesn't matter, Garrett's not in there. You've underestimated him."

"No, see you're wrong. I knew he'd leave you here. He underestimated me."

"Can't you let him live a peaceful existence free of your hatred? Whatever caused you to live with this much pain should never have been passed along to your children, let alone anyone."

Clapping sarcastically he proclaimed, "That's the Ms. Scott I want to get rid of. Always thinking of someone else. That's why you're here now."

"I'm here because you're a murderer and you crave destruction."

"You've been meddling somewhere you have no business being."

"Where?"

"In Garrett's life; turning him against me. They all turned against me and now it has to stop."

"Is that what you do when you're threatened by someone? Kill them? You act as though your family abandoned you."

"They did! Lauren left me a long time ago for God, so I thought I'd send her to meet him in person. Tess, on the other hand, has always favored her mother and I knew after Lauren's death she'd rather follow her than be with me. I only gave her what she wanted. Now Garrett, he was weak and afraid," he recited mockingly. "I was trying to toughen him up and turn him into a man! And here you are teaching him how to follow his intuition. You're dragging my son away from me for your own benefit. You women are all alike and Garrett, he should be more like me. I'd snap your neck right after kissing you."

"Garrett's not weak and he was never capable of being you. He was a child when you hurt him. All he wants is to live without the haunting memories of his childhood or threats from you."

"You don't know what my son wants!"

"I believe I do. The man you describe as weak is *far* from it and that's why you're angry. Garrett's getting stronger and you know it. He's nothing like you. The reality that you've lost your son to God is causing you greater self-destruction because it means your hatred didn't work."

"You have a lot of words for someone with a gun pointed at her head."

He was aiming directly between Marala's eyes and a half-inch above her eyebrows yet; Marala was as calm as she'd ever been.

"I am not afraid of you Robert. You may have murdered others in cold blood but only cowards do that. I will never answer to you for what I do here. I will only answer to God and so will you."

"I'm going to see to it that you answer a little sooner. Now get up!" Marala stood up with little strength using the sofa as a crutch. "Outside," he ordered.

They followed the wet path around back with rain beginning to fall heavily.

"Are you filled with so much rage you're driven to kill anyone who opposes you?"

"Yes. Do you think you can go around waking up people's conscious and disrupting their life? Some people don't want what you have to offer."

"You don't, but Garrett does. He knows who you are and what you've taken from him."

"I only took what he didn't need!"

"He's not trying to hurt you Robert. Garrett wants you to let him go. Let him live his life the way he desires. Why won't you do that? Your life doesn't have to be like this either."

"Haven't you noticed? I prefer my life just as it is. I didn't take Garrett's mother from him. Liam did that all by himself."

"Who cut her throat?"

"Well, I took delight in doing that," he boasted, dredging up a sick smile. "I was tired of her illegitimate son coming around."

Robert placed his gun in the back of his waist, pulled out his sheath and opened it. He slid the knife out exposing it before holding it against her ribs.

"I'm going to show you what I did to Lauren by butchering you the same way."

By the time Garrett, Liam and Lyss reached the house they realized Robert had taken Marala. They raced around to the back of the house to find Robert with Marala headed towards his boat. The drenching rain was still picking up force with heavy winds gusting out of control.

"Robert! Drop it," Liam yelled. Robert began to turn and Liam shouted again, "Drop it or I won't hesitate to shoot you!"

Robert looked up. His knife was jabbed against Marala's body but he realized Garrett's gun was aimed in his direction.

"Garrett! Shoot him!" Robert demanded infuriated by his hesitation.

"Mama!" Lyss cried out running towards her. Before she was able to take more than a few steps, Christian came running from behind and grabbed her securely slipping partially down the slight hill.

"Don't! He'll kill you, Lyss! He'll kill you!" Christian stated firmly while fighting to restrain her. This was a set up to get you and your mother together. Robert knew you'd come after her. He wants to kill your mother and you. He went to your hotel room to kill both of you that night." He looked up at Robert and shouted, "Isn't that right?"

"You're right young man and I just might add you to my list. Haven't you heard? I detest people who meddle in my business!"

"Garrett called his stepbrother, Liam to protect you. Only he hadn't seen Liam since he was a kid," Christian added, lending clarification to the situation.

"Liam?" Robert huffed.

"Garrett took your mother to keep her safe because Robert would've gotten to her at some point," Christian explained.

"Are you stupid? What do you mean I would have gotten to them? If you can't see, they're both right here," Robert gloated.

"Garrett's not trying to hurt your mother," he added convincingly. "He's been baiting his father out into the open, like this. Robert's in some of the audience photos at her last few speeches and so is Garrett. Garrett's been protecting your mother all along."

Lyss looked at her mother, Garrett and then back at Liam.

Without taking his gun off Robert, Liam admitted, "He's right Lyss. He's telling the truth."

"You've taken enough from all of us and it's going to end!" Garrett shouted angrily.

"You cowardly little—"

"That's all I've ever been to you! You murdered my mother! Tess felt your hate for as long as I can remember. You hated her even more for losing it over Mom. That's why you slit her wrist after you gave her those sleeping pills. I know all of your little secrets and I'm going to make sure you pay for them. You're sick! Back away from the boat and drop the knife or I'll kill you myself!" Garrett threatened.

"You don't know all my secrets son? You're so worried about her? What about him?" Robert shouted pointing at Liam.

Garrett lifted his head and sharpened his aim on Robert.

"No Garrett! You're not like him. He's not worth it." Marala said with little vigor.

Marala was broken and her frailty was showing. The painful thumping beating inside her head was taking charge.

Robert clenched his teeth and with a bloodthirsty stare dared him, "Go ahead and kill me because either way, she's going with me."

Marala quickly intervened with a pleading cry, "Can't you see he wants that? Then you'll be just like him!"

Garrett's rage was boiling over as he shouted back at Robert, "She'll never make it to where you're going!"

"Garrett," Liam said sternly, trying to reason with him, "Put the gun down. Put it down. Let me handle him."

"No Liam, he's my responsibility. I don't have anything left here. Marala, my intuition told me to protect you with *my* life. I'm being obedient—"

"No, Garrett. God doesn't want that. He doesn't. And neither do I," Marala begged.

"Trust me, Marala. I can't forgive myself for allowing him to kill my mother. I have to make this right. He'll kill you and your daughter if I don't stop him!"

"Garrett, I'm here to help you," Liam cautioned. "Robert took your mother away. She didn't deserve to die and neither did Tess. Marala's right. You're nothing like that man so don't do this," Liam stated boldly.

Garrett frowned, slightly confused by what Liam said.

"You mean he took *our* mother away." Garret said correcting him.

Christian glanced at Liam and then back at Garrett before revealing, "Garrett, Liam's not your brother!"

"Fish, shut up!" Liam yelled.

"Liam had been communicating with Ms. Scott for a few years," Christian told them, "But Robert—Robert killed your stepbrother a few months ago."

Lyss glanced at Christian in shock and returned an emotionless stare to Liam. A rapid linear motion formed in Lyss's feet and the chilling vibrations spread throughout her body causing instant paralysis.

"Very good," Robert acknowledged, addressing Christian. "Garrett, you'd be nothing without me. You don't even recognize your own family!"

"He's lying!" Garrett shouted. "Brother! Tell him he's lying!"

Liam never took his gun off Robert and didn't reply.

The storm worsened and the wind sent substantial waves crashing against the dock. Garrett's face was washed with disbelief. The man he asked to protect Lyss wasn't his brother. He didn't understand why he started the fire at the hotel and drove throughout the night to take antibiotics to Marala. Now, he wasn't sure if he was working with Robert.

"Who are you?" Lyss demanded. Liam didn't say anything. "Who—are—you?" Again, he offered nothing. "Mama! Who is this man?"

"He's to be trusted Lyss. Completely!"

He reached in his back pocket and tossed Lyss a black, leather wallet. It landed in the mud in front of her feet. Christian slowly bent down, picked it up and opened it. He held it in front of Lyss. He was FBI. His name was Michael. Michael Liam Christianson.

"How could you do this?" Lyss cried. "How did you know so much about Garrett's brother? Did you make it up?"

"No. He'd written his memoir and every detail that I told you was in it. That's how I knew. They found it hidden in his house but they never found his body. He loved you, Garrett. He had difficulty handling your mother's death. That's why he stayed away. He thought you hated him and all he wanted was for you to forgive him for being the cause of her death and Tess's."

"Why would you lie to me?" Lyss asked Liam.

"Lyss, let it go," Marala begged weakly. "It wasn't about you. He did what he was meant to do. It's his job. He was undercover as *Liam*. He couldn't tell you sweetheart. He couldn't."

Robert clenched his teeth and stared at Liam with his nostrils dilated.

Garrett glared at Robert like he couldn't wait to kill him and asked, "Is he right? Did you? Did you murder my brother?"

"Of course I did! He's the reason I had to slice your mothers throat. He wouldn't stay out of my life or yours," Robert confessed.

"So you took his life? The only family I had left!" Garrett shouted.

"Liam was trying to take your mother away. I couldn't let that happen so I killed her. Then Tess— she wasn't loyal. And that Liam, he tried to force his way into your life. Once you started changing, I went to find out why and the trail led straight to him. Who do you think was sending you her books? He'd been looking after you since I killed your mother, but you never knew. He was trying to help you by introducing you to the writings of our Ms. Scott here. Only, I'd killed so many people, I had to give it a break for a while so I left Liam on my radar until a few months ago."

"What did you do to him?" Garrett questioned, emitting a heavy wave of disgust.

"Like it matters," Robert replied callously.

"What did you do to my brother?" Garrett demanded, moving closer with his gun positioned securely on Robert's head."

Liam tightened the grip on his gun while heavy sheets of rain fell angrily from the black sky. He was prepared to shoot Robert at any moment; only he wanted Garrett to finally have the answers he needed.

"Let's see, I told him his mother left a letter for him and I invited him to come and get it. He was as dumb as he looked. He came up here expecting for me to hand him a sentimental letter so he could have some sort of closure. While he was in my office waiting for me to retrieve it, I walked up behind him and opened his throat, the same way I did your mothers."

"You're insane!" Garrett shouted.

Lyss observed her mother struggling to stand as Robert held the knife firmly against her side. Lyss grabbed her stomach and bellowed. "Robert, please! Take me and let my mother go! She's not well! Please! Take me!"

"I don't have to take you. I already have you right here. When I kill your mother, I will have destroyed you too," Robert spewed out hatefully. "Now kill that imposter and while you're at it, kill her, Garrett!"

"You tried to kill me by blowing up your house," Garrett replied.

"Let's attribute the explosion to being an error in judgment," he snapped pompously. "Now show your loyalty."

"I am loyal and obedient—to God!" Garrett yelled.

"Don't seek revenge. Garrett, you can trust Liam. He only impersonated your brother to save you. He's not here for any other reason," Marala explained.

"Drop it, Robert!" Liam insisted, pulling back on his trigger as his final warning.

Robert dropped the knife and pulled his gun out of his waist using the opposite hand in a subtle, swift movement. Before anyone saw it coming, he had the gun to Marala's head.

Garrett saw the hatred in his father's eyes and knew he was going to pull the trigger. He rushed towards Marala with his gun aimed at Robert shouting, "No! You're not taking her from me!"

Robert turned the gun on Garrett and the roar of thunder responded angrily.

"Please, Garrett! Please! Let God deal with him, He made him. This isn't your fight," Marala pleaded. She turned to Robert and stated confidently, "*God sees everything.*"

A blanket of lightning stretched eagerly across the ominous sky flashing brilliantly. Bending treetops and propelling branches, a corresponding powerful gust of wind forced Robert to loose his balance, falling against the aluminum boat. He grabbed ahold of the lift to avoid the rough water of the lake that became Lauren's grave. With little strength to combat what felt like a merciless gale, Marala fled towards Garrett and Lyss broke free of Christian's grasp to help her mother. Robert grabbed ahold of the lift and fired a single shot out of pure rage striking Marala. She drew in a short breath of air that didn't come back out. Robert's hatred caused him to quickly fire again, shooting Garrett. Liam returned two quick shoots back at Robert, shooting him in the leg and shoulder. As Robert tightened his grip to prevent himself from falling into the lake, an angry bolt of lightning violently struck the lift. A deadly surge of electricity was thrust through Robert's hateful body until he fell flaccidly into the lake.

Garrett reached for Marala before collapsing onto the muddy grass. Marala's eyes effortlessly fluttered shut and she fell off the side of the dock, plunging into the lake. The forceful waves began washing Marala's submerged, bloody body away from the dock dragging it closer to death.

Lyss released a terrifying scream that echoed throughout the very forest, hiding the secrets of the Rankin family. Her tears were lost in the freezing rain as she raced towards the lake. Lyss threw off her shoes and jacket then dove in the water searching for Marala; Christian followed. After several dives, to no avail, she called out beseechingly for her mother the way Tess had done.

Liam dropped his gun, pulled off his jacket and quickly removed his shirt. While applying pressure to stop the heavy bleeding, he called his backup. They should have been here since he notified them before he left his house. Yet, there was no sign of them. Garrett's barely audible words hidden beneath his maceration of pain met Liam's ears, "Marala—Help Marala," was all he said, before his eyes fell shut.

"Stay with me brother! Stay with me!" Liam begged.

The heavy rain and gusty winds continued as darkness took over.

~~~~~~~~~~

Forty-Four

It was unusually still. Garrett took his balmy hands and tried to wipe his nervous look away.

"Go ahead, Garrett. What happened was your past but this—what God is showing you now, is your future. It's your turn to share the reality of your life and inspire others," Liam explained, sharing a strong embrace with Garrett.

"Thank you brother," Garrett replied humbly, forcing a smile to his face.

"When I was going through your brother's things, I found the letter from your Mom, asking him to look after you. I decided I'd fill that role. We're family now. I'm not going anywhere. I know your Mom, Tess and your brother would be proud of you," Liam added.

Garrett walked over to Lyss and hugged her tightly before taking a deep breath.

"Liam's right," she said wiping her eyes. "I know for certain this is what Mama wanted. There was never a moment she didn't believe in you. I'll be waiting for you right here as I've always done for her. You'll do fine. I promise."

"I appreciate you being here, Lyss. It means more to me than you know. I look at you and—all I see is your mother. It's really hard for me to do this without her."

"I know. That's why I came," she assured him. "Garrett," she said, touching his cheek lightly with the back of her hand, "This is how her story began, with a lot of pain and many tragic accounts. She made a choice to share them so she could help others. Mama wanted to make a difference and I know she's proud of you for doing the same. Life is a continuance of experiences that are meant to help us learn, which will make us stronger if we choose to let them. Don't carry that luggage any longer."

"I won't," Garrett replied assuredly.

A beautiful young woman walked up to Garrett, blushing while admiring his good looks and said, "Are you ready?"

He nodded and said, "*I am.*"

The large theater was crowded but the room had a dead silence hovering above. The sound of his footsteps taking the stage was all anyone could hear. The typical cheering and enthusiasm that rang throughout the theatre when Marala spoke didn't exist. It was quiet, like a funeral. Garrett wrapped both hands around the microphone and began speaking with a renewed passion.

"Good evening." No one replied. "I know all of you are wondering about the stories in the media regarding Marala Scott and my father Robert Rankin. The reason I'm here tonight is to share with you a courageous story about a woman who cared more about others than herself. My name is Garrett Rankin and I learned from Marala Scott how to trust my God given intuition. Had I not done so, I wouldn't be here today. She had more faith in God's plan for me than I had in myself." Garrett's eyes clouded with tears before speaking her name again, "Marala showed me the value and beauty of the imprint inside of me, which will never be removed. It's called, *intuition.*

Everyone rose to their feet as an uproar of applause filled the theatre.

~~~~~~~~~

Forty-Five

The next morning Garrett arrived home, accompanied by Lyss and Liam. As soon as they walked through the door, Garrett dropped his bags to the hardwood floor. Her favorite fragrance lingered spiritedly in the air. He put his hands to his face and wiped his tears before going into the bedroom. For some reason, the smell of lavender and chamomile permeated his nostrils more forcefully. Garrett carefully sat down on the side of the bed and glanced around the quiet room. All he could think about was the unfaltering faith she had in him. His mind recalled the moment he fell in love with her and the persuasiveness of their first kiss. She was patient and believed in him without ever submitting to doubt. What they shared could never be erased from his heart.

Garrett gently brushed the hair off her peaceful face before kissing her delicately on her warm, soft lips. Gradually, her eyes blinked open and came into focus.

"There's my replacement. Hi gorgeous," she said reaching for his hand. "How'd it go?"

"He's not you, but he held his own," Liam interrupted, entering the room with Lyss.

With Garrett's help, Marala pulled herself to an awkward sitting position and smiled.

"I saw the comments about your speech online, Garrett. I'm sorry I couldn't be there but I'm really proud of you."

"This is right where you should be. Your body needs the rest. You're still healing," he said rubbing his hand along the side of her face.

"Unfortunately, I can't disagree," she said.

"How are you feeling beautiful?" he asked tucking the blanket snuggly around her lean waist.

"Better now that you're home."

"I'm just grateful you're here, with us. When I was speaking, I kept this vivid mental picture of you while reflecting on everything that happened. It was difficult to think about what my father tried to do to you. You weren't well when I kidnapped you and the shooting made everything worse. We nearly lost you because I thought I was following my intuition."

Lyss leaned her head on Liam's sturdy shoulder to conceal her sadness.

"Well," Marala began soothingly, affectionately rubbing her hand against the light stubble on his chin, "Following your intuition *did* save me because I'm here. Had you not made the choices you did, Garrett, things would be quite different. It's over and that means it's nothing but history now. Leave it where it belongs, in the past. You own every decision you make and your intuition will help you as long as you continue to trust it."

"Sweetheart, I intend to."

"There's too much negativity out there and allowing a little to get into the mix of your life opens the door for a lot more. Let's work to keep it away."

Everyone nodded.

Garrett studied the serenity in Marala's eyes. He thought of the words she kept trying to say at the cabin. He wouldn't let her because he didn't know where his fate would take him until now.

"Sweetheart, I—"

"I know. Me too," she replied sweetly.

There was a lingering silence before Lyss interjected, "Mama," she said walking closer towards her bedside, "I can't wait to fill you in on Garrett here. He did an amazing job last night. The audience couldn't get enough of his honesty and passion."

"I knew they'd see his truth," Marala admitted confidently.

"There's a need for people to have a continuum of encouraging stories. It's clear that it helps rejuvenate them," Lyss told her.

"Is that so?" Marala teased.

"Yeah and you're right, Mama."

"About what?" Marala asked.

"The male perspective. It's something people need to hear. It'll create balance in the comprehension of many issues between genders. It seemed to fascinate everyone last night, along with his apparent good looks. I think he has a new career, if he chooses," Lyss added winking at Garrett.

"I'm not surprised," Marala replied. "His story is another great testimony to God's love and power."

Liam patted Garrett on the back and told him supportively, "You have a lot to share and getting it out can help others take a closer look at their own reality."

Everyone agreed.

"Lyss, I know this might be a little too soon after everything that just happened, but while I'm recovering, can you work with Adam to reschedule the next set of dates and return my emails again?"

Liam smiled as he walked up behind Lyss and wrapped his muscular arms around her.

"Of course, Mama," she replied glancing back at Liam.

"Christian called to check on me. He said he'd see you guys this week. Something about a swim meet."

"Yeah, I told him we'd be there. Fish, I mean, Christian's a good kid," Liam added.

"All of you worked collectively and saved my life. I can't thank you enough."

"Mama, we weren't going to lose you."

"Thank you for loving me the way you do."

"I'm going to make you breakfast and a cup of tea."

"Thank you baby girl, but Garrett promised to make me an omelet when he got home."

Lyss leaned down, kissed her mother on the cheek and gave her a careful hug.

"Can he cook?" Lyss questioned.

"Absolutely," Marala replied.

"Sorry Lyss," Garrett added, flashing a smile.

"No problem. Just don't forget the raspberry jam on the toast," Lyss reminded.

"I remember everything you told me from the first time you replied for your Mom," Garrett admitted. "She always wondered how I knew so much about her."

"About that—" Lyss replied playfully.

Marala let out a muffled groan and squirmed painfully. Detecting her discomfort Garrett adjusted the two pillows behind her.

"Thank you," she said after leaning back. "It still hurts where the bullet went in."

"I'm sorry sweetheart," Garrett said consoling her.

"I'll manage. At least you didn't do it," she said smiling at Garrett. "I'm sure you know there's a reason we're all here," Marala began, reaching for Lyss's hand. Liam locked his arms around Lyss's waist while Garrett sat lovingly next to Marala.

"I'd say so," Garrett acknowledged looking up at Liam and Lyss.

"We were brought together because each of us knew there was something we were intuitively driven to accomplish. Although we didn't exactly know what or even why, we were obedient to following our intuition," Marala explained.

"I didn't know what the outcome was going to be. I thought it was my responsibility to bring my father to justice. My intent was never to kill him, although I was capable of it when I saw him with that knife against you."

Marala lightly ran her hand down the side of Garrett's face and released a smile full of peace and grace.

"God made sure it wasn't an option because as I've said before, He knows your heart and He allowed me to discern your spirit from the beginning. My intuition, regardless of the case that was building against you, *never* changed," Marala confessed. "And as for you beautiful daughter, your obedience kept you alive and I had no doubt that you would only believe in what you felt intuitively. What hurt me is that I was certain it was hurting you. Liam, thank you for being resolute in trusting Garrett while protecting my daughter."

Liam smiled and said, "I plan on doing that for the rest of my life." Lyss's eyes sparkled.

"Mama, I remembered everything you taught me and my intuition was right. Now I know the result of unwavering faith. Working together allowed us to share our experiences and change lives. Thank you for teaching us to trust our intuition."

"Oh sweetheart, I didn't teach you, God did."

About The Authors

Marala Scott is the Best Selling Author of the memoir *In Our House: Perception vs. Reality*, *Bad to the Bone* and *Surrounded by Inspiration*. She is Oprah's Ambassador of Hope, a Motivational Speaker, and Ghostwriter. For more information about Marala Scott, visit: www.maralascott.com.

Alyssa Curry embarked on this heartfelt project in an effort to help her mother recover from a craniotomy, due to multiple brain aneurysms. Alyssa is a young woman illuminated by her passion for life. A recent college graduate in the field of Psychology, she is a copyeditor and graphic designer that spends her free time engulfed in music. Her goal for now is to meet Ben McKenzie!

Intuition
Trust It!

www.ingramcontent.com/pod-product-compliance
Lightning Source LLC
Chambersburg PA
CBHW030646260626
47157CB00007B/2517